Praise for Cody Goodfellow

"Cody Goodfellow's imagination is a freeway flyer, and his prose is a ride on a rocket-sled. He's one of the two or three god-damned best writers in the Genres today." --MICHAEL SHEA, World Fantasy Award-winning author of *Nifft the Lean* and *Copping Squid*

"Goodfellow's voice sweeps you away like the undertow of a tsunami, and once you're in, he's got you pinned." —MICHAEL ARNZEN, author of *Grave Markings*

"One of the best writers of our generation." —BRIAN KEENE, author of *The Rising* and *Dark Hollow*

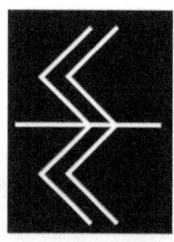

A Broken River Books original

Broken River Books
103 Beal Street
Norman, OK 73069

ISBN: 978-1-940885-10-0

Printed in the USA.

REPO SHARK

CODY GOODFELLOW

BROKEN RIVER BOOKS
NORMAN, OK

For Tim,

Ali'i of Agoura

"It's a pity you can't savor a bit of their very sweet language. They sing, 'Welcome, welcome, strong and handsome white man. Welcome, welcome, seductive and beautiful white woman. You will teach me the secret of your elegance, wherefore you can seduce your men. I will teach you the secret of my dance, wherefore I seduce mine.'"

— Narrator, *Mondo Cane* (1962).

Aloha ino oe, eia ibonei paha oe e make ai, ke ai mainei Pele.

("Compassion great to you! Close here, perhaps, is your death; Pele comes devouring.")

—from "Pele And Kahawali" in *Elliss Tour Of Hawaii*.

1
SPOUTING WATER

The kid in 318 was making the whole hotel nervous.

Horse-faced, whippet-skinny, with a brackish accent like a blend of Australian and Dutch via extensive and inexpert orthodontic surgery. Jailhouse tats on his knuckles and slithering up his wrists like toxic smoke from a plastic fire under the cuffs of his Upper Playground hoodie. Room reserved for a three-day stay by somebody local, premium no limit high roller treatment in the third cheapest hotel in Waikiki. Only chumps and crooks and diehard fans of *Dog The Bounty Hunter* stayed at the Illikoi, and nobody ever, even at the peak of tourist season, made reservations.

He coughed an ugly noise for a name and inked an illegible graffiti tag on the register. Took his key-card and a pair of bulky but suspiciously light suitcases and went to his room, then around the corner to the nearest ABC Store. Returned a half hour later with two deluxe shopping bags and holed up in Room 318. An hour later, one of Wo Fuk's third-string girls slinked through the lobby and up the back stairs. Half an hour later, the furniture started flying.

* * *

Awakening a sleepwalker was once widely supposed to be dangerous, but no such helpful old wives' tales exist about interrupting a man engrossed in what the kids call "pillbugging," or giving himself a blowjob.

The prostitute was trying to break down the hotel room door with the fire extinguisher. Drunk, dumb and clumsy as she was, her aim was bad. Huge wrecking-ball holes in the plaster. A day-glo slanderscape of Diamond Head fell to the burnt orange shag carpet. If she wasn't so wasted, she might have noticed that the door was unlocked. Bitch polished off a fifth of Malibu and a sickening vanilla cigar before she even quoted him a rate. Zef should've got off the bed and let her out, but he was busy.

He had to get off, and she was just smothering him. When he shoved her off the bed and threw her clothes at her, he meant for her to take her cash and leave, but she sloshed into the bathroom to top off her sinuses before the next john. When she came out and saw him curled up in the winter lotus position in the middle of the bed, she quite understandably freaked out.

Zef was well aware he was tweaking out the whole hotel. You don't become a living weapon, an elite repo ninja, without noticing your effect on regular people on the rare occasions when you must slip out of the shadows. It's so easy to forget that the natural abilities you've come to take for granted are extraordinary or even frightening to others. In many parts of the world, he could probably still be burned as a witch, if suckers could catch him.

For instance, most men in a similar predicament would probably finish themselves off manually or perhaps into the stolen underpants of the source of disappointment and frustration. But few men were as resourceful as Zef DeGroot, or as limber.

So, confronted with the sight of her disgruntled trick rolled up like a garden hose and somehow deep-throating himself, she must've thought he was having a seizure. She picked him up by his ophidian hips and shook him.

Zef bit himself where he could afford it least. Arms and legs windmilling, he caught a dresser with one foot and sent them careening backwards into the window air conditioner, which popped out of its housing and fell three stories to smash on the concrete apron just short of the pool.

By now, a crowd had gathered on the surrounding balconies and around the pool, even the semi-permanent inhabitants of the swim-up bar. When the hooker came out cursing in Cantonese and a pair of coral pink stirrup leggings, the whole hotel gave her a standing ovation.

Zef watched through a slit in the curtains. "Fok," he grumbled, "bitch blew my cover."

The whole point of holing up in the Illikoi was to be invisible until he leapt out of the shadows to strike. Such was his reputation that no one would dismiss his appearance in Honolulu as just another badass on vacation. Zef DeGroot had been summoned by the powers of darkness to execute a commission of the highest urgency. Hawaii wasn't shit but another job. Everybody in America dreamed of blocking a toilet in Hawaii, but everybody in Hawaii wanted to go to Vegas.

But ever since he got off the plane, he couldn't so much as think about the mission. He couldn't get his nut off, couldn't even pass the vacuum-sealed plastic bag lodged somewhere in his lower intestine, not even after popping enough Maalox to move Gibraltar.

Fok.

The Christmas tree in the Illikoi's lobby didn't look decorated so much as it seemed to have lost an ornament fight. Lopsided garlands of gold tinsel made the flocked Douglas fir look like it was slowly tipping over, and the tacky tiki ornaments had been fired into it at high velocity with clear malicious intent. With a tree that nice, Zef could understand why they'd want to leave it up halfway through February.

He took a deep breath of the breeze, trying to have a vacation moment. The air smelled nice. Low tide added a gamey bite to the desert-clean air rolling in off the waves, and some sweet yet tangy floral aroma gave it a lovely tropical flavor.

See, was that so hard? He felt so relaxed he could hardly hear his own pulse drowning out the surf and the slack key guitar muzak and the tinnitus from the fucking flight over.

He asked the bellhop about what kind of flowers made the smell in the lobby and he just gave him a weird look. "Those flowers don't smell, brah," he said, pointing to the elaborate helliconia and bird of paradise displays on low tables throughout the lobby.

"But the smell, it's like perfume," Zef said, waving his hand around and trying not to look like a fag. "It's, you know, pretty…"

The bellhop nodded and winked and went away. He came back with a dishrag that he was pouring something on. The perfume smell came on way too strong. It was tile sealant. Winking again, he handed Zef the folded rag. Zef gave him five bucks but threw the rag in the trash.

The guy at the bar didn't want to tell him where to find a decent whore, and he didn't even know what Ecstasy was. A leathery old Jersey Jew covered in melanomas, he had that spacey passive arrogance of all the old-school island transplants.

"You came here on a jet, right? When I came out here, when I was still a *haole*, people still did the cruise ships. That way was better. A whole week of nothing but a blue void, man… you need that to clear your mental palate, to be ready for *this*."

Zef looked out at Waikiki, as dirty, loud and crowded as the Strip. "It has its peculiarities, but big cities are all…"

"I don't mean Honolulu, man. I mean the islands. They call it America, but it's *soooo* not. America is a layer of plastic shrink-wrap over the islands, but you can wander off the tourist track and fall through a hole into a whole other world. It's like getting trapped under ice, but you won't ever want to come back."

Zef finished his drink and noticed people staring at him. His stomach rumbled, bitching about the syrupy booze and the blockage and the shitty airplane Salisbury steak that still hadn't found its way out of him. He was a skinny guy with a metabolism like a coyote.

"Relax, brah," the old Jew said with a horrid fake island accent. "You on island time now." A stupid capped grin split his death-freckled face. His teeth looked like they were carved out of soap.

Eyes left, right, and nobody was looking. Zef tossed a twenty on the counter and left a finger on it. When the bartender came in to snatch it, Zef leaned over the bar and headbutted him so hard he rebounded off the sink behind him and dropped out of sight like a hand puppet.

He left the twenty. He wasn't a dick, or anything.

In the lobby, when he asked for messages, the Hindi desk clerk tossed him a cheap cell phone.

"It's been ringing for an hour," the clerk said. Zef frowned. There'd been a smiling Hawaiian *wahine* working when he checked in. This guy had the give-no-fucks attitude of an owner's immediate family, and now the lobby stank of curry.

Zef hit redial. Harv answered, "Howzit?"

Harv was one of Zef's dad's mates back in Johannesburg. Old-school uniform cops, all less than five years from their pension when the shit hit the fan in South Africa. Apartheid got scrapped and they emigrated in a group, pooled their resources and bought Nevada businesses and real estate with Springbok gym bags filled with Krugerrands. Harv ran the top towing and repo outfit in Vegas that wasn't Mob- or Mormon-owned. He was one of those jolly, giant guys who's always super nice and helpful because he once lost control so bad, he still scares himself. Like his hands could go berserk at any minute and start breaking people like eggs for no fucking reason. Like he's trying to keep an angry dog in the back of his head from biting your hands off.

The agency didn't have an office in Honolulu, and if they could work with the local repo men, they wouldn't have had to send out for Zef. Shit like this wasn't supposed to be a problem on an island.

"Where's my car?"

Harv was probably dicking around with Google Earth. "Across the street, in the lot, but you won't need it. Look at the phone. Familiarize yourself with its functionality." Like a lot of old-school Afrikaaners, Harv dug over-pronouncing Latinate diction, and like most dumb cops, he thought big words made him sound smarter.

The map had a bunch of icons on it, little digital pins spread all over Oahu. Outside the city, there was nothing but Army bases, tract homes, golf courses and cane fields and country. Zef groaned. His quarry had a lot of friends in the middle of nowhere. "Those are his known associates' localities. He seems to not have a permanent address. He was born in the Waipio Valley on the big island."

Outside, the air was two parts tropical perfume and four parts auto exhaust and diarrhea. The lot across from the hotel had nothing but rental Mustangs and minivans. A huge banyan tree sprouted from the ruined pavement and cast the whole lot in a green, sweaty shade. It was practically raining pigeon and parrot shit.

"Which car?"

"Yellow Mustang. Key in a casket under the rear driver's wheel well, or else somebody..." The thought terminated in a crush of gritting teeth.

"Relax, unclefucker. It's here." In the car on the street, he asked, "Why did somebody have to come all the way out here, dick?"

"We needed a rock star."

Zef hung up.

Dad could give him the really real, but Dad was currently facing off with the LVPD over the apparent suicide of Doug Zweibel, the douche who owned the hotel chain that ran the Illikoi.

Zef didn't really need to know why, but it did give him pause that nobody local would touch the fucking guy. It was an island, for fuck's sake; soap in a bathtub. Zef knew only as much as he needed to. Curiosity seldom paid off in this business. Get in, get the goods, get out... but you don't steal somebody's car without getting a taste of their life.

The deadbeat's legal name was Pauwalu Don Nanaue—54, no criminal record—but everybody called him Donny Punani. He came out to Vegas the month prior and stayed at Caesars for the long holiday weekend. High roller suite and food and everything, and they never billed him for any of it. He bought the Harley in Vegas and drove it to LA, then sent it air-freight back to Honolulu. Somewhere along the line, his credit turned out to be fairy gold, and the dealer wanted the bike back.

Easiest kind of grab, but apparently, this Donny Punani was some kind of big deal in the islands. The locals were scared. Fine. Zef DeGroot didn't run on island time. He'd have it done and be back at the airport before the fat pineapple-head knew it was missing.

He thought he could unwind and enjoy a vacation, but this place had his ass puckered even harder than home. It came across all syrupy and serene like, but little things snowballed into big things until the whole place seemed out to fuck him over. He didn't like the way they said, "on Oahu," instead of "in." Nobody lived *on* Los Angeles or on New York. The subtle distinction made it feel like he wasn't *in* a place, but on top of something that could get washed away or just sink back into the sea.

The language wasn't doing him any favors, either. It sounded pretty exotic at first, but the fuckers only used like half the alphabet, so the words stuttered and repeated like a baby babbling—Wai-napanapa, Havapipi…

OK, some of them were kind of dope.

Nobody hung a *lei* or planted a kiss on him at the airport, either.

Before he started the car, he thought about it for a few minutes, then switched to a prepaid phone and called Primo. Fuck it. He always worked better under a deadline.

Primo came to Vegas to deal cards, but like a lot of transients, he was less than religious with paying his bills. Zef's colleague Finley snapped up his Corvette in front of Primo's condo in the north end, and Primo came after him on a little 500cc dirt bike. Pacing him across the golf course, jumping the fence and passing him on the freeway at four thirty in the fucking morning. Got sideways in front of the 'vette so Finley had to stop, and this crazy fucking Hawaiian rolls up to his window and goes, "Hey, you like to party?"

He wasn't sore about the car at all, but he really needed the briefcase full of weed and blow under the spare tire in the trunk. Finley let him take it and Primo hooked him up, which he knew would be no fun without someone to stay up with, so he hooked Zef up, too. Primo stayed in touch with Finley for a couple weeks before he went back home, but Zef only met him once. He fronted all kinds of shit for the hotel trade, but harped on how they couldn't get decent E in Hawaii. He may or may not have fucked up a transaction with the Mexicans, so he was the only Hawaiian who didn't want to go back to Las Vegas.

"Yo, Primo."

Dope-addled pidgin English, thick with sleep. "Eh, brah. Who this?"

"Zef, man, like... Finley's friend... He told you I'd call, you know... when I was, like..."

The silence was like thick, sucking mud. "Right, when you comin' out? Soon, yeah? We get fucked up then, I promise."

"Yo, I'm already out here now, man."

"Fuck... really? No way! Did the Fin come with you?"

"No, I'm here for work, but like... yo, did he tell you what I was bringing?"

Zef could practically smell the burning gears through the phone line. The sleepy accent dropped like a mask. "How many you got? How pure is it?"

"Two hundred stamped tabs of pure from Amsterdam. Can you move that weight?"

"Not right away... You brought it with you?"

"Yeah. It's... close by."

"Alright, listen... yeah. I get one bad feeling about you, I don't just walk away. I'm not a guy to fuck with on this rock, you know?"

Zef's voice snuck out of his mouth. "Yes—Yeah... Fok, man... I want twenty each."

"Get fucked, you think I'm Japanese? Twelve."

"Yo, I'm not paying you to take them. I'm wise to how much it fetches, over here. Eighteen or go to hell—"

"Shit, who else you think you can sell this shit to? You know anybody else in Honolulu, white boy? You don't even know *me*."

Zef waited for a counter-offer, but the sleepy breathing on the other end was like a saw on his nerves. "Sixteen," he finally said.

"Do better."

"Fifteen, and fok you, fokking fok."

"Tomorrow midnight, for shuah. I let you know where later."

What did they think he was going to do, set up an ambush? "And I'll let *you* know... uh, when it comes out."

2
OCEAN ROAD

Kalakaua was like a midget Vegas Strip on steroids, with the neon and casinos and stripclubs and everything else worth doing squeezed out. The designer boutiques like embassies from hideous alien worlds, the huge hotels like filing cabinets that made the body-farm towers in *The Matrix* look like country bed & breakfasts. His Mustang faded into the crush of identical rental cars in primary Lego-block colors, Mustang convertibles for couples, PT Cruisers or Navigators for families. This part of Hawaii just made him lonely for home.

Check the phone. Your prey has many watering holes and hides.

Ala Moana shopping center was like twelve blocks long. The parking lot alone had its own zip code. It was like *Blade Runner* with more rich Japs. So many in the endless mob were pale people buried in brand-name merchandise who seemed to have come to Honolulu and never left the mall.

He bought an aloha shirt, Billabong board shorts, Oakley shades, bright orange Crocs and a UNLV Rebels cap on the company card. Some of that white shit on his nose and a hotel towel swiped from the Surfrider's poolside lounge, and Zef was ready to work.

The beach was the first thing to stop him and shake him and make him forget about the job. Las Vegas had no shortage of sunlight, but stand still in Vegas, and you could feel it starting to kill you. Here it was actually somewhat pleasant.

Beyond a desert of powdered sugar, the ocean was a glistening azure abstraction, the waves impossibly wide and smooth as a bedspread being turned down. Kids with dark skin rode the waves on short boards like birds on a telephone line, swiping at each other and darting back and forth until the wave played out and they dropped out of sight under the next one. White kids and women knelt on trainer boards the size of canoes as smiling surf instructors pushed them down the faces of the puny in-between waves. Like clockwork, every third wave was a modest shelf suitable for riding.

Zef had actually only seen the ocean once on a trip to LA with his family, but he considered himself a fucking excellent surfer.

Parking in a pay lot across the park from the beach, he walked past rows of cars, as many local as rental. He ran a few plates through an app that checked them against bank and federal hot lists, just by force of habit. More than once, he'd come across a cherry hidden in plain sight while doing something else.

This job, in and out. Ten percent on the bike's sale price of $72,890, plus the side action, if he ever passed it. He tried to clear the known-associate addresses and look for a pharmacy.

The little differences. Even the grocery stores had tikis and Hawaiian shirts and impulse gift bullshit in the front, where they had slot machines in Nevada. That's all Hawaii would ever be to a lot of people, just a lot of tacky shit somebody else brought them from the Vons in Honolulu.

The ocean shut him up and made him forget his plans. It was like the desert, but way more empty. The sky and the sea were mirrors reflecting each other, sandwiching infinity. He was looking at this shit and getting lost in a postcard when he saw the motorcycles.

It couldn't be this easy, could it?

A line of them parked in the front row. Harleys or old Hondas, with a vintage Husqvarna dirt bike for wtf value. No rice-rockets or organ-donor bikes like the young guys and squids favored. A line of those stood across the street with the aggressive separation of a blood feud.

The sunlight off the chrome was so dazzling that he couldn't tell anything else about them until he came up among them. A lifted midnight blue Toyota pickup with knobby tractor tires, a roll-cage and a camper shell was parked beside them, sitting crookedly on what must have been royally fucked-up shocks. An empty catamaran trailer was on the other side.

Nobody was around. Looking out at the waves, he spotted a couple of big native-looking guys standing on their longboards on the lip of a lazy wave wide enough to carry ten riders.

Shading his eyes, he approached the row of bikes. Seven of them. One was a tricycle thing with a little ice cream freezer on the back. Another had a sidecar. And in the midst of them, shining so hard it made the sun look dull, a cherry chopped, chromed 1962 Harley-Davidson low-compression 1200cc police bike with raked, extended fork and ape-drape handlebars and a custom stars-and-stripes motif on the teardrop tank.

He stepped off the curb and turned sideways to squeeze in between the bikes. He was looking at the bike like the guy who owned the thing would look, not like a guilty geezer checking to see who's looking. The dick who owned it was out on the ocean and nobody could stop him.

His outstretched hand was an inch from the handlebars. The other was in his pocket, fingering the ignition key. His right foot was an inch off the ground, cocked to go over the teardrop tank and sit his skinny ass on the leather seat, which looked like a huge pat of black butter. The ignition lock did not appear to be engaged, but there was a padlock on the neck that would take a few minutes to pick.

"Eh *haole*, you got one lighter?"

He froze and looked up with an idiotic half-smile. "For real? Yo, sure, hold up…"

He'd been spotted, but had he been made? He could just walk away and try again later or he could offer some bullshit about how he had a bike just like this at home and, *whoa, brainfart…* All of this ran through his mind in less time than it took for his forebrain to think, *Fok.* Such are the ways of the ninja.

Ice cold yet supple as a rubber, he turned and said, "Sure, brother…" and he didn't even scream when he saw them.

They were sitting on the tailgate of the Toyota. The one who held his hand out for the lighter was about Zef's height and had maybe fifty to seventy pounds on him. But he looked like a ventriloquist's dummy next to his friend.

The big one was close to seven feet and weighed at least three Zefs. Naked to the waist, he wore a sarong, but his epic belly more than hid his junk. His whole right side was tattooed dead black with little designs and symbols in it. Even his face, which was the size of a goddamn frying pan. He had a trash bag full of Mc Rib sandwiches under one arm. Blinking at Zef incuriously, he cracked the cardboard boxes and gobbled sandwiches like he was shelling peanuts.

The "little" guy wore a faded red T-shirt that said I NOT LATE… I STAY ON ISLAND TIME and a ratty pair of board shorts. His hair was prematurely silver, his skin ashy and oddly wrinkled all over. His left arm was in a fiberglass cast from shoulder to fingers. In his free hand, he held a three-sheeter joint the size of a burrito.

Slowly, feigning lazy unconcern, Zef patted himself down. He never smoked tobacco, but having fire handy got him into interesting conversations. He found his new tiki lighter with blinking red LED eyes and tossed it to the little guy. Sidling out from between the bikes, he slouched over to stand before the two and watched wistfully as the little guy turned the tapered prow of the joint over the flame like a fine cigar. The big guy just looked at him, not because he gave a shit, but his head was pointed that way and he couldn't be bothered to move it. A snake on a hot rock had more initiative.

Just smile and nod like he's fascinating. Talking right now wouldn't make these guys like him.

But he got bored. "You know these guys with the bikes?"

"Buncha pussies, I promise," the little guy said, sucking the joint tip to a fiercely glowing ember. He stuck out a hand and took Zef's in a sandpaper grip. "Kewalo, brah. Welcome to my islands."

Something about the way he said it told Zef he was being fucked with. Kewalo let out a huge gust of smoke. He looked like one of the Four Winds on old maps, blowing up a storm.

"ZzzzZebediah, yo. Thanks." Zef kept out his hand for his lighter, but Kewalo passed him the joint, instead. Zef was apt to turn it down, but the big guy rumbled so Zef decided to push back. One hit on a blunt wouldn't dull his edge, and what was the fucking hurry? He wasn't even here eight hours yet and *damn* it wasn't a blunt and it tasted like pineapple and it filled up his chest until his lungs reached down to his knees.

"Holy shit, yo," he croaked, coughing so hard he threw up a little bit and his eyes felt like they were melting but these guys didn't care, they were awesome, fuck a lei and a kiss, this was how to welcome weary travelers to the mighty Sandwich Islands.

"Eh, you like da kine, yeah?" Kewalo laughed like he had maracas and rattlesnakes in his lungs.

"Smooth," Zef managed. The big guy took the joint from him and hit it hard, eyes nailed to something over Zef's shoulder. Zef turned around, suddenly sure he'd see a cop car—what did Honolulu five-oh cars even look like? Shit, this shit was making him paranoid.

"Better than Maui Wowie, I promise," Kewalo said. "Old-school strain, yeah, but we made it bionic." He hit the joint and blew oily liquid smoke rings, then passed to Zef. "How long you on the island, Z?"

Zef totally forgot the question halfway into his second hit. "Holy shit," he coughed, "it's really fokking beautiful here. You guys don't know how lucky you are, to have this all the time…"

The big guy growled, crushed Zef's hand in his paw when he took the joint.

What… was the… question…? "Oh yeah… Just a week. Here on business, actually. *You* guys here for business? Cos I know a guy, yo, who's looking to move—"

"Mind your own fuckin' business," the big guy snarled, blasting smoke out his flaring nostrils like live steam.

"Be cool, Peapea," said Kewalo. "He not even passin' out."

The joint came around again. Zef took a good look inward before he took another hit. The last two (or three…?) were sitting on his skull like a thirty-pound steel helmet. He was worried about being out in the open, he wanted to crawl into a crack, was that a thing? Claustrophilia?

Anyway… *what*?

Right… the bike… It was ten feet away and he had the key and lockpicks in a trick pocket in his sneakers. The owner was somewhere nearby and these fuckers might not care if he took it, hell, they might even be cool with it, maybe they hated… what's his name… Punani.

When he was done coughing, he tried to steer the conversation back to the motorcycles, but talk turned to surfing.

The waves on Ala Moana this time of day were regular as clockwork and just as exciting, but they had plenty of stamina, and many of the tourists who bought a longboard after their first surf lesson took them out here to discover that they had no idea what the fuck they were doing. When they dumped in the shallows a few hundred yards out on the coral, they often ditched their boards and everything else in a panic to get to land. And the five o'clock swell, when the trade winds turned, was something to see. Behind the little guy sat a box filled with designer sunglasses, watches, cell phones and hotel key cards.

"Peapea," Kewalo said, "you goin' out for the swell, brah?"

The big guy got off the truck, which bounced up on its shocks, and pulled a surfboard down off a rack atop the camper shell. The board was a fucking canoe. Nearly twelve feet of ugly black resin like it was made of tar, fitted with skegs like fucking scimitars.

Zef said, "You guys going out right now?"

Kewalo looked at him like he was a dipshit and wiggled his busted wing. "No, I going to stay here and jack off."

Zef had one of those flashes he always got with pot—call it *pregret*—when he knew that something he was about to say was fucking retarded, but he couldn't stop himself. "Longboards are like training wheels," he said.

"Eh *haole* boy, you ride the wild surf on a little trick board on one wave machine back home?" Kewalo cackled and Peapea joined in.

Zef said, "Yo, I cut up the waves on Malibu, bitch," which wasn't strictly speaking true, unless one afternoon of bodyboarding counted. But Zef was an excellent waterskier and a champion indoor surfer, and it suddenly seemed important as hell that he prove it to these tubby island punks. "I could outride tons-o-fun here, if you had any real waves, and if I had my—"

"Use my board," Kewalo said, and the big guy put a board in front of him. Shorter than Peapea's, it was still big enough for three guys to use for fishing.

"I only use a short board, yo. Too bad, too, 'cos I could show you some mad Cali style, like…"

"He want a *short* board, Peapea." Kewalo smiled real big as Peapea took down another board and dropped it on Zef. It was just over seven feet and ridiculously wide. Gorgeous unpainted koa wood under layers of resin polished until it shimmered like a mirror. Shit, why not? He wasn't going to get the bike away from the little guy, anyway, and hey, the little shit still had his lighter…

"Bet you a hundred you don't get up once," Kewalo grinned. Half his teeth were gold.

Zef snapped, "Keep my money dry," and shouldered the board. The weight almost threw him backwards into the row of motorcycles, but he tilted the huge board and chased it towards the ocean. Suckers didn't know who they were messing with.

Zef didn't like to spread the word around, but he was the champion surfer of Las Vegas. He rode the nose of a short board continuously for three hours, thirty-eight minutes, twenty-nine seconds in the Wave Tube at Circus Circus Adventuredome. His record there was still unbeaten.

He kicked off his Crocs and dropped his beach gear in the sand. Hot MILF tourists watched their kids cry and flail through surf school. Too-tan, leathery *wahines* on all fours showed the kids how to get up on the board on the sand. Zef marveled at their asses in the air and walked through a Japanese couple's wedding photo shoot with a raging boner tenting his shorts.

The water was warm but not uncomfortably so, not like the Caribbean, which felt like a huge basin of sweat. He stepped out into the water and did the sting ray shuffle until the spent waves came up to his knees. Then he gratefully dropped the board in the water and laid down on it.

It felt bloody ridiculous, but paddling out, he found that the board sliced through the waves and glided over the fields of coral to where the bottom became ridges of soft sand and dropped off into a bright topaz void. The board was magnificent, fully fucking rude. Embedded in the wood, he now noticed, here and there, crystal clear within the resin, were shark teeth.

The waves were crap. A few other riders sat astride their boards in the dazzling spray of scattered sunlight off the water. Zef could already feel his Euro-honky skin crisping.

Way off on his right, he saw the SS Peapea wallowing out against the rollers, making little headway. The fat fucker wasn't even going to get out there before Zef was headed in to collect his winnings.

He could barely make out more than stick figure silhouettes of the people on the beach, but he could see what he figured was Kewalo in his red T-shirt. He was standing next to a big guy with long black hair that shone with silver in the sunlight. The guy tore off his shirt and headed down towards the water when somebody behind Zef shouted and he turned around and son of a bitch, a real wave was rearing up out of the placid sea, gathering mass and rising until it blocked out the setting sun. The water was so clear that he could see through it like green glass. Twelve feet tall, and the crown of spray shaved off by the wind seemed to double its height.

Suddenly, Zef was very cold, but that wasn't why he shivered. Even peeing his suit didn't help much when the wave started to drag Zef into its yawning maw. Furiously paddling and trying to turn around with his feet, Zef had just laid down and closed his eyes when the wave passed beneath him, lifting him eight feet and then dropping him behind it as it pounded closer to the shore before reaching critical mass and breaking. A few junior surfers rode it in, but the bulk of the riders, the natives, ducked it and paddled even further out. Even Zef knew that every third wave was the keeper.

The next one was even taller, but it threw Zef over its shoulder and raced for the shore, breaking on the coral fields and wiping out a platoon of tourists.

The next one would be the one, and Zef would ride it in. He searched for Peapea in the coral field, but was shocked to find the giant way out past zero break, laying prone on his longboard like a walrus on an ice floe.

He looked to the shore once more and scoped out the little guy, who was jumping around and waving his arms, trying to get his attention, or somebody else's...

The sun went out. A chill wind rasped over the water, sucked into the vacuum as the ocean seemed to turn sideways. Zef looked up at the wave but he couldn't see the top of it without rolling off the board. He began frantically paddling, chanting, "*Fok fok fok!*" to keep from hyperventilating.

He was shooting down the face of the wave and he could feel rather than see the tube closing in all around him. He remembered what to do, what he did at Circus Circus and at the water park, but the worst thing that could happen there was that girls would point and laugh when the wave machine spat you out.

He gathered his legs under him and crouched on the board. It held his weight and didn't wobble and if he closed his eyes, he felt like he was in a boat, not plummeting into the trough of a wave that was closing over him like the jaws of a monstrous garbage disposal.

He stood up. And it was easy, for a glorious, pregnant second. He twisted his body on the board as he stood and the board pivoted under him to shoot for the mouth of the tube, picking up speed until the wave itself seemed to freeze over and he was out in the sunshine again for just a second and he was searching the shore for that little guy with his lighter and his hundred bucks.

And then, just like that, his surfboard was gone. His feet clung to the waxy deck but his body rolled off and smashed into the collapsing tube of the wave. The initial impact was like hitting concrete. The water gave him road rash before it swallowed him.

These waves were not like the ones at the Adventuredome. It was like falling headfirst into an industrial washing machine on the rinse cycle. He rolled with it like an empty suit, seeing only bubbles and thinking only to close his mouth and try to find the surface. There was no surface, there was no bottom, there was only the wave and it would never end, because even if he escaped it, he would be in bed somewhere in his old age and awaiting death and when he closed his eyes, he would still be whirling in the grip of this fucking wave.

Zef curled into a ball and tried to ride it out, but something snatched him out of his death spiral and seemed to be pushing him up, no, it was pulling him down, and he couldn't tell much but he knew from the burning in his lungs that he was about to inhale a lot of seawater, and something was *riding* him.

He felt feet planted in the center of his back, between his shoulder blades, and he felt a grip like steel manacles on his wrists, pulling his arms back and driving his body down towards the sandy bottom and they were still hurtling on in the teeth of the breaking wave and all he could see was foam and he plowed sand with his face but somehow clung to consciousness long enough to see the coral reef rushing at him, and then all was a merciful blur.

Foamy waves lapped at his face like a dog. He rolled on the sand, then kept rolling until he was well away from that fucking murderous ocean. His face and chest burned and his hand came away bloody when he touched his face, and empty when he touched where his gold chain was supposed to be.

Touching his nose made him scream into the sand. He started to get up and dizziness sent him sprawling back on his ass. Nobody was looking at him. The surf classes were all gone. A few surfers straddled their boards beyond the waves, but they couldn't see him. He should get the fuck out of here before the little guy showed up. By rodeo rules, he should be wearing a ribbon.

Yo, where was his board? He got up and scanned the waves and up and down the shoreline, but the board was gone. The surfers out beyond the waves: One of them was a huge lump, had to be Peapea. He was huddled close to another surfer who had long black hair. It might have been the same one Kewalo was talking to before, but how could he—

Zef threw his arms out in frustration and winced at a sudden shooting pain in his back that cut through the medley of discomfort.

When he touched it, he didn't know what the hell it was, at first. A foreign object embedded in his skin, a lot thicker than a tattoo needle. It hurt more taking it out than when it went in. He had rash on his chest from getting slammed into the bottom. He'd even felt like someone was standing on his back, but that was fucking impossible…

The object in his hand was a bloody shark's tooth.

Somebody had taken Zef's towel.

They left his Crocs.

3
SHELTERED HOLLOW

In his short yet already somewhat legendary career, Zef had stood out early on because he did not focus on the debtor. He didn't do confrontation. He was a champion bullshitter, but he was a better thief. He focused on the car. But Donny Punani, he already knew, was going to require a radical departure from the formula.

He drove up Queen Street into an appropriately shady commercial district, fooling with his phone, looking for a cheap clinic to get his nose reset. A pin dropped in the map only a mile away.

He called Harv.

"Fok off, you. I'm busy." In the background, a murmur of indeterminate gender, and the fuzzy rumbling of a hot tub.

"Then I quit."

"Alright, fok, don't drown in your own period blood." A long, clumsy pause forced Zef to picture Harv buck naked and slipping into an animal print bathrobe. "What's the predicament, butterfly?"

"I think I just got rolled by the debtor."

"Fok me. What'd you get entangled with him for?"

"Didn't try to… I don't think he made me, but he's surrounded by big fuckers all the time. It's just gonna get messy if I can't involve the cops."

"You seem to have grown quite a pussy already, on your vacation. I've never known you to shrink from an opportunity to distinguish yourself. No local police interference will be tolerated." Harv's Afrikaaner accent went into overdrive when he got torqued.

"Yo, how'm I supposed to track him when he got no home, and take it when he got a fokking posse?"

Harv sighed but Zef knew he was just stringing it out. Something juicy was stuck in his throat. "OK, but you tell anyone—"

Dropping the car in a Puumano Pay Lot, he crossed the street headed for Dr. Tung's clinic in the Kamehameha Corner Mall. "Just drop it, uncle."

"It isn't for the bank." The Harley dealer in Vegas was out of town when the debtor bought the bike. Rally touring across Australia. He never would've agreed to the sale price and never would've carried the financing himself, but somebody at the dealership did, letting this fat Hawaiian fuck take off with a one-of-a-kind bike for a song on the dealership's account. When the owner returned and went through the paperwork, he quickly sized it up.

His wife was the finance manager, and she also worked the floor. She played the dumb blonde to the hilt and usually made commission more often than most of the sales staff. She wasn't his first wife, either. He punted the old one for this young thing and installed her at the dealership. They'd been together for almost ten years and he'd never had cause to mistrust her before...

Long, elaborate sigh to build drama while Harv sniffed a line or got a blowjob. "So, to find out that she had fraudulently financed the nicest bike in the store for some Hawaiian smoothie who took it halfway across the Pacific inflicted serious cracks of doubt in the façade of his matrimonial bliss. And when he rushed home just in time to cut her off in the driveway as she was pulling out with the back of her Escalade full of suitcases, he was shattered; his faith in his marriage, in love and trust itself, lay in ruins. With his heart broken wide open, it was all he could do to beat her half to death."

By the time Harv paused to catch his breath, Zef was pretty sure the story itself had given him an orgasm.

"So," he puffed, "the police should not be informed of the repossession."

"But I have the papers..."

"They're illegitimate. There'll be questions. We just want the bike. Don't make excuses like some *kaffir* whore. Just get it, hey?"

Something landed on Zef's shoulder and sank claws into his flesh. Powerful feathered wings battered his face. He stumbled off the curb, waving his hands, when a flash went off in his face.

"Beautiful shot! Welcome to the islands, your family back home is gonna love it, print and email, only ten dollars."

"What the fok?" A scarlet macaw perched on his shoulder, nibbling his ear with a beak like a tiger claw. A geek with long, kinky brown hair and a Members

Only jacket held a digital camera with a printer on his belt that spat out a print of Zef being assaulted by the parrot. He had another parrot, a big blue, on his guano-caked shoulder.

"I don't want a picture, fokker, I know what I look like…"

"But the birds, man, they're expensive, do it for the birds…" The geek pushed the picture in his hand. Zef looked like he was about to burst into tears in the picture. His nose looked like a smashed tomato. "Show some aloha, brother…"

Zef took a swing at the photographer. He easily dodged, and the blue parrot went after Zef's face. Claws raked his cheeks and a godawful squawking filled the air. His hands went to his face, his phone slipping out of his fingers. And suddenly, the scarlet macaw was gone. It flapped off and disappeared behind the strip mall with his cell phone in its clutches like a baby mouse.

Zef grabbed the photographer by an epaulette. "Your fokking bird mugged me!'

"Bullshit, man! *You* assaulted me and scared my fuckin' bird away! I'm calling the cops right now, man. That bird was worth a thousand dollars…" He held his phone to his ear, but he was angling for some kind of payoff, and then he'd get the phone back from the parrot and sell it…

Zef looked around. He saw no cops, but cars were slowing down to look at the two street freaks grappling on the corner. Zef deftly hoisted the man closer and headbutted him just as the photographer scooped his groin, which sent him to his knees in the gutter.

"'Aloha' also means 'fuck you,'" the photographer said, and hocked a wad of bloody snot on him as the blue parrot took his picture back.

Zef pled emergency priority and bypassed the other vacation casualties in the waiting room. Stingray Butt, Terminal Sunburn and Hysterical Miscarriage all gave him the gas face, but they weren't dripping blood on the carpet.

Dr. Tung didn't think there was anything funny about his name. He took three hundred to reset Zef's nose, which was broken in two places and required splints. He disinfected and dressed the abrasions on his face and chest from the macaw and the coral and hooked him up with some topical ointment and heavy-duty antibiotics ("Call or come back immediately if gangrene sets in") and some weapons-grade laxatives. Zef declined a shot of avian flu vaccine.

In the car, he slammed half a bottle of the chalky shit and a double shot of the stuff that tasted like crankcase oil. Squirming in tourist traffic for most of the rest of the drive, he left the Mustang in the Illikoi driveway and threw his keys at the desk clerk, who shouted that they didn't have valet parking.

Prairie-dogging it all the way down the interminable corridor, he ran past a Filipino maid who should have known better than to park her supply cart so close to the stairs.

His key card was in the front pocket of his trunks, but thrusting his battered junk at the door did nothing. He backed up to kick it down. He bounced off the door and nearly went over the railing. Cursing, knees knocking, he wrapped his fist in his shirt to smash the narrow window beside the door. The maid jumped in the way and opened the door with her key. He pushed past her, grunting gratitude all the way to the bathroom.

He hit the seat and he was like a tube of toothpaste getting stepped on. It felt like a subway train coming out of his ass. The satisfaction was better than an orgasm, which made him worry for a moment if it wasn't gay to get off on a good bowel movement, but then he started to get alarmed because it wasn't stopping.

His guts twisted and wrung themselves out. The pain dropped him off the toilet and wadded him up into a ball for a half hour. When he finally got up and crawled to the toilet, he had a rush of pure satisfaction that numbed him to the discomfort of shedding three percent of his bodyweight in one sitting.

It didn't last long. His throat closed up and his last meal tried to escape. The smell was so palpable he could *feel* the huge, awful brown molecules caroming off his cheeks in the insufficiently conditioned air. He had no idea what shape his cargo was in, but it wouldn't do it any good to soak in the toilet, though it had built up a nice shell of solid waste while blocking up his large intestine. The soupy mess in the bowl hadn't had most of the water extracted from it. All his holes tried to close up against the horrible stench, the awful, intimate warmth of the mess, the sickening viscosity of it squishing between his fumbling fingers. The cold kiss of the bowl brushed his knuckles. He swiped his hand around and around until he'd made a whirlpool of his own filth.

It hadn't flushed. The bag hadn't come out and dissolved. It was a double-hulled, vacuum-sealed Mealsaver pouch. The outflow conduit was so narrow it'd take two flushes to dispose of a tampon.

He probed his belly, palpated his pelvis, his prostate. He couldn't feel it, but he knew.

It was still in there.

Zef wondered if Harv was trying to get ahold of him. He wondered if the parrot could answer the phone.

The bartender came over with a fresh piña colada. It wasn't the same guy he'd butted the day before. That guy held down the far end of the bar next to the TV with a worried, lost expression.

"I wouldn't drink all those fruity drinks, if I were you," said some guy on the next stool.

Zef spun to check out the next guy he was going to have to beat up.

A lumpy, vaguely Asian-looking guy wore an amazing aloha shirt with volcanoes with gigantic hot chicks coming out of them to claim virgin sacrifices all over it. His arms, neck, everything but his face were even more floridly inked with crazy Japanese tattoos: giant octopi raping Marines in Okinawa surf against rising suns studded with kamikaze lightning bolts. He was chewing gum and looking at Zef as if he'd just had to clean up Zef's bathroom.

"Your uncle said you needed a local guide. I'm not touching whatever you're doing. Don't want to know. But I can run a skiptrace on your guy and show you around, if you don't turn out to be too much of an asshole."

The bartender put a straight shot of vodka in front of the stranger. "On the house, Phun Boy." Phun Boy flipped him three or four different varieties of the bird.

Zef slurped his drink too fast, brainfreeze like an icicle driving up through the roof of his mouth. "What the fok, man? Who the hell are you?"

"Jimmy Phun. People who want their asses kicked call me Phun Boy."

Zef could understand why he would want to be covered in tattoos. Not just to want to have something beautiful—and the snake sleeve down his left arm was all that, with emerald scales so brilliant it looked like powdered bottle glass embedded in his skin—but to have something intentional about his appearance, when everything else about him was a sad accident.

His face was mostly forehead, and most of the rest was chin. His wildly asymmetrical features were squashed into a concave space between them. He was not quite ugly enough to make a living off letting people gawk at him, but he was pretty close.

Jimmy Phun stared at his neck. Zef checked himself in the bar mirror. The tattoo on his neck, in letters meant to look like a scar from a hangman's noose, said REPO NINJA. Jimmy said, "You do that yourself?"

Zef smiled and blushed. "Yeah, I do all my own…" His voice trailed off as it sank in he wasn't being complimented.

"Jesus, what is that?" Jimmy pointed at Zef's mouth. "Do you have something…?"

Zef smiled wide, skinning back his lips to show off the only tattoo he'd paid someone else to do, and yes, if you must know, it *was* on a dare.

Inside his lower lip, in letters big enough to read from across the bar, it read, WISEBLOOD.

"You gonna buy me a drink or something, or…" Jimmy's forehead and chin almost met as he scowled.

Zef ordered a Jack and Coke "and something with an umbrella in it for my excellent friend."

Jimmy took out his phone. "Why don't you tell me who you're looking for, and I'll get started while you finish your drinks?"

It almost all came out, but Zef bit his tongue. *If Harv didn't tell this prick anything, then why should I?* "Yo, why don't you just drive? I got a list. When we find his, uh—the vehicle, you'll drop me off."

"Whatever. Who you think gave your uncle that list in the first place?" Dropping cash on his tab, Jimmy led him out to the turnaround. Zef tried to hide his boner. A cherry '69 Shelby GT-500 convertible in metallic flake crimson with gold detail, like a giant Hot Wheels car.

Zef climbed in and immediately started twiddling the stereo dial. No hip hop anywhere, just shitty classic rock and reggae. "How much this set you back?"

The engine was rebuilt to street racing specs. It felt like an earthquake. "Seven hundred." Jimmy laid a patch burning out of the driveway and onto Kalakaua, cutting between a tour bus and a honking herd of minivans. Zef was pressed back in his seat as they kept accelerating. He could not reach out to change the station to save his life.

They leveled out and crossed a canal on a bridge and then executed a series of jack moves down alleys and side streets to lose whoever might be tailing them. "Got it at an auction. Nothing ever leaves an island. A sailor who never came back from 'Nam left it in a storage space. A Marine who bought it at auction in '86 was one of a couple dozen who got killed in Just Cause…"

"What?"

"Panama, Wiseblood." His widow kept it in a garage for over a decade, until she remarried and went back to the mainland. The last owner was sent to South Korea, where he bought it in a student riot while guarding an Army post in Seoul. The car sat in a storage space until Jimmy bought it.

"Asians are real superstitious," he said, "islanders even more so. And sailors? Nobody else even bid on it."

Outside, the hotels turned to motels and massage parlors and sushi buffets. Zef said, "Cos it's a fokking death-car, yo. It's like, cursed…"

"Not for me. I'm not in the military. Where are we going first?"

"Take me to a Verizon store first. I need a new phone."

"Okay, man. Whatever you say." His rolling eyes laid out the subtext: *You some detective, white boy.*

"I didn't lose it, Phun Boy! Fokking parrot stole it!"

4
DA KINE

Once you got to know Jimmy Phun and got past his unlikable exterior, he wasn't just abrasive and abrupt. He also became aggressively morose and boring.

"Three days. That's how long civilization would last out here, if the ships stopped coming. Three days 'til the gas and the fast food get used up, and the lights go out."

Zef poked at his confusing new phone, bouncing unanswered texts off Harv. "Good times, for sure. You a native?"

"Like, was I born here? Yes, but I'm not a pineapple. I'm *hapa*." Heading off the next dumb question, he added, "Half Chinese, half Portuguese, and I don't have acromegaly. I'm just supernaturally handsome." He didn't explain what the fuck aquamegaliens were.

"Half the native Hawaiians can't even swim. A lot of them, they hate the ocean. It used to protect them from the world, but now it's no protection from all the bad things, so it's just a prison. The outside world's like outer fucking space to them, man."

Seen in this light, Honolulu was like Vegas with an even bigger desert and no fucking action. It had no recognizable spine like the Strip, but the jumble of towers and the shelves of greenery-infested hillside studded with gleaming estates like the displays of a jewelry store—it had the same feel of a fragile bubble in an alien and hostile environment. He saw the same look on many people's faces, the same face you saw everywhere in Vegas or LA when they got bit in the ass taking it for granted—pockets picked, luggage swiped, cameras, iPhones and iPods and wheelchairs, when they realized that this splendid, beautiful place where so many lived was nobody's home.

"So they try to be Americans, but they're fooling nobody. Or they play native for the tourists. Or hit the bottle or the bong or the ice… Shit, you wouldn't believe the meth problem out here… But some folks, they hold to the old ways for real, see? They do it when nobody's watching. You never see them, less they want to see you. And you don't want them to see you—"

A green Challenger cut them off and a siren wailed and threw off a strobing blue light from a dome on its roof. It had no other markings, but the driver was in a uniform. Zef hated asking Jimmy about it.

"Cops here get an allowance to use their own cars, and they've only got one chopper. Lot of them have shitty sedans you could lose on a scooter, but that guy probably wrote off most of that fucking Dodge."

Zef figured they must be in Chinatown, since a lot of the signs were in Chinese. He scanned the curbs and saw a lot of bikes, but they were all rice-rockets. They'd been to five locations on Harv's list and found nothing.

"Look, Vanilla, I don't give a flying fuck who you're looking for… no, *you* shut up. I've lived here my whole life. I'm not afraid of anybody. Long as I don't have to get involved, whoever you want to fuck with, that's your business…"

Still looking out the window at a light, watching a couple choppers pass by, Zef said, "The natives got gangs and like, mobbed-up gangster shit?"

"Of course they do, but except for the ones that're connected to the Yakuza, they're strictly local. They steal from tourists, do burglaries and deal ice and outdoor weed, but they don't hardly use guns, 'less they on the ice. Can't get too big out here, can't really hide, but if they get off Oahu, the other islands are still pretty country…"

They turned right off King at the bridge across a dark, defeated little river and turned back into Chinatown to do Hotel Street. The Challenger was parked on a side street behind a Lexus. Just as they passed, Zef saw the officer jump back from the luxury sedan and run back to his car with his mouth wide open in a scream.

Jimmy Phun snorted as they passed. "Nice to see them bust somebody who deserves it for a change."

They could do this shit all night and come up with nothing. "Donny Punani mean shit to you?"

"Never heard of him," Jimmy said, looking real hard at his sideview mirror. "I don't suppose that's his real name…"

Zef checked his texts from Harv. Nothing new, but back a week, he found the name he kept forgetting. "Nanaue. From the big island… Fok, I don't know."

At the next stoplight, Jimmy punched the name into his phone. "He probably cooks ice or grows weed up in the hills. A low-grade gangster. A lot of them like to play outlaw, but they don't have the sack for real trouble. If he's in Honolulu, he probably won't be too conspicuous unless he's looking to fuck somebody up. Then he'll be in Waianae."

"What's that?"

"Polynesian ghetto on the leeward side. It's not a safe place to be after dark. If he's out there, you're probably not going to find him."

"Don't need *him*, yo. Just need to know where he's parked. He's got mad cribs up in Whateverville, homes."

Jimmy checked his phone one more time. Whatever he saw made him scowl and suck his teeth. "Not going in cold. Here, lemme…"

He executed a tight U-turn in the middle of the narrow two-lane street. A few street freaks hung out in front of a dive bar. An ancient Chinese woman rolled down the bars in front of a tiny market. It wasn't a tourist trap Chinatown like in San Francisco. It didn't care to put on airs for tourists. "It's still a dump," Jimmy said, "even though the mainland Chinese are trying to buy up downtown. But the Japanese aren't ready to sell."

They swung into the gutter to park. Jimmy got out and told Zef, "Just be a few minutes. I got a guy who knows all the island lowlife."

Jimmy and Zef went around the dismal pack of smokers and panhandlers outside Da Kine Karaoke Bar. A tiny Vietnamese hooker in a blond wig braced

Jimmy, but he shook her off. Zef couldn't get her to look at him. The bouncer was a sullen, tubby Chinese guy with a wide, thick face on a head shaped like a huge toe.

Everything in the club was black lacquer and glass. All the lights were red, except for a warm white spotlight on a Japanese salaryman torturing the Piña Colada Song. A sullen crowd of every color but white packed the narrow space between the bar and a wall covered in bug-eyed, fanged masks and pictures of dragons in Chinese New Year's parades.

Zef felt eyes on him but he tried to play it cool, hanging just close enough to Jimmy as not to seem like his date. It looked like a service industry night at any cheap off-Strip club in Vegas. Some of the Hawaiians in the crowd still wore their hotel uniforms.

Jimmy leaned over the bar to talk into the bartender's ear. She shook her head and tapped her watch. Jimmy ordered drinks and came back to hand Zef a big glass of melted rainbow sherbet with a parasol and whipped cream and a cherry on it.

"Fok you, man."

"Guy I need to talk to should be in any minute. Why don't you just…"

"Way ahead of you, Phun Boy." Zef knocked back half the frothy, icy drink, wincing at the cold and the overpowering volume of dirt-cheap white rum and the aftertaste like cherry cough syrup. He slithered through the crowd, wary of starting trouble, well aware of forbidding glares from all around the room as he went to the DJ booth. Instead of a sign-up list, they had a brass urn filled with paper slips next to the fat songbook. Zef scribbled his name and his song on a slip and dropped it in just as the song ended and the Japanese guy bowed off the tiny stage.

Jimmy shook his head. "Your uncle was right," he said. "You are an idiot."

Zef ordered a rum and coke. The DJ drew the next name and was about to read it when the back door opened and a bunch of huge Hawaiians came in.

Zef shrunk down behind Jimmy and watched through the hideous *hapa* dick's receding hairline.

Four guys came into the bar and the crowd made room. Older women shouted and threw arms around one or another of them as they passed and guys hugged them, so it was almost impossible to see them. But when the crowd parted and the DJ came down from the booth, one guy in the party stood out as the star. He was about six-eight or more, maybe two-sixty, not much of it fat. Fifty, with a finely creased, crudely chiseled face, and silver streaks in long black hair pulled back in a loose ponytail. A black dress shirt and charcoal pinstripe slacks made him look like two Hong Kong gangsters trying to sneak into a movie in one suit.

Zef stared at the guy for a full fifteen seconds, watching him endure a sloppy hug from the DJ and take the mic to politely frightened applause from the crowd, before he realized he was looking at Donny Punani.

"Oh fok... dude... it's the motherfokking debtor."

"Where?"

"The guy on the fokking stage, yo."

Jimmy just shook his head sadly and tried to act like an ugly tiki.

The other guys… oh shit, the little guy he owed a hundred bucks blocked the back door. The fucking giant wasn't here, thank fuck.

What was the fuck going to sing? "Tiny Bubbles?"

The music started. A homely, parched sounding cowboy violin blew through the room like a wind off the desert, driving tumbleweeds and the shadows of circling buzzards.

And with a voice like leather worn and battered to a creamy softness, he totally fucking owned "Cool Water." When Zef closed his eyes, it sounded like Marty Robbins, with the slightest tinge of Lorne Greene.

Zef slid down the wall, headed for the front door. The fucking bike was somewhere nearby. Game, set, match, motherfuckers—

Jimmy grabbed his sleeve and jerked him back. "It's really bad manners to walk out when somebody's singing."

"But that's the fucking mark, yo…" He stopped dead when he looked for the front door and couldn't find it. There was a huge Hawaiian in the way. Peapea looked around the bar, nostrils flaring like he could *smell* that Zef was here, but did he see him?

Jimmy pinned him to the wall until the last haunting coda of "Cool Water" died away to ferocious applause. As sullen as they seemed when Zef walked in, now they didn't want Donny to leave the stage. Donny Punani assayed a lazy bow and scanned the room with his sleepy eyes once before he went to sit down.

Zef broke free and moved for the back door with the hood of his sweatshirt pulled up. Peapea reached over the bar to grab a bottle of rum. The bartender strenuously avoided noticing. The way looked clear. Zef got three steps towards the door when they called his name.

He kept going, but hands trapped him and pushed him back towards the stage.

Okay, this was nothing he didn't ask for. He knew "Follow The Leader" by Eric B and Rakim better than he knew the National Anthem. Classic old-school shit, also the newest hip hop on their catalog.

Even if this pineapple-head motherfucker knew what Zef was up to in the islands, what was he going to do? *How many repos have you failed to bring in?*

Zero.

Is this the motherfucker who's going to get the best of you?

Hell no.

Donny Punani was talking to a sturdy native girl in a waitress's uniform. He took her hand and sat still when another one slapped his face.

The crowd was getting ugly.

Zef took the mic from the DJ and stepped onto the little platform. A monitor on the ceiling would show him the lyrics, but he wouldn't need them. Shaking off the tension like a boxer, tugging the drawstrings of his hoodie tight to hide his face, he got into character and waited for the crushing bass pulse he knew so well.

But instead, a whiny slack-key guitar riff echoed out of the PA. The natives went apeshit. They loved this song like it was *their* national anthem. Even as they clapped, he saw dull, drunken eyes blink clear and blaze with fierce intensity as they took in his every gesture.

Walking out on your own song was probably the apex of antisocial behavior in these parts.

The DJ had his back turned and was sweating a pretty *wahine*. Donny Punani leaned back in his chair and steepled his fingers under his chin. A waitress put a bottle of Everclear and a tumbler on the table and sat on his lap.

The words started to roll across the screen. Zef couldn't recognize a single syllable. It was some kind of Hawaiian gibberish like a cat walking across a keyboard with only half the keys working. Trying to sound the lyrics out on the fly made the crowd come to its feet hooting and spitting. Bottles flew at his face.

The crowd dissolved into knots of internecine brawls. Dodging while bottles shattered on his arms and ribs and the side of his head, Zef ran for the door, but he didn't get off the dance floor before he ran into Peapea.

"*Haole boy!*" In the deep red light, Peapea's left half was a shadow of a ghost, except for his glittering, hungry eye. Half the bottles thrown at Zef bounced off Peapea's back. "*You owe my cuz one bet!*"

Zef punched the man-mountain in the mouth. The punch was swift but weak, barely splitting the thick lips, let alone denting the big grin. Peapea was just opening his mouth to give his frank opinion of said punch, when he got hit six more times before he could raise a tree trunk arm to block the rain of blows to his face. The cumulative effect put out the lights, but he was so fucking big, he couldn't find his way to the floor. Zef shoved him back and ran up his falling body to leap on the bar.

Running down the bar, kicking drinks into the crowd, he sprang like an unarmed samurai onto the nearest *kanaka*, planting a foot on his shoulder and launching himself over the next three to come sprawling down on two more with his elbows and knees flailing like a tornado full of doorknobs.

They parted under the full force of his wrath and suddenly he was throwing elbows at the door. He kicked it open and hit the sidewalk, sweeping the bouncer's barstool so he dropped into the doorway to trip the first of the mob coming after his ass.

Jimmy's Shelby peeled out into the street and rushed at him. Zef jumped back across the hood of a Honda as the Shelby screamed past him and out of Chinatown. *Fokking coward—*

Zef was in the street with his back turned when the Harley passed by and the rider kicked his legs out from under him. Zef landed on his bony ass and rolled under a car as three more bikes tore off after Jimmy's vintage muscle car.

As soon as the sound of motors faded, Zef rolled out from under the car and checked the street. A bunch of irate Hawaiians in front of the bar saw him and began to give chase. Whooping with exhaustion, Zef ran down the street, and still somehow found the dexterity to answer his phone.

"Smooth move, shithead. You just got us Custered."

"Custard? What the fok you mean, us? You better come back and pick me up..."

"Your friends aren't letting me turn around. Tell your uncle not to expect his deposit back."

The line went dead.

At the next intersection he saw nobody was chasing him, but off down the alley, he saw a shitload of random cars with blue lights parked around that same Lexus. Oh shit. He kept walking, totally casual, totally cool, and then he started running, because he heard motorcycles coming from everywhere but directly overhead, and then the drugs they put in his drink back at the bar started to kick in, and he forgot where he was going.

Then he forgot who he was.

Then he forgot that he was forgetting.

5

THE CALLING

"Maple syrup," he said. "Everything... that isn't something else... is maple syrup."

When Zef came to, or suddenly became able to think and act and remember, he was sitting in a booth in an Original Pancake House, mopping up the last traces of something he could just barely taste from a platter the size of a hubcap.

His brain and body convulsed like when the power comes on after a blackout, when all the lights and appliances kick in.

His mouth was full of food. It was running like he was talking to himself, but he had no idea what he'd just been talking about. It was like walking into a room where strangers stopped talking about you and just stared, waiting for you to leave.

Blood on his knuckles, and his right hand screamed a little when he did anything with it. His nose was still broken. His dummy wallet was gone from his hip pocket, but his lock picks, hotel key, billfold and his real ID were still in his shoes. His cash was light almost a hundred. Grime and mud on his pants and shirt, like he'd been rolling in the gutter, or worse.

Sun just coming up outside and the street was filled with rush hour traffic. About ten people, some of whom looked like they had jobs to go to, were still enjoying breakfast and the paper. A little round mailman at the table next to him was reading the *Advertiser's* local section. On the front page was a color picture of a car being hauled out of a canal by a crane while cops and firemen watched. The car was a red Shelby GT convertible. CHINATOWN STREET RACE TURNS DEADLY, said the headline.

Zef held out a dollar. "Yo, yo… lemme buy that paper off you…?"

The mailman turned away in his seat, wrinkling his nose. "They sell them up front. Get your own, yeah?"

Zef slouched out of the booth. The manager hovered around the door, smiling but fully expecting him to dine and dash.

"Yo," he said, "newspaper?"

The manager sold him one for a dollar. He found change in his front pocket and shook it out in his hand, then hid it and choked back puke.

Among the quarters and dimes and loose breath mints was a little silver barbell-shaped thing that was sticky with blood. He figured it must be some kind of nipple piercing, because it still had most of a man's nipple attached to it.

Also, he had never in his whole life seen these pants he was wearing. They were baggy houndstooth slacks with a cracked leather belt as slim as an extension cord. A thrift store tag was stapled to the zipper.

He wiped the blood off four quarters and took the paper. Reading the same way small children type, he stitched it together, but he had to go over it three times before he realized how little anyone else knew.

This sweet '69 Shelby GTO was doing "in excess of 90 MPH" westbound on North Kukui Street while racing with one or more motorcycles around eleven last night, when it broke the railing and went off the bridge into the Nu'uanu canal, taking one of the bikes (*oh fok no*) out with it. No bodies recovered, no survivors expected. The car was, oddly enough, not registered and had been inactive with the Hawaii DMV since 1989. HPD were hopeful that someone could ID the current owner. The motorcycle, a late-model Honda (*yes!*) was registered to an unidentified North Shore resident who reported it stolen a week ago.

Zef went to sit in his booth and only then noticed the used plates and coffee mug across from his.

He'd been eating with somebody, just before his brain started working again. Maybe two or three, by the extent of the wreckage.

The remains of an omelette and some blueberry pancakes and some sticky rice and Spam and some purple shit that looked like if you ate the sticky rice with some beet juice and then puked it up into a side dish.

Only one set of silverware, though. Big eater.

There was deep burgundy lipstick on the mug. *Zephyrus, you dog, you...*

A check was tucked under his plate. It was for forty-two bucks, and he only had thirty-three. Figuring there was a better than even chance he would get rolled or arrested last night, he'd only brought a hundred and forty bucks, and he didn't remember paying for anything at the... that place where he... did he sing a country song last night?

The last thing he remembered was that ugly private dick blowing him a kiss as someone put a microphone into his hand and he finished a drink...

Someone slipped him a fucking date-rape drug.

Looking around guiltily, he stuck his hand down the back of his unfamiliar pants. They came up stinking but not bloody and he appeared to still have both kidneys. Thank Christ for small favors.

He remembered... that grizzled, sleepy-eyed Hawaiian motherfucker sneering at him over the waitress's shoulder, like he knew.

Donny Punani.

It felt good to have an enemy.

When you had an enemy, someone who hated you as much as you hated them, you knew they were thinking about you. So you lived your life as if you could almost see each other by some kind of telepathic hate rapport, as if some curtain would occasionally pull back in their mind's eye and they'd see you when you were living extra large. It forced you to step up and take shots you never would, otherwise.

To show them.

It was what would make him get his shit together right there. He didn't have enough to pay the bill. The manager was already on his ass. Whoever ate all this food already skipped. He doubted he had a car outside. He would just have to run for it. Head for the restroom, just past the cashier counter, and hit the doors and sprint for the far side of the parking lot.

Easy. Simple. *So get up and do it.*

Suddenly, he found himself sitting in a deep, dark shadow, and cold... He shivered and slid out of the booth with his eye on the front door. He ran right into Peapea's belly.

He fell back into the booth.

Kewalo slid into the seat across from him.

"One thing about Hawaiians, yeah? For real, we the only Polynesian people who gamble. Our *aumakua*, you know, our ancestors? They bet on everything, and they take it *too* serious. Like, *Aztec* serious, you know?" He drew his finger across his throat, pointing to Zef's gold chain hanging around it, and grinned. Too many teeth for two mouths, stuffed into dead gray pincushion gums.

The giant's stomach made angry dog noises. Kewalo picked at the purple shit on the plate and passed Peapea a menu. "Bet their lives on surfing contests. Loser get cut up for sacrifice, maybe baked alive in an oven. Some say we pick it up from Japanese fishermen, but that a lot of shit. We learn it from our gods, I promise."

"Um, yeah," Zef said, "listen..."

"You owe Kewalo one hundred dollar," said Peapea.

"Bullshit... Look, that was just... yo, we were fokkin' high as shit..." He pointed at the necklace and bling around Kewalo's neck. "Anyway, we're fokking even right there. Where'd you get my fokking chain?"

Kewalo fondled his bling and grinned crooked teeth, all canines. Weren't half of them gold before? "Ocean gave it to me. Now, for the last time, I promise—"

The harried-looking waiter came back over. Peapea growled at him in Hawaiian and he wrote it down. Kewalo said, "And one country breakfast, yeah? Don't burn my Spam, brah. Put it on his tab." He slid Zef's check across the table.

"And more coffee," Zef said, "fokking fresh and hot, this time, please." When he was gone, Zef leaned in close and said, "Yo, I don't have the cash on me right now. I was out late drinking and like, I hooked up with, like… this hot bitch… but I can—"

"We can take you to your hotel," Kewalo said. "Where you staying?"

"I… Yo, look… I'm just a little prick with, like, a shitty job, like, on vacation… I was just fokking around on the beach… I'm not rich, I'm not looking to start trouble…"

"Please," Kewalo said, leaning forward to whisper, "*start trouble*. We *love* trouble."

Peapea added, "We *eat* trouble."

The waiter came back and reached around Peapea to fill Zef's coffee cup. He was still foggy in the head, but the narrow window of opportunity was like sunlight in his eyes.

Grabbing the waiter's wrist and twisting it, Zef upended the coffee pot and dashed the piping hot coffee in Peapea's face.

Peapea rolled out of the booth squealing. Kewalo reached across the table, then jerked back when the hot coffee splashed him. Out the corner of his eye, Zef saw the cantaloupe orange laminate surface of the table shred and fly apart under Kewalo's palm like a belt sander had gone over it. Kewalo jumped up and stabbed at him with his fork as Zef tried to get out of the booth. Zef smashed the coffee pot in his face. The tempered glass shattered on his chin. A backhanded swipe with the jagged edge gave his screaming face a harelip.

Zef leapt out of the booth and threw his shoulder into the groin of the roaring, blinded giant. Peapea sat down hard on the next table and it collapsed onto the mailman's lap. Zef threw the rest of his change and the pierced nipple on the table and bounded for the exit. His crazy legs were a blur. Linoleum tiles ripped off the floor and flipped away under his heels, but he went nowhere. A huge, brown horny hand was wrapped around his ankle.

Still roaring, still apparently blind, Peapea jerked Zef off his feet and snapped him like a locker room towel in the greasy air, then smashed him to the floor and dragged him backwards.

Zef mule-kicked Peapea in the face, grabbed a chair and smashed it over his head. The cheap aluminum chair bent and flew apart. Anything and everything he could grab, he threw—silverware, menus, plate shards, napkin holders. The Eureka moment came and went almost unnoticed. A syrup jug broke on Peapea's forearm and cheap imitation maple syrup sloshed out, covering his skin. Suddenly, he simply let Zef go.

Zef crabbed backwards away from the giant, almost paralyzed by what he was seeing.

Peapea spastically bit into his own arm like he meant to eat it. His eyes rolled back in his head, the sugar somehow pushing out all awareness of the outside world and the fight he was in.

Kewalo was under no such influence. The table parted like balsa wood and he came running. The mailman tried to grab him by the arm, screaming, "Hey, this ain't right…" then he fell down holding a wet red mitten to his chest.

The manager cowered behind the register, screaming into the phone. Zef hit the doors and ran for the parking lot.

A couple classic Harleys were parked at the curb. Their steering locks weren't on. He thought about jumping on one and riding off when an old mail delivery Jeep covered in bumper stickers swerved into the lot and crashed into both bikes.

"God damn it, why didn't you follow me, you stupid *haole*?" A husky Hawaiian grandmother leaned out of the wrong-side driver's seat and pulled him into the Jeep. She wore burgundy lipstick.

Kewalo came boiling out the door of the pancake house and sprinted across the lot after the Jeep. Zef tumbled into the back and rolled in a mound of rotten flowers. The overripe perfume outraged his nose like a long feather shoved down his ticklish throat, and something underneath it was so ripe he almost puked up his breakfast. A big canine travel carrier sat amidst the junk piled against the back doors, with a smaller one on top of it. Something inside the smaller one was clucking, while the bigger one was the source of the smell.

"You one stupid fucking operator, you know," said the local lady he apparently just had breakfast with.

He was all set to rank her out, when he remembered seeing her before. She was the one who slapped Donny

Punani at the karaoke bar. Holy shit, all he wanted was the fucking motorcycle and a satisfactory bowel movement...

The Jeep swerved off the street and into the parking lot for a beach. *Kewalo Waterfront Park*, it said. *No shit.*

"This is where they used to drown the *kauwa*..."

He looked around, at an ocean liner and harbor cruise boats docked at a pier and a clipper ship that was a nautical museum. "The what, now?"

"The outcasts." She killed the engine and wrung her hands. She was short and he didn't want to say fat, but her curves would have made a goddess of a taller woman. Zef knew he had a sickness for the thickness, but could he have gotten so out of his head...?

"You think this a pretty place," she said, "with pretty, simple people. Like the Indians back home, but dumber. You think this one big theme park. You come take what you want and leave a mess and we just sweep it into the sea, no problem, yeah?"

"I don't know what you're talking about, uh, ma'am... I'm just, uh, here on vacation, and... yo, seriously, thanks for picking me up back there, but... Like, don't take this the wrong way, but... Do I know you? Like..."

"It still hasn't wore off, yeah? Cut the shit, I know why you're here. You let some shit slip when I picked you up."

He shook his head, punching his stupid brain. "Listen, I was fokking flying last night. Somebody..."

"They do that to tourists, sometimes. But you walked right into his face. Either you one stupid motherfucker, or you the one who's gonna do it."

He said, "Do what?" but she didn't hear. She jumped out of the Jeep and opened the back. She dragged the carriers out and then pulled the tarp out onto the tarmac, and then she took out a big, cheap Styrofoam bodyboard. "You can help, you know…" When he reached for the carriers, she nudged him away and gave him a shovel.

They dragged the pile to the edge of the lot and across the lumpy lawn to the rocks jumbled up at the edge of the water.

The lady looked around, muttering under her breath so Zef thought *shit, she's a crazy bitch*, but she was chanting something in Hawaiian. She opened the big carrier and a little black pot-bellied pig trotted out. She caught it by the collar before it could escape. She did something with her hands in front of its face, and it stood there like a windup toy.

Zef was standing by, too, waiting for the right moment to beg off and walk away, wondering just what he must've told this lady. "So you know him pretty well…yeah?"

She unrolled the tarp and threw an armload of flowers into the sea. "Get to work, already," she said.

"Doing what? I don't—"

"What you think the shovel is for? Start digging." He started digging a hole where she pointed, looking around for cops. This was some sort of voodoo bullshit, but weren't you supposed to do animal sacrifices in the dark?

"Blood made nature tame in these islands, long before any white people came. Blood made the gods our slaves. Up on Punchbowl," she pointed at a hill directly inland from where they stood, "there was a great heiau—a temple, you know—where people were sacrificed to keep the seasons turning.

"Now shut up." Kneeling on the rocks, she started chanting a little louder, but still way deep down in her throat. She set the bodyboard on the gently pulsing water and piled rotten flowers on it, making a bed. Then she put the pig on the bodyboard. They watched the tide pull the raft out over the aquamarine sea, and then a whirlpool sucked it out of sight, pig and all.

"Hey, goddammit, what the fok—"

She turned and her hand whipped out like she was going to slap him, but landed on his face like a hummingbird to cover his mouth. "You need to stop saying that."

Her hands smelled like flower perfume and pig shit. "What, goddammit—"

"That. You go around calling it down like that." She stopped, still staring into his eyes for a moment, and then her head cocked like she was looking down a hole. "You were all over it, like one hour ago. What happened?"

He looked around like he had somewhere else to go. "Fok you, whatever…"

"You better fix your attitude before it gets you killed. Gimme that shovel." She jammed it into the turf and ripped it out. The earth underneath was redder than blood.

"Anybody who don't like my attitude can…"

She finished digging the hole and opened the smaller container. She reached in and took out a red hen. "This part is for you, stupid. Hold out your hands."

He looked at her, thinking, *Fok you, peace out*, but when she locked eyes with him, he couldn't walk away. He held out his hands and let her put the hen in them.

He gritted his teeth, expecting her to take out a knife and cut its throat or something, but that was Santeria... Mexicans did that, but what did Hawaiians do? Everybody but honkies had black magic to protect them from honkies...

Chanting, she did that thing with her hands that was over before he noticed it, and the chicken just sat still like his palms made a fine nest.

"What the fok...?"

"Put it in the hole."

He looked down. It was a chicken-sized hole, about two feet deep. "No way..."

Do it, or you not getting Number One massage."

"So what? I didn't want a..."

"Or your drugs."

He grumbled, but he put the hen in the hole. It stood there stock-still, staring straight ahead while he shoveled dirt on it and tamped it down and covered it with the displaced chunks of turf.

She chanted something else and bowed to the ocean, then picked up the animal carriers and scurried back to the Jeep.

Zef followed, circling round and climbing in on the wrong side and the smell without the flowers was like a porta-shitter in summer. He would've walked, but where would he walk to? Catch a cab, but then he would never find out what was up with this witch—

He leaned forward and rested his head on the dashboard. A bumper sticker on it commanded, COOK RICE, NOT ICE.

"Everything out here is attitude, fool. That not a line to sell surfwear, I promise. And attitude isn't about swinging your *ule* in the world's face." She slammed the Jeep into gear and gunned the engine to make it buck and leap the curb before she wrestled it into the street. "This new land, yeah? Bubbled up out of the ocean yesterday, in the big scheme. Islands got made one at a time. Oldest, Nihau, is seventy million years old, and already going back to the ocean. The big island still getting made. When a place is old, it's marked by all what happened in it... but when a place is so new... no lie, there's still magic here.

"If you belong to it, then it'll act like a live thing. It don't like anger, and it *hates* fear. Islands *love* to punish fear. You think island people go around smiling all the time, happy and gay because we love you *haole* fuckers fucking up our home? It because you can't be negative here, fool. Bad attitude like a lightning rod in a storm and it's always raining somewhere.

"The people here almost two thousand years ago, they didn't wear no clothes, and they didn't worry about who was making babies, but before long, they had *kapu* everywhere. Some fish kapu for women, some only the *alii* could eat. Places only the *alii* and the priests could go. The smoke from the temple pass over your shadow, you got to die. Every temple had a *mu*, who had to find the sacrifices. Any excuse, he trap a body for to cut up for the gods. We not stay cannibals, but our gods were hungry."

"Yo, this, all this… I don't, uh, know…"

"You don't know history, do you? When they came out here, the missionaries, there were four hundred thousand of us, and just a couple hundred of you, but within forty years, there were only eighty thousand of us left, and the missionaries' kids owned all the land. Wasn't no war…just muumuus and smallpox, the white god and all his laws, and the white way of life. They came preaching sin and death and didn't know their words out here were magic. Death magic worse than germs, worse than alcohol and Spam and Mickey D's.

"Lot of Hawaiians still believe in one god, but when they need something done on this side of the grave, they still leave treats for the *menehune*, they still make offerings to the gods."

"You keep telling me all this shit, but I don't, uh… I don't think I'm gonna need it, to…"

"You don't need to believe, but if you don't respect it, if you don't fear it a little in your head, then in your heart, when you see what you're really into, you gonna remember what I said."

He squirmed in the seat, wondering if he shouldn't jump out and run for it, when she turned and took his hand. "I trying to help you."

"Great, that's great… Just… I never work with help… but I'm totally down to do this job…"

"So, how you going to do it?"

"Um, what?"

"How you wen kill him?"

He bit his lip and looked away. Shit, what did he tell her when he was blacked out? The idea that he'd been up and around and bullshitting fat old chicks and ripping off nipples for several hours with no memory of it made his asshole eat his jockeys.

"I need to know more about him first," Zef said, "like... is he into drugs? Does he like to party?"

The sigh she let out went on for a minute and left her an inch shorter. They stopped in the turnaround in front of the Illikoi.

She said, "You don't know what they were, back at the pancake house?"

He got out of the Jeep and turned to walk away, but then leaned in the window. "They're nobody."

She snapped her fingers in his face. "You don't wise up, you just one sacrifice. Feed his fat belly, that don't never get full."

He said, "Yo, listen..."

"Shut up, or I knock you down, I promise." She gunned the engine and lurched forward, but then stopped. "You should go home. Whatever you think you wen do... he going to eat you up."

"Alright, great, thanks! I like you, really, but like, I think we should see other people..."

A valet came over and offered to take the Jeep. Zef feigned like he was going to punch him and the guy went away.

"You got like a shadow or something riding you. It wasn't there before." She made gestures like a crazy person, or like somebody casting a hex. "You go catch bus and pack bag, but you not get your money back."

His hand went to his cash, which was still light a hundred dollars. "What'd I pay you for, yo? I get paid for what I do on ladies your age..."

She spat out a bug. "Not! I not a whore, stupid *haole*. You paid for Number One *lomi lomi*, fix your problem."

"Well I don't remember any of my problems getting fixed…" He stepped to her in a halfass boxer's stance. "You owe me some fucking *lomi*, yo."

"You get yours so good you shit your pants, *haole* boy!" She caught his hand in an odd grip, like they were going to thumb-wrestle. She pressed her thumb into the back of his hand hard and hit some mysterious button that cut the bloodflow and nervous control to his legs like a karate chop to the kidneys. He swayed and almost sat down when she released him.

As the Jeep peeled out of the turnaround, Zef was doubled over by a shooting pain in his gut.

Legs wobbly, he ran for the elevator and jumped in with a Korean newlywed couple. Bent over in the corner with his back to them, he clenched his asscheeks together, but it was starting to come.

The newlyweds hit the emergency stop and got off on the second floor. Weeping, Zef banged his head on the door until it opened. He waved his shoe with the key in it at the door, ran into the room and dropped on the toilet.

The bellhop came running to the room with his cell phone, ready to call the cops or paramedics at a moment's notice, calling out, "Sir, you alright?" when he waded into a brown wall of stench like a river in monsoon season. He turned and fled, holding back vomit with his fingers.

Zef DeGroot screamed, "TOUCHDOWN!"

6

DEAD MAN'S HEAD

Running the fan and the shower to cut the smell, he lifted a rubber tube, nine inches long and an inch in diameter, out of the bowl; a double-hulled condom stuffed to ribbed rigidity with Schedule 1 psychoactive substances.

All the shit he'd gone through, from the indignity of inserting it into his rectum and the ensuing, deeply humiliating multiple orgasms, and the fear that it would burst open or work its way back up to his stomach and dissolve, unloading enough MDMA in him at once to make a dubstep rave bearable, to the ungodly yellow mess of it coating him up to his elbow. All of that was behind him now, already eager to be forgotten.

He checked the room for any signs someone had been there in his absence... like himself. But nothing seemed different, except for the general tidiness, the made bed and the purple orchid on his pillow.

He changed into trunks and went down the back stairs to the pool. His neighbors laughed and made hysterical Chinese hooker noises when he passed by.

The drunks in the swim-up bar told everyone who sat in their pee about his exploits. "*Don't shit in the pool, too, pally!*"

When he didn't know what else to do, he went back up to his room and did a whole lot of pushups and thought about throwing the TV in the pool. He didn't even know what he was thinking. So he called the one person who always knew.

"Enjoying your sabbatical, boy?"

"Dad, yo… It's alright…"

"Hula girls give you the clap yet? You remember never to leave your wallet—"

"Dad! I'm here to work…"

"And yet you overindulged on your first night, and you've done regrettable things. And now you're sitting on the loo because one of those regrettable things is in your bed."

Geezer always knew. His mates wouldn't play poker with him. Back in South Africa, he never even needed to beat the truth out of the blacks. He just did it to keep up appearances. "It's a flash bike, y'know, but this fokker is hard to pin down, and I don't know the town—"

"Harv said he had retained a local authority. Did you alienate him already?"

"No, he… uh, like…" What could he say on a cell line? "This guy, right, he up and left *me*. I think he's scared, right?"

"And now *you're* scared."

"Erm… Nooo…"

"And thinking you can't fulfill your contract because this client will always be one step ahead of you, until he gets irritated enough to kill you."

"Yo, I'm not afraid of nothing…"

"Alright, fine. Did 'nothing' break your nose?"

"No, it was…I wiped out surfing…"

"So you are getting some vacation in. So wonderful that, even on such a difficult assignment, you're finding the time to enjoy yourself at Harv's expense."

"I didn't…it's not like I wanted to…"

"You think you've got difficulties, you don't even know. This cont Zweibel…"

"Your boss…?"

"He's not my fokking boss, boy. He was a client, and now he's a headache. Jumped off the roof of his own casino, as if he had any real problems—but now he is *my* problem, because his security cameras went to shit right before he jumped, and the fokking police are crawling up my ass to cover their own fok-up. These cocksockers wouldn't survive a day patrol in Soweto. Lost track of half the Jew's head, and trying to make something more out of it than it is."

Like a magnet, Joorgen DeGroot had pulled his son's thoughts into a neat alignment. He knew what to do, but not how to get his father off the phone.

"Look, Dad…I got a masseuse coming, so I gotta get in the shower. You know how those bitches…"

He bit his favorite bait. "They'll pick your bones clean, those despicable whores… You know, one fokking time, Harv and I—"

The phone trilled in his ear, drowning out Dad's rambling. "Look Dad, someone's ringing through."

"Oh, that's fine then, but mind your wallet and watch out for Bat-Kaffir, boy—"

He should call Primo. Show some initiative. Don't wait for that punk to put him on island time. Take the bull—

His phone rang again. It was Primo.

"Yo—"

"I'm real pissed you stood me up last night."

"I did what? I didn't even—"

Last night.

Fok.

"I don't know who you talked to last night, but it wasn't me… I mean, I was mad fucked up, like…"

"Well, you got one chance and you fucked up royal, you know?"

"Yeah, I, um…" Was it a pimp move to apologize to Hawaiians? Apologizing was almost universally for pussies. "Listen, yo… I don't need this shit from you, if you don't want to do business…"

"Twelve."

"What?"

"If you still want to sell to me, that's all I'm paying, I promise."

"Oh, fok you! Listen, I got fokking doped at—"

"Like I care. Tonight, same place at eleven…"

"Yo, what place? Shit, I don't remember, and I don't see how you called me…"

"You called me, dipshit, from a fucking pay phone in Chinatown."

"OK… where do we meet?"

"Punchbowl, on the overlook. Don't fuckin' forget again, brah, or I won't forget *you*, I promise."

"And I promise *you*, broo—" Zef started, but he was ranting at a dial tone.

He flopped on the bed and turned on the TV. A fat native guy—Jesus, the fattest guy he'd ever seen—was singing Hawaii's favorite song, a cover of *It's A Wonderful World* where the big dope forgets the words and starts mangling the Wizard Of Oz song. Zef cut a hole in the condom and started counting out tablets into his palm. He fell asleep before he got to forty.

They threw him out of the hotel bar and he was cruising the deserted moonlit beach wasted. He was naked, but he found hats, sunglasses, snorkels and flippers and tourist shit everywhere. He wrapped himself in a hotel towel, picked up a Titleist golf cap to find a skull underneath, half-buried in the ice-white sand.

He couldn't go off the beach, for someone was waiting for him in the alleys between the looming, windowless tombstone hotels. The black glass surf pounded up the shore to smash into a palisade of sinking sand. Zef walked along the eroded edge, looking for his pants. The cold wind stung him with flung sand, scouring his naked ass. He picked up a surfer's shirt, but it clung to the sand, wet and filled with driftwood bones. A human ribcage.

Slipping on the shirt, he stumbled along the seawall, thinking, *this is no place for a vacation*, until it crumbled under him and he rolled ass-over-head into the mud. Sinking into frigid quicksand, he clawed at the wall but only pulled it down on his head, burying himself waist-deep in instant concrete, and the wave was coming and the wind so cold blew down from the dark side of the moon, and the sound so loud, he couldn't hear his own screams when he looked back and the wave rearing up behind him was not a wave at all, but a vast cavern of teeth.

He got three Red Bull and vodkas in and went out in the Mustang. He cruised the beaches and the clubs and got as far west as Pearl City and found no Punani before he had to go to Punchbowl.

The spot was the same as in every town with enough young single people living with their parents; an unlit dead-end road with a soft shoulder or a parking lot and a view of the lights, where the cops didn't come by too often and everybody was too busy to mind anyone else's business. Fourteen cars and a couple monster trucks were lined up and discreetly spaced, facing the city and the sea.

It seemed like a good place to meet, until he actually pulled into it and turned off his engine. Almost ten minutes early because for a change he was actually able to find the place without losing his shit and throwing the map out the window.

The radio was tuned to a reggae station, the least annoying thing he could find on the radio, the lazy-tongued singer warning him that love is contagious. The cars on either side of him had their windows fogged up. He reclined his seat. He didn't want to get out and go peering in at fat *wahines* getting drilled by pimply flat sailors' asses.

This was only one of the many reasons Zef never tried to make a career or even a hobby of dealing drugs, the primary one being that his Dad would literally kick him to death. Somehow, whether you were buying or selling, you always ended up waiting. In the repo game, you often had to stake out a debtor's place, but it was a whole different situation when you were the hunter.

He called Primo.

On the fifth ring, "What?" Deep, labored breathing. It didn't sound like Primo came alone.

"I'm here... Is this Primo?"

A low, long growling chuckle. "For shuah, brah."

"Where are you?"

"You figure it out, I promise." Laughing, he hung up.

Zef stuck the bag of pills down his shirt and tucked his shirt into his track pants.

It didn't take a detective to figure it out. The iridescent green Nissan Cube seven cars away had vanity plates: PRIMO1. It was one of those boxy minivans that looked like a French police truck. Lights and engine off, stereo playing the same reggae song pretty loud, all triple-tinted windows rolled up. Primo was slumped forward against his steering wheel with his head at a funny angle, like he was puking on the floorboards, or getting some head.

Zef tapped on the hood as he went around the front of the Cube, opened the door and climbed into the passenger seat. A palpable cloud of stale pot smoke spilled out like snow.

He knew something was wrong before he reached over and turned on the light. It was such a powerful flash that he almost just got out and walked away, but what the fuck was he going to do with this shit? He couldn't just put it on Craigslist or cram it back up his asshole when he went home.

He turned the light off.

Even in the dark, he could still see it. Probably always would.

Primo's neck was snapped. The jaunty angle of his head and discoloration around his throat looked like he'd gotten whiplash while breaking the sound barrier in a jet. And his face was gone.

The skin and most of his facial muscle was flayed cleanly off his head in a starburst shape—but really, it was the shape of a hand, the stripes of naked skull on the forehead corresponding to a set of fingers. His naked eyes, stripped of lids, stared wonderingly at him as if waiting for the answer to a Really Big Question. It looked as if someone had simply ripped his face off with one sweep of a razor-clawed hand.

He was starting to get out when he saw the blue light flashing, way off down at the end of the line of cars. A cop sat in the driver's seat of a pimped-out El Camino while his partner went down the line peeking in windows with a big flashlight.

Right now, he was looking into Zef's empty Mustang and wondering what the fuck. The road ended at a trail that went up into the shaggy green hills above Honolulu. He could report his car stolen, but there was no getting out. If he took off now in the Cube, they'd pull him over. Even if he ditched the tabs, he'd have a shitload of fun trying to explain the faceless dead drug dealer whose car he'd stolen.

The cop walked on to the next car, knocking on the roof with his light and giving a big thumbs-up.

Do you want to go out like this? he asked himself.

Do you have a better idea?

And just then, he had a perfectly horrible idea.

Primo must've been dead when his face was torn off, because the steering wheel and dashboard were only dappled with blood. Most of it had pooled in his lap and on the black rubber floormats.

Work fast. He got up and dragged Primo into the passenger seat. The Hawaiian was big, but he was able to do it once panic set in, though something in his back and something else in his abdomen snapped like cheap shoestrings.

Sitting in the pool of cool, half-clotted blood in the driver's seat and trying to look relaxed took a whole different kind of resolve.

The cop was only two cars away.

Zef kicked off his shoes and ripped off his socks, used them to wipe the blood off the steering wheel, then rolled them up and stuffed them in his pocket.

The cop was looking into the next car.

Zef lifted his hips off the blood-slick seat and slid his track pants down to his knees. The best disguise is something nobody wants to look at.

The cop tapped on his window.

"Go away!" Zef shouted. "It's a free fokking country, ain't it?"

"Roll down your window, sir. You've got nothing I haven't seen before…"

Zef cranked the window halfway down and handed over his license.

The cop choked up. "Put that shit away, I don't want to fucking know you."

"Do you mind, officer?" Zef put his hand on the back of Primo's head, which was buried in Zef's lap. Shivering with terror and barely-contained panic, he made Primo's head bounce in his lap as if he was hard at work, and tried to look like a man getting a blowjob.

"You're over eighteen, right?"

"I'm twenty-four, and, um... so's he." Zef rolled his hips to make Primo's head nod. "He's, uh, pretty wasted, like... but like, he's not gonna drive."

The cop's nostrils flared, hoovering up the pot smell. He flicked the flashlight over the Cube's interior, clearly not wanting to see anything more. "Goddamn perverts," the cop mumbled.

"Yo, we're not doing nothing they're not doing. It's all just love, yo..."

The cop's furrowed brow and sunken, lost look made Zef forget the cold, dead man's face seeping blood into his crotch. "Shut up, fucko." In a local tone, he shouted, "After all she got to deal with, Primo, I just hope yo auntie not find out. Nice night," he said. He went to the next car.

Zef watched him walk away. It took a year off his life, every second he let Primo rest on him. His jockeys were soaked through with tacky, lukewarm blood, his hoodie plastered to his chest with sweat.

Only when the cop was in his own car did he try to move. His legs had gone to sleep. His fingers were cold and clumsy. Primo slipped out of his lap and fell facedown on the floor between the seats.

Tears tried to come out when he ripped off his pants and shucked off his boxers. He looked around for something to put them in, but the car was clean. Primo had no wallet on him, certainly no envelope with his money in it.

"How're you gonna fok me now, Lord?" he asked the ceiling.

Two or three cars pulled out and took off. The cops in the El Camino finally kicked on their lights and rolled. "Go home, Primo," he shouted as they passed, then turned down Nuuanu Road to Honolulu.

Fok me, the cop knew him, his auntie and shit. He'd sure remember the face of the stranger Primo was blowing, when they found Primo's faceless corpse. This was so much worse than getting caught with drugs. This was just… The whole thing was supposed to be so easy… just a quick meet and he'd make some extra scratch. It was hardly Scarface; just some pocket money, who would kill over something like that? How could his luck have gone so fucking bad, since he came here?

He took a deep breath of the fresh night air from the open window. The Cube smelled like Primo must've shit his board shorts. The weed stench was familiar— pungent like overripe fruit and brown flowers, and it was so familiar because he'd smelled it and smoked it only yesterday.

Pineapple—

Old-school strain, yeah, but we made it bionic—

Zef flashed on the scene at the pancake house. Kewalo's hand shredding the laminate off the table like his hands were made of razors…

Zef climbed out of the Cube and walked around behind the other cars to the Mustang. He climbed in and stuffed his bloody socks and underwear into a McDonalds bag in the passenger footwell.

The car started right up. Peter Tosh wanted to legalize it. Burglars shot him dead in his house in Jamaica. Burglars in the Caribbean traditionally went to work naked and covered in grease or chicken fat, so nobody could catch them. Anything on earth was only a fleeting refuge from what he was living through.

He drove well below whatever the speed limit was. An oncoming car flashed its brights at him. He swerved and hit the gas, whimpering with panic until he figured out his lights were off.

He had to pull over to cry. It wasn't some sissy thing at all, but full-on thunderous soul-rending *crying*. His hand found the bag filled with MDMA in his shirt and he pulled it out. He wanted to chuck it into the canyon plunging into blackness just beyond the shoulder of the road. Wanted to forget the whole thing, maybe forget the Harley, too.

And that's when the cop pulled up behind him and blipped his siren.

"Oh fok, no no no." He twisted in his seat, looking at the lights, kicking the sack of bloody clothes under the seat and the bag stuffed with Ecstasy was suddenly very heavy, twenty to life in the palm of his hand, and the bag of bloody underclothes just gravy, if they could pin it on him. Thank God this wasn't in Nevada, where they still did lethal injection…

"STEP OUT OF THE CAR, PLEASE," said an amplified old cop's voice.

His body knew what to do to save itself, even if his mind still couldn't accept that this was happening. With a disturbing feeling of routine, he leaned forward and slid his hands down and grabbed his pants.

"NOW, SIR," said the cop.

Zef slowly got out, wiping off his hands with a moist towelette thoughtfully provided by National Car Rental. It was a different cop in a Camry, Asian and older than his Dad.

The cop looked at his ID, gave him a desultory pat-down and shone his flashlight under the seats.

"This car was reported abandoned up at the Punchbowl," he said.

"I was, like… hiking, you know. I got lost." The key to lying to cops was not to go overboard inventing shit. You'd only cross yourself up. Keep it simple. *I was trying to sell drugs, and the guy I was meeting got murdered by some Hawaiians who think I owe them money from a stupid bet.*

"Shouldn't go hiking alone. Or parking, either," he said with a brief gesture that might be stifling a yawn or miming a blowjob. "Have a nice night, sir."

7
MULLET WATER

The rain shut Honolulu up tight. He rolled over and over in bed until the sheet wound around him so he couldn't get out when the tidal wave sirens started up. He got up when the people running past his door started screaming.

It was hot outside, but the rain was cold, and came down in dense gray sheets that ran in his eyes in streams and overfilled his pockets. The people were running into streets choked with cars, headed for higher ground but going nowhere, waiting for the tidal wave. Zef raided the minibar, shotgunning the tiny vodka shooters and hell, the tequila and the gin, too, since he was going to die before he threw up, anyway.

The wave still caught everybody with their pants down. It came down from the hills at their backs. It came rushing down from Diamond Head and all the rust-red, mansion-encrusted mountains overlooking Waikiki in a roaring red floodtide that combed the tourists out of the traffic jams and sluiced them out of the hotel ghettos like fleas, swept them out of the shopping malls and swimming pools and into the sea, where the sharks packed the churning water so densely you could almost walk across them.

He was laughing his ass off at this jackoff who rode his Waverunner into the lobby and got boxed in by a swarm of hammerheads. He leaned out over the balcony to see what happened to the idiot when the whole railing sagged under him, struts popping out of sodden, substandard concrete to dump him into the red flood and he thrashed around in the water trying to get onto a second-floor balcony when both of his legs were jerked out from under him in opposing directions. Two sharks had him, and they split him like a wishbone.

He jerked awake to sirens. He leapt out of bed and crouched in the doorway before the smoke overtook him. Coughing and sicking up on himself as he crawled for the door, he tried to remember if he smoked anything, lit any candles, did anything that could have burned the place down... and came up blank.

Did it happen again? Did he black out? He remembered...

Oh Christ, he thought, as it all came back. The dream with the sharks had been better. Tied into a drug dealer's murder in the worst possible way, on the cops' radar as a sex tourist sleazebag, and after much ballyhoo and tribulations, the sack of Ecstasy had found its way back to its home in his colon. His last memory before passing out was drunkenly trying to rip the weird coat hangers out of the closet to make a hook to pull the big dildo made of drugs out his asshole.

His room wasn't on fire, but it was filled with smoke. When he tried to open the door, the palm of his hand practically came off on the knob. Red fucking hot. The door was on fire, on the outside. Swearing, Zef dove out the window and into the corridor.

Two bellhops and a manager-type and a security guard were standing by the door, all of them holding phones except for the security guard, who was spraying a fire extinguisher at the burning door.

Zef was in his jockeys and a tank top. The palm of his hand screamed agony so bright and pure it emptied his mind. He held his mutilated hand out to the manager, who shook his head, unable to look at Zef as he pressed an itemized bill into the smoking blisters. "Just get out before the fire department gets here, and we won't press charges, okay? Aloha."

Getting his bags down to the rental car and peeling out of the lot, he berserkered into the dazed Waikiki traffic fully expecting a souped-up hot rod with a blue dome light on the roof to cut him off and the cops to drag him out and cuff him and, after a brief, thoroughly professional interrogation, throw him into a volcano. How many local celebrities' untimely and fucked up deaths could he get away with being involved in?

And *why* was he involved? None of this shit had anything to do with the job. He came out here to get a fucking motorcycle and turn it in at a tow yard in Pearl City, get paid and go home. He could still do that. He could still do his fucking job... couldn't he?

* * *

He parked in a mall lot off the street and checked his map while he slathered anesthetic cream and bandages on his toasted hand from the first aid kit thoughtfully provided by the rental company.

If anyone asked, Zef would say he ran down the skip trace himself, but he owed his breakthrough to a phone call that woke him up last night.

"He's in Waianae, dumbshit, on the leeward side, if you're still looking."

Zef was still rubbing his eyes and pinching his nipples. "Who the fok…?"

"He's getting a tattoo tomorrow. Should be there all day. Take the bike then. Do it before tonight."

"Jimmy? Yo, like—"

Dial tone.

The snarl of traffic around downtown was like a kiddie pool version of real urban traffic, but they'd made all the worst urban planning mistakes on a smaller scale. Outside Honolulu, the urban landscape subsided into the same kind of creepy mass-produced sprawl that choked Las Vegas half to death. Costco, outlet malls, waterslide parks and tan tract homes with fake tile roofs shit out on grids with putting green lawns and two or three SUVs or monster trucks blocking every driveway. The rust-red dust all over everything made it look like the suburbs of Mars.

When even that had fallen behind, the northern mountains pivoted to the east and the last traces of green disappeared, except for the golf courses. Suddenly, it looked more like Nevada than Nevada did. If he didn't look to his left and the infinite blue horizon, it could be Palm Springs or the Australian outback. He thought tropical islands were supposed to be tropical, with banana trees and perfumed flowers and shit. It made sense this was the part they'd let the natives keep.

Waianae looked like a seaside Indian reservation, the sad kind without a casino. The churches were Pentecostal and Adventist and looked like rocketships or waffle houses. The cars were all shitty and ten years old, at least; the houses were tin-roofed drywall and cinderblock shacks and trucks with ramshackle camper shells on the beaches. Some dumb Hawaiian law said you could camp on the beach here, if you were *kama'aina*, local.

He buzzed a public basketball court and watched some guys playing way too hard for a pickup ball. Bodies slammed in midair, war-whoops were cut short by larynx-crushing elbows. He had to honk twice to get their attention.

Two motherfuckers had those weird spiral tattoos on their faces, and flicked their tongues at him like fucking snakes. The rest popped knuckles and ground their teeth, tears of venom dripping from their poverty-hardened bodies. Yeah, this was gangster country.

"Can any of you guys make change for a hundred, and tell me how to get to the Makaha Valley Country Club?"

They came after him like he was pussy. He let them reach the parking lot before reversing the Mustang and laying a patch and flipping a bootlegger reverse and standing the car up on its front wheels in a brutal braking maneuver that actually caused two of the pursuing basketball players to crash into the back bumper.

Zef peeled out cackling like Woody Woodpecker on nitrous and ran the red light to turn north on Farrington Highway, cutting off a trash truck.

Reconning downtown Waianae didn't take but a few minutes, and before he was even sure he had ditched the basketball court gang, he had cause to look in the rearview mirror and kiss himself.

Da Hui Tattoo Parlor was a cinderblock bungalow on a side street with no sidewalks and wild dogs slinking in the gutters. Between Ahuna's Party Rentals (2 FA 1 XMAS BONCE HOUS3 SP8CIAL!) and a Bible college. A line of bikes was parked in front, a blinding picket line of chrome and custom paint jobs. A couple locals were sitting on a bench on the front porch of the place with a trash bag from McDonald's between them. He noticed one of them glaring at him before he recognized them.

At least he knew it was the right place.

Peapea pointed at him, rubbing his gut with his other hand the way some guys polished their Camaros in their driveways on a Sunday afternoon. If he was any good at reading lips, Zef distinctly made out the words, *Get in my belly, haole boy.*

Zef DeGroot was working on his own tattoo when he heard the unmistakable seismic growl of the vintage Harley. Lying on his side on a grimy futon with a mirror propped against the cinderblock wall to see the work in progress on his tailbone, he was almost finished with his masterpiece, and nothing else would have broken his bubble of perfect concentration.

The needle skipped and stabbed a Hitler mustache on the angel's beatific face. "Fok me," DeGroot snarled, but he leapt off the futon and peeked through the blinds.

The plate didn't match, but the bike itself was more familiar to DeGroot than the taste of his own dick, as was the slope-browed profile of the motherfucker who straddled it, rolling a cigarette and soaking up the giggling worship of the tubby wahines who came out of the hotel bar.

Donny Punani was back.

One at a time, he took them round the parking lot, their drunken war-whoops like a seasick siren while the others shrieked and burnt each other with cigarettes.

They were all very impressed with the bike. But none of them knew. Maybe Donny didn't even know about what Zef DeGroot had found out, today. It had given him new eyes, new resolve, a whole new set of balls.

Harv called him in the car. "Having a nice vacation, Zephyrus?"

Not even his fucking parents called him by his full first name. "Yo, I'm on the fokking case, but there been, like... obstacles."

Harv made a sound that couldn't find a way out of him in words. Almost chewing the receiver he said, "You just keep fokking doing what I'm not paying you to do, boy, and see what it gets you."

"Look, Harv, I'm on his shit like a sunburn, but he's got people..."

"Alright, fok it. Maybe there's no alternative to make you understand the urgency… Fok, I tell you, Joorgen would never let affairs get so sideways…"

Zef knew this was no time to talk back. Harv was always intense, but he never sounded scared. "What's the real deal, Harv?"

"This bike is worth a lot more than the Hawaiian put up for it. It's not just some custom bike made up like the Captain America chopper from *Easy Rider*."

"OK…"

"You fokking nitwit, it is the fokking *Easy Rider* chopper."

Zef sat down and took a deep breath before he meekly asked, "Who the fok is the Easy Rider?"

The growl came back, more exasperated than ever. "It's a wonder your generation doesn't drown in the fokking shower, boy. *Easy Rider* was this hippie movie from the 60's about some drug smugglers who get done for, hey, but the bike in the movie… you say you saw the property, over there?"

"Fok, Harv, I been closer to it than I ever been to my mother, but…"

"And you say it didn't look familiar to you?"

"Uh… maybe a little? Like, I seen choppers before and I seen 'em with, like, the flag shit on the tank like that…"

"That's the most recognizable motorcycle in the world, boy. I can't believe you didn't…"

"Well, if it's such a famous fokking bike, then why am I the only one looking for it? Why ain't it on the news? Why am I only getting…?" He trailed off not because he ran out of breath, but because his brain finally caught up to his mouth and he figured out his own answers.

"You're too dumb to know this, so you'll probably forget it… They bought two LAPD bikes at auction and chopped them in '69. One of them got sorted in the movie, but the other, this hippie actor put it in storage, but somebody broke in and took the bike."

"So, like… the dealer…"

"*Nobody* wants to know how he got it. The hippie actor, he figured it got stripped for parts, since the movie hadn't come out yet, when it happened. It never resurfaced. In '93, they made a perfect replica for the silver anniversary. It's in the Harley-Davidson Museum, but it's only a fake.

"So this bike is worth, like…?"

"It's an old piece of shit police bike, but if it's verified, it'd probably go for more than five."

"Five…?"

"Million. Dollars. Shitforbrains."

"But, like, it'll never go to auction, because it's hot, right, so, like… it's worth a lot less… and a whole lot more, ain't it?"

"First half-smart thing I've ever heard you say, boy. So, you starting to see how important it is that you stop fokking about and deliver the property?"

"Uh, like… yeah. But…"

"But what?"

"But if it's, like… you know…"

"Yes, your fee. Right… Triple it."

Zef let the pause go sour and stink up the air between them. Finally, he said, "Five times."

"Boy, you're not irreplaceable…"

"I'll have it tonight. You can pay me two hundred thousand for it, or we can all see what kind of reward the hippie actor will put up."

"Pretty sure he's a poor motherfokker now. Adverts for hippie rock music compilations, and whatnot. Put it out of your head, Zephyrus. Somebody else would clip you before we could even get to you, if you were to show the wrong kind of initiative. That's the kind of game this is. Everybody plays their part, everybody wins."

"I'm a player, Uncle Harv."

"I have faith in you, nephew. Call me soon with good news. I'm going to go sodomize someone."

Though it was late at night, Zef went through his morning meditation ritual before he left. This consisted of cleansing his mind and focusing on his goals for the day before he emptied his mind of everything and projected his excess *chi* energy into the vagina of every beautiful woman in the world. It would be a hell of a thing to deny them, if he didn't come back to pleasure them in the morning.

He polished off the leftovers from *New No. Two Chinese BBQ* and checked his kit one last time before packing it into his knapsack and strapping it tight to his back.

The Holokai Seaside was indeed a beachfront hotel at stunningly reasonable rates, probably owing to its proximity to Oahu's largest sewage treatment plant. He had cruised the area looking only for a cheap place to drop off his shit while he looked for Punani, but then he saw the three-story pale pink horseshoe around a sad, leaking swimming pool, surrounded by miserable plumeria trees furry with whitefly infestation. It still might have gone unnoticed if not for the huge, dark blue Toyota monster pickup in the parking lot.

Checking in using his ID and credit card for Robert Saber, his luck turned out even better. The gregarious old hag who ran the front desk was the owner's widow. She fed a small army of feral cats that lived in the office and the lobby; they wouldn't go outside because of her dead husband's "stupid birds," and because "the Flips" were eating them when their welfare checks ran out. Draped in a knee-length cable-knit cardigan seemingly knitted out of cat hair that screamed *shut-in hypochondriac* over flannel pajamas, she had come out of her shell to natter like a magpie as she followed Zef to his room with the commanding view of the parking lot and highway and treatment plant.

Much that weighed on her mind had to do with those people in three adjoining rooms on the ground floor facing the ocean. With little urging, she went on to describe how they came and went at all hours and threw wild parties and left unspeakable messes in the swimming pool. Their "ringleader" was pretty *nohea*, she admitted, but they were involved in drugs. She had a nose for such things. Anybody local who threw money around like they did had to be dealing "ice" or cheating the federal government.

Peeking through the curtains, he watched Punani drop off one tittering butterball and pick up another. Zef came down the stairs but took the beach door and circled around the building. The parking lot was less than half full and there were three bikes against the curb. He assumed Holokai Seaside didn't have a valet lot.

Zef crouched between a sickly hibiscus bush and a beater Mazda pickup with a shell that he was pretty sure had someone sleeping under it.

Ever since he got off the phone with Harv, Zef had been unable to resist picking at the scab.

The most expensive bike in the world was some fruity Ecosse bespoke superbike that tops out at 250 mph and sells for 3.6 million. The most anyone ever paid for a Harley was some custom rubbish called the Cosmic Starship. It fetched a million at auction. This piece of shit CHP-surplus chopper was worth more than both of those, just because of some shitty old hippie movie?

He'd endured the trailers and some scenes from *Easy Rider* on YouTube, but was unable to get into it. It wasn't even good bike porn. No chases, no decent fights and the only sex scenes were all fucked because everybody making the film was clearly tripping balls the whole time. But then he watched the last two minutes of the film. He'd watched the end a dozen times or more, and he watched it again, right then.

The end of the movie *was* the movie, no need for all that happy hippie horseshit before it. Open on two longhaired freaks riding high through Dixieland, and a couple shitkickers show up to push their shit in where nobody will ever know. That shot of the wreckage of Captain America's bike flying off the road onto the grassy knoll, followed by the camera lifting off and flying away like an untethered soul—that shit meant something his blood understood, even if his head couldn't fathom it, yet. But now it made a little more sense that some cunt would pay five mil for the chopper.

This shit had to end soon. Motherfucker had been under the needle for at least eight hours continuously, and the fatties were drumming on his back. He was wearing shades and his hair was wind-whipped and hung down over his face when he stopped to switch riders again. His grin was tired but infectious. The girls wanted to go back to his room. He stood up on the pegs and took off. A porker clung to his thighs with her face pressed into his ass as he roared out of the lobby turnaround and into the parking lot. Zef ducked into the hibiscus under the sweep of his headlight. Whiteflies fluttered out of their flossy nests and went up his nose, but Donny Punani was long gone and didn't hear him sneeze.

The other three local girls scooted into the lobby on awkwardly high wedge heels. Zef rolled his watch cap down over his face and booked across the lot ninja-style, hugging cover when he passed under the stationary security cameras and parkouring across the lawn to the shrubbery surrounding the pool.

A couple was skinny-dipping in the shallow end and a few surfers on their balcony were staring and pointing. When he saw what they were marveling at, his heart sank. He saw through the open sliding door of Donny Punani's lanai, lit up a garish red from the taillights of his Harley, which was parked in the living room of his suite. The engine snarled once more, loud enough to backfire and make the surfers hit the deck, then it cut out and someone yanked the curtains and slammed the door.

Well shit, this fucked up everything. How the fuck was he supposed to…?

Harden the fuck up and hold tight, rude boy.

In the adjoining room, he saw Peapea and Kewalo and two more local thugs sweating the other three Hawaiian chicks, playing some kind of drinking game around the table and smoking a joint like a turkey drumstick.

Kewalo's braying laughter when Peapea had to empty his cup seemed to set off a car alarm in the parking lot. The girl in Punani's room squealed even louder, making a song out of his name. The skinny-dippers got out and ran for their room, turned on or terrorized by the sounds. The surfers tried embarrassing them with catcalls and whistles, but the noise just got louder and they went inside, chanting, *Punani, Punani.*

Zef crept around the lawn, staying in the bushes and down on his belly, until he crouched behind one of the lounges on Punani's lanai. Nobody pointed and screamed. Ninja. He turned and ran into a face full of feathers. Dazzling metallic blue, golden iridescent green like an array of gaping, hypnotic eyes. In any other place, he'd be wowed by their beauty, but he nearly shit himself and choked back a high, hysterical scream. The manager said something about her husband's "stupid birds." She didn't say *peacocks.*

The big, stupid horny bird rushed at him with tail fanned out and quivering beak parted and hissing like it was fatally aroused. Zef shoved it away but it nipped his fingers and let out a fearsome falsetto shriek. Zef punted the bird away and dropped on his belly in the bushes. The peacock limped across the lanai, wailing pitiably. A goon opened the sliding door and threw an empty rum bottle at it.

One of the plus-sizers took her drink and shambled for the next room, where the squealing subsided into even more provocative moans and whimpers.

Breathing harder than when he was running, Zef crawled around the edge of the light spilling out of the living room, his keenly honed senses picking up the telltale brown aroma of the bike's exhaust mingled with the spoiled tuna stink of a porno set. The curtains were drawn over the sliding door, but they weren't quite closed on the window. Zef inchwormed over to the wall and skulked up to peek sideways over the windowsill into the darkened room. He stood up once real quick, snapping a sight picture and dropping to process it in his head.

His boner somehow figured it out before he did. The window offered a panoramic vista of the bed and the bodies on it entangled in a hot, heaving 69, and neither of them was Donny Punani.

The chubby girls were working each other like maniacs, like they were trying to climb into each other tongue-first and become one really huge Hawaiian girl. The girl on top squeezed her partner's face with her thighs like she was still riding the motorcycle, crying into her friend's snatch and screaming Donny Punani's name.

And where the fuck was Donny Punani?

Zef cautiously peered over the windowsill again. The only light came from a bedside lamp and the bathroom, so most of the room was in yellow shadow. But there he was, in a chair at the far corner of the room from the bed, sitting fully clothed with his fingers interlaced in front of his face as if he was contemplating a hospital emergency room, instead of a girl-on-girl bonanza. He didn't look like a man who'd just had sex. The weird, faraway stare captivated Zef for a while before he even realized Donny wasn't wearing his sunglasses. But he was looking past the banquet of flesh on his bed, and whatever he was seeing made him unutterably sad. Worst of all, he didn't look like a man who'd be passing out any time soon.

Maybe in the morning, Zef thought. He'd just stake out the view a little while longer, to make sure…

The Hawaiian girls just kept on going. Whatever the fucker did to women, he was doing it to them in spite of himself. The look in his eyes seemed to say that he'd take them, he'd have them inside out, but then he'd have to kill them and eat them.

Maybe the drugs were slowly leaking into his bloodstream from his rectum. Fok, thinking about that shit just got him depressed. If his mood lightened even a little, it would only mean that he had maybe an hour to live.

He was just thinking about taking off when Donny abruptly leapt out of his chair and barreled out of the room. He said something in a low, gravelly voice that cut the party game off and sent the four thugs scurrying. The other two chicks were already passed out. Within a minute, they'd all cleared out carrying surfboards. Zef was rubbing his hands, wondering if maybe those thick chicks would still be in the mood, or maybe he'd just ride off with the bike…

The bike raged at being kickstarted indoors. Zef barely had time to roll away with his hands on his head before the sliding glass door shattered and the Harley roared across the lanai and shredded the lawn, fishtailing and and hitting the parking lot with a scream of vaporized rubber.

Zef pounded the dirt and pressed his forehead into the grass. *Think, don't fokking blow this, don't do what you always do. Listen—*

The bike was headed north on Farrington. There was fuckall past Waianae, unless Punani was going night-golfing. Makaha, then campsites and Kaena Beach, where the highway just ended. Zef was arsed if he could figure it, how they couldn't even get one road to go all the way around the fucking island.

Spring into action.

Ninja!

He jumped into the Mustang and gunned it backwards out of the parking space. It felt like he was driving on four flat—

Fok. He rolled out of the Mustang. His tires were not so much slashed as shredded, steel belt dangling in springy ribbons from the gutted rubber.

He whirled and jumped out of his crouch, but they had the drop on him.

The grotesque face hovering over his own was even more off-putting than the Glock lazily aimed at his head. Jimmy Phun shook his head and tucked the gun in his leather jacket. "You starting to see how far over your head you are, now?"

8
THE HEAT

The moon over the water chased them up the highway, unnaturally full, its overripe umber light picking out the quicksilver foam on the breakers slamming into the rocky shore.

In a shitty old Hyundai hatchback, Jimmy cruised slowly, scanning the beach and looking for cops who might harass them on the return trip. Past Waianae's despair, separated by a brown canal in which he saw boys fishing pull up something as long as they were tall, like a cross between a lobster and a tapeworm. Makaha was slightly gentrified, with tiny art galleries and other vanity businesses instead of liquor stores and fast food, but still funkier than the Navy-flavored sprawl around Honolulu.

After Makaha, civilization gave up. Jagged ridges of lava rock loomed up on their right and crowded down against the highway, threatening to shove them into the ocean, but then they receded and the lunar landscape was exactly like the desert, except for the deeper, darker emptiness on their left.

"That car was worth more than your fucking motorcycle," Jimmy bitched.

"Nobody told you to…"

"Save your life? Yeah, I'm not gonna try to bill your uncle for it, don't worry. I'm just saying…"

"They thought you were dead… But how come nobody knew it was your car…?"

"It was a fucking special car, okay? It was never put into the system. Untraceable."

"So what happened last night?"

"I don't want to talk about it."

"No really, like… did you see me again, after the bar, where you totally fokking ditched me…"

"I came back, didn't I? Your uncle's credit line is maxed out, by the way. You fucked up big time. You were supposed to do like I told you…"

"His fokking posse was sitting on his bike the whole time he was in there… why you care about it, anyway?"

"Didn't Auntie Kalei let you know what you're fucking with?"

"You said you didn't buy all that Hawaiian voodoo bullshit…"

"Fuckin' aye I don't, because if you believe in it, then it works!"

Jimmy slowed down and passed a shantytown on the beach, dug in among the spiky stands of hala trees and scrub brush, a *mauka* turnout for Satellite Tracking Station Road, with a handpainted sign pointing in the other direction that said PRAY FOR SEX.

They turned off on a dirt road just before the three-row parking lot at the end of the highway, where the end of the island sported a perfect little beach with bone-white dunes in the lee of the ragged edge of Oahu. Kaena Point State Park.

A bunch of cars and trucks lined the front rows of the shallow, poorly paved lot, thousand-candlepower halogen headlights trained on the monster waves stacking up on the soft white beaches. A few fire rings burned and maybe a couple dozen people stood around drinking and smoking and watching the waves. And yet it felt nothing like a party.

They turned up the sloping road and Jimmy pulled over and got out. Zef tried to open the door but he couldn't find the latch, because there wasn't one. Jimmy yanked the door open and circled back around like he was going to push if Zef didn't get out. He shouldered his knapsack and started to get out, but then Jimmy got back in and started the car and pushed in the cigarette lighter button. "Get out."

"What the fok is that, down there?"

The lighter popped out of its socket, but the heater coil was cold. Jimmy tossed it out the window with a disgusted hiss. "Night surfing."

"How come?"

"It's… the waves are bigger, how the fuck should I know, do I look full-blooded Hawaiian to you?"

"Fok, man… I'm sorry… Look…"

"I don't want to hear it. Just go, okay?"

"No, like, no… but like, listen… I don't know what the fok I'm doing, out here… They're fokking playing with me…"

"You just now figured that out?" Jimmy lit the cigarette off a kitchen match. "Who sent you? Your uncle is fucking clueless. Who paid for this bullshit?"

"The Harley dealership owner. He just, really likes that bike, I guess…"

"It's personal, then? Donny Punani gets 'em wet wherever he goes. Your friend shouldn't get so twisted up. Probably nothing happened. He never fucks what he can't kill."

"This the same motherfokker you never heard of, day before yesterday?"

Jimmy just shrugged and shook his head.

"OK, I'm going." Zef got out.

"They hired you for a good reason, whatever it is. Just take the fucking bike and go home. He's just a man… until he's not."

The Hyundai coughed and stalled when Jimmy put it in gear. Zef took off running down the road towards the parking lot, then hit the ground and lay on a bed of lava rock as the headlights of the Harley and the Toyota passed over him headed into the lot.

They made a big detour, if he beat them here. The Toyota parked on the sand, blocking the view of the rings. The thugs went around back and got out a trashcan full of palm liquor. Kewalo shouted something that made the crowd drop their drinks and gather into a tight circle.

Carrying a ten-foot longboard on his shoulder, Donny Punani strolled out of the parking lot and into the glare of the headlights. Some in the crowd cheered; others made noises like catcalls. Zef wasn't sure which were which.

When Donny Punani set down his board and turned his back to Zef where he crouched in the bushes, the repo man forgot for a second why he was here.

The tattoo covered most of his back in blood-streaming scabs. A parabolic slash that rose up from just above each of his hips to touch the base of his neck, it was insanely ornate, crazed with patterns, but from this distance, it was clearly a mouth filled with jagged, triangular teeth.

A shark's mouth.

And he was going in the ocean with that shit?

Motherfucker was hardcore.

But not too bright. Liable to get infected.

Also. His bike was parked in the lot, and unattended.

After a final check on his gear, Zef prepared to move when he heard more motorcycles coming.

A swarm of rice rockets in lurid candy colors with blinking LED's all over them screamed into the lot and swooped like one huge, glittering wing to alight on the edge of the lot and gun their engines in unison like they'd just got done watching *Mad Max* and smoking crank.

As they got off their bikes and shucked their helmets, Zef crept up closer to duck behind the back row of cars, and his heart sank. Eight or ten Jap bikes were parked in a hedgehog formation around Donny's Harley, hemming it in to make sure there'd be a confrontation after whatever the fuck was going on out on the beach.

The biker gang took the beach to loud, barking cheers from the crowd. In colorful rashguards and baggy black boardshorts, they filed through the crowd hitting high fives and accepting paper cups of the shit from the trashcan. A longboard with an island sunset airbrushed on its deck was passed over the heads of the crowd until it came into the hands of the tallest of the bikers. In the harsh halogen lights, his face was a sculpted study in perfect proportion: cheekbones like straight razors, wide high brow unwrinkled by any trace of worry, and a strong, outthrust jaw that framed a wide smile that seemed to throw off its own light. No doubt, he was one beautiful motherfucker.

While Zef was reevaluating his heterosexuality, the others stood apart from the surfing stud and the crowd fell silent as Donny Punani came out to stand chest to chest with him. Shorter, thicker, gnarled with scars and oddly overgrown knots of muscle, Donny looked like a tiki chopped out of red lava rock with an axe, his grim face hidden by a veil of unruly obsidian hair.

A short woman came between them and held up a smoking bunch of grass, making a net of smoke to bind them as she chanted something in a low growl lost to the hammering surf. Zef wasn't sure, but he looked around the lot and spotted the postal Jeep.

No way, she was much too old. In a crow's croak, she called out something and the crowd repeated it and both men charged down the beach with their boards under their arms.

The waves were breaking almost right on the shore, but they rose up in fearsome, foaming walls several hundred yards out. Tube city, a traffic jam of perfectly formed deathtraps. Even from up here, they looked twice the size of the men who disappeared into the breakers, so he had to figure they were well over twenty feet high.

The whole crowd was watching them. He saw nobody in the lot. Crouching, he jogged over to the cluster of motorcycles. They were on the near edge of the lot to the crowd but screened by a couple pickups with their lights on, so he figured he'd be well covered. The other bikes would be a problem for a lesser repo man, but he'd assembled a crack field kit and he was prepared for this eventuality.

Kneeling down beside the outside row of rice rockets, he went through his knapsack and took out a jug of mineral oil, cracked the lid and started pouring it around the wheels. It was a lot easier than messing with the steering locks and as a bonus, it'd make chasing him a lot more interesting.

Peeking out from the bikes, he heard the crowd roar to drown out the ocean. The rider in the fiery rashguard come down the face of a wave like a scalpel carving God's ass cheek, slicing back up the wall to ride just outside the mouth of the tube.

Something came shooting out of the tube like a moray eel out of a reef and intercepted the other rider. Maybe Donny hit him, maybe he just cut him off, but the other rider seemed to fly apart, body and board flailing and flying and smashing into the rushing black water like eggs on concrete to vanish down the tube.

The crowd erupted in cheers and outraged shouting. Shoving and flying fists split the group.

Work faster. Zef rocked the first bike back and forth in the mineral oil until it came loose and slicked any way he pushed it like it was on ice. It was a tricked Kawasaki racer with a sweet cardinal red and gold paintjob. Across the red teardrop tank in discreetly ornate gold script, it said KAMEHAMEHA IX. He moved it aside and did the next one and the next with one eye on the crowd.

The fighting had settled down, the old witch yapping at the kids to keep them in line. It looked like the lady—Auntie Kalei—from the pancake house, but this one had white hair and her back was bent almost into a shepherd's crook. Maybe it was her grandmother.

Move move move.

The last bike was clear. He got out his pick and went to work on the padlock, which came open almost instantly. The key went into the ignition lock perfectly. He straddled the bike, the final objective of his mission, the key to getting on with his life and off this motherfucking island.

He took one last look down at the beach.

Donny Punani came striding out of the surf and dropped his board on the sand. And held up the head of his opponent by the hair.

The crowd went berserk. People turned and ran for the parking lot. People rushed Donny or ran down the beach or just fell to their knees like their whole worlds were suddenly, irreparably fucked.

Donny came up the beach, shoving aside fools with economical gestures from which they'd probably never recover, and tossed the head into the nearest fire ring. The bikers rushed him, but Kewalo and Peapea drove them back. Peapea picked one up and threw him into the fire ring with the blazing severed head. Kewalo fought like a pussy, but he bitch-slapped a guy a head taller than him and the guy went down screaming. His face, the whole left side of it, was just gone.

Nobody seemed to notice when he rocked the bike off its stand and stood up on the starter. This part was tricky, because Harley starters were engineered for a heavier brand of rider than Zef DeGroot, who, for all his uncanny flexibility and wiry physical prowess, weighed less than some people's dogs.

He stood up on the starter. A couple people noticed him as they ran by, too panicked to do anything about it. Donny Punani was maybe a hundred yards away, and nobody was stopping him.

The bike seemed to slip out from under him like soap in the shower and smash into the nearest rice rocket. Flailing to keep the huge, heavy bike from tipping over, he jumped off and threw his meager weight against the chassis, but his feet landed squarely in mineral oil. He danced and fast-pedaled just to stay on his feet, pushing the Harley like a plow through the pack of bikes. He'd taken pains not to get the mineral oil anywhere near the Harley, but the fucking lot was on the slightest of inclines, so it had run everywhere. The rice rockets all tipped over and skidded across the lot to logjam Kewalo's Toyota.

People noticed Zef.

In the midst of the mass exodus, one of the bikers who had been fleeing Donny Punani now shouted at him and came running.

Zef jumped on the starter and got the Harley to fart.

The biker slipped in the mineral oil and sprawled chin-first on the asphalt.

Donny Punani seemed to hear the sound of his hog and knocked Kewalo down running for the lot.

Another biker threw his helmet at Zef, who ducked it easily as he kicked the starter.

The engine caught and let out its trademark drowsy growl, bitching about having to work twice in one night. Donny Punani was maybe a hundred feet away and closing. He pointed at Zef and shouted something. Zef honestly wished he knew what it was, because it set his stooges to whooping like gladiator dogs in a pit fight.

Zef dropped his card, the one that said, "Your vehicle has been repossessed by an agent of AAACE ASSET RECOVERY SPECIALISTS. THANK YOU FOR YOUR BUSINESS!" He put in his earbuds and hit his secret car chase playlist, straddled the seat and jerked on the throttle, crying out as the blisters on his palm burst.

The bike lurched and spun on the lake of mineral oil until two more bikers got close enough for Zef to see they were crying, then the slick tires finally bit into naked tarmac and jolted in the wrong direction. Wobbling, straightening out with more throttle, he found himself soaring down the line of cars as several of them tried to back out of their spaces in a drunken, terrified panic.

It was a magical moment, and would've been sheer perfection if he could steer the fucking thing. The ape-drape handlebars were higher than his shoulders and he practically had to stand up on the pegs and throw his weight over the tank to get it to change course at all. He glanced off one truck bumper, throwing out a foot to fend it off, and veered between a camper and a huge local lunatic who tried to tackle him off the bike. That idiot got a ninja hand chop across his trachea as Zef passed, almost bowling over two wasted *wahines* and crashing sideways into the postal Jeep before he found the access road to the highway.

Zef felt steady enough to look over his shoulder at Donny as he shifted and opened up the throttle. Donny was standing there in the parking lot with his arms out like he was trying to call down lightning or something and it made Zef want to laugh, but then he heard thunder. It was kind of flat and muted. Donny went down holding his chest.

The narrow two-lane highway barely contained the runaway Harley. He knew the bikes he'd knocked over were twice as fast, but at least he wouldn't have to worry about Donny fucking Punani anymore.

Nobody had a gun on the beach or they would've shot Donny when he came out of the waves with their champ's head. And the sound of the shot was distant and almost seemed to come after Donny got hit. It had come from behind him, way up the slope, where the dirt road turned off the dead end of the highway.

It didn't matter. Nothing did, but what he had between his legs.

The first Harley-Davidson was designed as a racing bike and it swept the first American Motorcycle Association races, but by World War Two, the Wisconsin company had ceded the racing field to the Europeans and opted instead to make the heavy, loud, intimidating bikes that cops would ride to catch them. The 1962 FL was an awesome touring bike, built to cruise the wastelands with minimal pit stops. On Oahu, it was like keeping a bald eagle in a canary cage.

It was truly an amazing bike. But it sure as fuck wasn't fast enough…

He climbed jerkily through the gears on the silver, moonlit road, looking over his shoulder. The waves rose and pounded up the beach to send walls of spray arcing over the road. The ocean looked fucking pissed.

A monster truck with a bunch of screaming locals in the back flew past him, swerving all over the road like they were fighting over the steering wheel. He topped out around sixty but kept braking when the road got squirrelly. Nightmare flashes of laying five million dollars down on a flooded hairpin turn made him ease up on the throttle, but he kept looking over his shoulder. No one was coming. The darkness just rolled up the road behind him. The lights of Waianae hove up around the bend and he passed a couple trucks at an intersection and they honked at him friendly-like. They recognized the bike. Zef sped up, ran the red light. Nobody was going to mistake him for Donny Punani, even at this hour.

It was another twelve miles around the island to the lockup in Pearl City. After Waianae, the road passed a strip of resorts before it turned into a proper four-lane highway. He'd seen cars that could only be unmarked cops on the overpass in Kapiolani, near the Costco-Target complex. One was there now, but he was cool... did this stupid state have a helmet law?

He was cool, everything was cool. He passed under the bridge and he was passing a garbage truck on the right shoulder when the Harley's liquid growl was unceremoniously drowned out by a wailing, whining rocket thruster blue-hot with crumpled Doppler effect as it flew up his ass.

Zef stood on the pegs and looked over his right shoulder just as the rice rocket overtook him. Zef felt whipped by the wind of its passage. It seemed to rip right through his leather jacket, his tracksuit and his undershirt to peel his back down to his last layer of skin.

The pain of it was so total it almost sent him forward over the handlebars. The Harley swerved left and clipped one of its many superfluous turn mirrors off the rusty hull of the garbage truck.

He elbowed off the truck and accelerated to clear it and swoop into the fast lane. The faster bike's taillights described a waggling crimson trail as it whipped around another car and then flipped a retarded U-turn in the opposing traffic lanes and came back at him.

The wind howled on his back, an icy saw across his naked shoulder blades. What the fuck was that? He thought of Primo's faceless skull in his lap...

The bike blipped its horn at him as it passed, Kewalo straddling a red Kawasaki Ninja. His arm came up to wave, red palm outstretched. Zef flinched away, but just as Kewalo passed, he jerked into Zef's path and touched his sleeve. *Tag, you're it.*

Zef's jacket and shirt sleeves came apart and slid down over his hand. Zef flinched and skidded within inches of the concrete center divider.

The wailing of the Ninja's overtaxed engine faded into the slipstream, but before Zef had caught his breath, the fucker was back.

Zef hung from the handlebars,throttle wide open, the Ninja right at his back and whooping like it was laughing at him. Zef tried to put a contractor's pickup truck between them before the next pass, but the Ninja clung to him. Zef looked back.

No.

He wanted to call time out and just refuse this. The Ninja was popping a wheelie at seventy-five and coming up behind him with the front wheel upraised like a huge hammer. Zef gunned the engine and hugged the truck. His knapsack slid down his arm, and then it occurred to him and he knew it probably wouldn't help, but it was so dastardly and stupid and wrong that he just had to try it.

The contractor's truck was loaded with racks of huge mirrored glass panels. Averting his face, Zef swung the knapsack at his reflection. He jerked the bike hard to the right as the walls of glass came tumbling off the truck. They smashed into the pavement like the raw ingredients of the Big Bang. Flying shards of dazzling moonlight danced in his wake, bouncing and becoming smaller and sharper and turning into a hurricane by the time the Ninja flew through it, still balanced on its back wheel. Both tires burst at once and the bike seemed to try to trade places with its rider. Coccooned in broken mirror glass, Kewalo tumbled onto the highway and came to rest under the wheels of some unfortunate in a rental minivan, with the cartwheeling Ninja hot on his heels.

Zef took stock of the situation. Shock was already setting in, along with the endorphin rush of somehow continuing to not die or wreck the bike, to alleviate the pain of his back, his hand, and his face. He took it up to eighty when the highway allowed for it, thinking, *this is my bike, now. I have paid for it. I own it. Nobody else is going to try to take it from me.*

They tried to take it from him again.

The monster truck came up on his left and Peapea was standing up in the bed, hanging over the side like he was going to scoop Zef right off the Harley.

No way. Zef braked and tried to scrape them off against a dump truck, but the Toyota recklessly crowded him to the edge of the road, snapping off his remaining side mirrors.

The highway was getting too crowded for this Road Warrior bullshit. The truck pinned him against the wall but had to relent and swerve around a poky Pinto in the slow lane. Before he could change course, the truck pinned him again and Peapea caught him around the neck and lifted him off the pegs. Some kid in the passenger seat hung out the window to try and grab the handlebars to keep the bike from going under the truck. Zef, slapping and scratching the meaty, monstrous eel of an arm clutching him in a sleeper hold, started to see spots. Nothing he did seemed to faze the fat fucker.

Zef was not strong, or heavy, or particularly blessed with much reach or dexterity. But when pressed, a man capable of otterpopping can summon all kinds of unusual physical resources.

Squirming around in the sweat-slick cave of meat, Zef fumbled until he cupped the man's exceptionally small genitalia and honked them like an old-timey automobile horn.

Peapea folded and dropped him, but a reflexive deathgrip closed on his hair, which was maybe an inch long on top and pink walls of sunburnt dandruff everywhere else, but just long enough for him to dangle from over the wobbling Harley. All bodily control went straight away and he was a ball of white fire, so intense was this new outrage. But through his own screams, he heard someone in the truck roaring at the kid not to drop his bike, and he felt the Harley just beyond his flailing feet like a botched hanging feels the chair just out of reach underfoot.

His hand chopped out at the same place he'd grabbed before, and suddenly he was free.

Falling. And then he was on the bike and he hung on for dear life and Peapea fell on his ass in the truck, sending it careening into the oncoming traffic. Zef fishtailed to the right and bounced off a bright orange Dodge Charger.

The driver was a balding white guy who looked somewhat out of place with a two-foot waterpipe clamped to his lips, but then he dropped the bong and slapped a blue flashing dome light on his dashboard, which made total sense.

"PULL OVER," the cop said into a PA so loud it gave Zef's ears a black eye. He swerved away from the car and yanked on the throttle. The Harley pulled away from the Charger just as the monster truck swerved artlessly into his lane from the left, intent on smashing him into the cop car. Even at maximum acceleration, only half of him was going to clear the truck's front bumper. He could see the stupid punk hanging out the window with a wooden Louisville Slugger baseball bat cocked, the whipping wind making a floppy, moronic mask of his teenage face.

The cop looked like murder with hemorrhoids, and his partner, a big Asian woman, looked even more pissed, but at least patient enough to fire a warning shot with the pistol she was pointing at Zef.

For once, the bike's sturdiness worked in his favor. At the first touch of the handbrake, he didn't lay the bike down and go skating across the grooved roadway like cheese across a grater, but merely lurched up against the handlebars and seemed to be yanked backwards and out from between gnashing steel walls.

The kid's baseball bat smashed the cops' windshield. Truck tires ground against the Charger like it was going to climb right over the muscle car. The cops slewed sideways off the shoulder and out of sight with horn stuck on and airbags deployed.

The truck seemed to hover in Zef's path. The bike was squirreling out under him. He let off the brake and seemed to shoot forward into the arc of the baseball bat. He leaned way back, his fingernails digging into the rubber grips on the handlebars. It passed right in front of his face and smashed the speedometer. The kid was overextended and hanging out the window by his knees.

Zef had the merest glimpse of the driver's shaggy silhouetted profile.

He was still staring when the bat clipped the side of his head. Not much force behind it, but the blow fell on his ear, which seemed to fill with fire and melt off his head. Blind reflex lashed out to catch the bat and rip it free of the kid's hands. The Harley swerved into the truck again and Zef felt rather than saw Peapea diving against the bed of the truck and reaching for him with a paw like a pie plate.

Ducking under the crook of the handlebars, Zef licked out one-handed with the captured bat and caught the kid across the back of his head. He went ragdoll and slipped right out the window into the rushing river of concrete beneath them.

Zef swung again and caught Peapea across his forearm, sending him tumbling against the cab. The truck rocked on its shocks. Zef hit the truck and his hand went numb. The bat split apart like a Barry Bonds roidgasm. The truck seemed to pivot towards him and bounce alarmingly so that its spinning right front wheel came up on him like a buzzsaw.

He didn't know what to do and nothing would save him, so he just stabbed the wheel with the shiv of shattered bat in his hand and the whirling blur of knobby tire ripped it out of his hand and he was shoved away so hard his right peg struck sparks off the concrete. He fought the Harley to bank away from the shoulder. He didn't dare look but the truck was flipping end over end alongside him and then he was shooting down a canyon of backed-up traffic and the truck smashed into the back end of a dump truck.

"Boo-yah!" Zef flipped the bird over his shoulder. Suddenly the traffic was gone and he shot through the frozen street theater of a five-car pileup with police cars, ambulances, tow trucks and even a news van with its antenna tower fully extended. Cops turned to look, paramedics cursed him and horns honked in long blaring stabs that could only be salutes to his untameable glory.

The freeway was preternaturally clear past the accident. He made it to Pearl City in three empty minutes and swooped down the offramp to slalom past stopped traffic and run the light.

The tow yard was at the end of the street, the only lights that were on in this godforsaken industrial backwater. *At least they left the gate open when they ran out to the accident*, he thought, seeing the outer gate hanging wide open and the garage at the back of the lot that history would remember forever as the place where the world's greatest repo man presented the world's most valuable motorcycle for field appraisal.

He wasn't really watching where he was going as he roared up the driveway of JGA Towing, but he somehow saw it anyway—a shiny seam in the world that shone in the light from the tow yard's halogen spotlights, a spiderweb stretched taut across the entrance at the height of his collarbone. He studied it long enough to wonder what it was, but not long enough by half to do anything about it.

It felt like fire across his chest and the Harley ripped free of him and he was flying backwards. He heard the bike hit the curb and cartwheel across the lot and some part of his brain, he would later insist to himself, was calculating the cost of each echoing impact right up until the moment he landed on his head and everything went black.

9
THE LONG POINT

He awoke to a concerned face endowed with big brown eyes so clear and bright and lustrous, he was sorry when he realized they belonged to a man.

"You had a pretty gnarly accident tonight, my friend. Do you know where you are?"

Ambulance. He was in the back of one and this fresh-faced local kid was a paramedic. They weren't moving. There were no sirens. Was he dead?

He had to think, which was harder than usual. He hurt all over, like lying on a bed of sharp teeth, and his neck ached and burned like he'd been hanged. Just beneath his skin, a cold bubble of numbness quite unlike anything he'd ever pay to experience hid a world of grievous bodily harm, so he clung to it like death doing taxes.

"What happened to me, please? Am I…can't feel…?"

"You're restrained. We gave you a local anesthetic for the road rash. You really should've been wearing a helmet, brah. Do you know what day it is? Can you follow my finger?"

His mind shook itself down for clues, not to answer the paramedic, but for himself. The motorcycle—the last thing, he was riding the motorcycle and those fuckers tried to take it back, but he dusted them. He remembered reaching the lockup, but he couldn't figure how he got here, unless the getting away was a dream.

"Yeah, you were going pretty fast and you would've got there, too, only somebody strung this angling line across the gateway. Twenty-pound testline, brah. You're lucky you were standing up, so you didn't get decapitated."

Maybe it was *all* a dream. Maybe he was still in Las Vegas. That would be fucking tits. "So I'm gonna be alright, right?"

This other guy pushed the paramedic aside, leaned down to drip sweat in his eyes and fill Zef's world with his shitty hungry breath. At first, Zef didn't recognize him, but right away he caught on that this was no paramedic. "Sorry, buddy," the new guy said, "but no, I'm afraid you're fucked."

White, mid-forties, pattern baldness buzzed down to bristly white-blonde stubble over a fierce terminal sunburn. He looked like a plainclothes cop who got busted down regularly. His jaw muscles bunched up like he had nine-volt batteries wadded in his cheeks. His lime green Adidas golf shirt reeked of bongwater.

Oh sure, he remembered now... This guy was driving the car he'd bounced off on Queen Lilioukalani Highway, causing him to drop his two-foot bong just before that shithead kid did in his windshield with a baseball bat.

"Okay," Zef said, "I feel fine, like, ominna get out..."

Detective Bongwater pushed him down and tightened his straps. "Hey Doris, I think this guy, he's having a heart attack."

"No, I'm good, fok you..."

The cop menaced him with a pair of defibrillator paddles. Looking at them cluelessly, he said, "So, do these things work like jumper cables, or what?"

Zef tried to scream, to tell them everything, but the cop behind him stuffed a wad of gauze in his mouth. In a deep, tired voice tinged with a slight local accent, she said, "What you mean, like, do you gotta ground it, or something?"

"Yeah, it don't even say which one's the negative..."

"Fucked if I know... I'm no fuckin' doctor."

Rubbing them together like a doctor on TV, Bongwater shouted, "CLEAR!"

Zef was struck by lightning. He felt the paddles like the entry and exit of the bolt that tore through him. He convulsed so hard he could've snapped his own spine, if he wasn't restrained.

He felt sick and strange, but not altogether bad. His mouth was dry, except for the freshet of blood from where he'd bitten through his tongue. And his heart... it wasn't beating.

Sick and dizzy. Shuddering, coughing up the gauze, spraying foam from mouth and asshole. Trying to speak. Trying to say, *Please stop.*

His heart rolled in his chest and twitched. He gasped burning breaths of luscious air through bubbling rivers of snotty tears.

Paddles rubbing together like eager steel hands, the cop said, "You ready to talk now?"

Zef tried like hell to make his shivering head go up and down.

The male cop tapped him on the forehead. "So you're the piece of shit who clipped Primo Waialani. Smooth stone killer shit, sticking around to fuck with the body. Hawaiians are crazy for open-coffin funerals, brah. What'd you think, nobody was on your ass after that?"

Zef fumbled with a couple mouthfuls of answers. "Yo, I don't know nobody named Primo, and omma sue your whole fokking city—"

The cop started laughing. The quiet bitch behind him let out a brief, snorting laugh. "Homeboy, you're so fucked we don't even *want* to arrest you."

"No way, Five-O! No fokking way, I didn't do nothing to him, man!" He tried to get up, but the restraining straps gave him not an inch of space. "I'm just a repo man, shit, I only came out here to run down a dead skip..."

Detective Bongwater picked his nose, admiring the booger for a moment, and flicked it at Zef. "Did he burn you on a deal? Primo does that a lot, especially to fuckers from the mainland who try to play the locals."

"Yo, like I don't even know him, hardly. He's trying to front me on some kind of side deal, he said it was legit—"

Bongwater stood up. His head hit the ceiling, then he jumped on the gurney, straddling Zef. Took hold of his ears, pinching the lobes so hard the rush of blood made Zef feel like he was drowning in his own skin. Then he yanked on them like he was trying to tear them clean off. The whole time screaming, "Bullshit. Who d'you work for, the Mexicans? Is that who's coming in here, trying to start a fucking ghetto drug war on our fucking tropical island paradise?"

Zef tried to answer. Would say anything, given half a chance. The cop's partner pulled him off. Doris was a chunky Hawaiian woman in her late thirties with bad acne scars and sweating like a lawn sprinkler. She wore a smart suit with a blouse and a string of real pearls. She looked more like the bald cop's superior than his partner. They whispered for a minute while Zef tried not to puke and drown in it.

Finally, Bongwater got off him. Doris loosened Zef's straps and mopped his face with a cool towel. Bongwater said, "We don't really like you for the murders, okay? Maybe you telling the truth and you just came out here for this bike... Or maybe you're one of Primo's fucking drug mules."

Doris said, "He bunched up his butt when you said that."

"You saw that? I saw that, too."

"Whatta you think?"

"I think maybe you should see if they got an enema kit."

"No way! I'm not holding..."

"So talk."

"What happened to it? To the bike?"

"It was totaled out, dipshit," Bongwater cackled. "You wrecked it good, brah."

Doris ripped open a big plastic pouch. Rubber tubes and a sack of saline and mineral oil spilled out. Zef stopped trying not to puke.

"Come on, don't make a fucking mess in here." Bongwater headlocked him and clamped his jaw and pinched his nose shut. It backflushed into his lungs, burning like Tabasco sauce. He thrashed fit to bust the straps. Drowning in his own puke.

"Jesus, let him go," Doris said.

Split lips and tongue added briny red broth to the vomit that came out his nose, scouring his sinuses with acidic Hawaiian barbecue.

"So what's so special about the bike you couldn't go through normal channels? Just 'cos it was the bike from the… what's that fucking movie, Doris?"

"*Easy Rider.*"

"Yeah."

"No, (choke, spit), it's just (snort, gag) a real fancy replica, like… Anyway, (gag, spit) fok, you don't need to fok with me no more, it's fokkin' Donny Punani, that's who you want…"

Now Doris got in his face. "Don't tell us fucking bullshit ghost stories, boy. You operated on my islands, it's GTA at least, I promise. Whose bike did you take?"

"I told you already, it was Do—"

Zef couldn't see what the big Hawaiian lady cop was doing, but apparently neither could her partner, not until it was too late.

When she leaned over Zef, he shrieked at her empty eyes and the cloth in her hand, but she pressed it over her partner's face and slammed his head into the row of lockers behind him so hard he left a red star on it.

"Hey," Zef said, but she didn't answer. She got up and opened the back door, and grunting with effort, dragged her partner to the threshold and dumped him on the shoulder of a road with only infrequent streetlamps to show it was anyplace at all. She closed the doors and bent down over him like she was going to kiss him, but then out came the rag and he was breathing ether and blackness.

10
BAMBOO HUSBAND

Dark room.

Black walls, no windows. Red light from a slit under a door. Hot like a sauna, wrapped in steaming sheets and turning over to get up only tangled his legs and he wasn't going nowhere but his head was floating away...

And the heat... the heat was coming from *her*.

He thought it was the cop at first, but no, not unless she'd been wearing a fat suit. Her naked back, rippling muscle trimmed with baby fat, falls of ebony hair plastered to golden skin slick with sweat, hair down to the floor crowned in plumeria and hibiscus flowers hiding the better half of everything.

Head bowed, she rocked ever so slightly, voluptuous golden curves glistening like honey, cocked a round, bounteous hip and made him hear music. Waves raced down her spine to break on the lithe, chiseled pillars of her legs.

He reached out for her, but he was handcuffed to the bed frame.

Don't scream, don't give her the satisfaction, but he made the frame shriek, made his wrists slick with sweat and slimed with blood, but they just bit deeper.

She turned and he saw her face for just a moment before her hair blocked it, her eyes gleaming like something wild on fire inside, like something only superficially human. It was the stare of a bad man getting dragged out of the strip club at last call, a wolf in the zoo before feeding time. It scared the shit out of him, but it made the blood rush to his cock so hard he damn near came red.

Undulating, and now he could feel the rhythm that throbbed from deep within her, heavier than the heat. She ran her hands up her inner thighs and parted her sex with both hands and then brought her fingers to her lips. The smell of wine and blood spilled on hot coals filled the room.

She fell across his lap. Hair washed over his legs like a wave of hot sand. Her full, strong lips were like a branding iron. Her kisses raised blisters on his thighs.

He closed his eyes and held his breath and bit into the meat of his biceps to hold back the screams.

Her mouth was first a jet of live steam bathing his cock, then a fiery vacuum singeing the hair off his balls and making his hips buck and arch to get himself deeper into her. It burned and blasted and broke him, worked his whole body, every last drop of his life into his erection. He tried to force himself to ejaculate. Even dying like this would be better than burning to death on the edge.

It was more involuntary twitch than act of will that made him open his eyes and look down.

She wasn't even touching him. Her breath twisted and warped the air and played over his skin. Thick curls of smoke trickled from her lips and nose as she rose up, climbing to squat over him. Her skin glowed dull red, her face in shadow from the crackling torch of flowers ablaze in her obsidian hair.

Deep inside her, the tree of her lady parts glowed right through her skin like veins of magma in a glass volcano. The heat from her belly and breasts made his skin bubble and crisp. His vision blurred as blisters erupted on his eyeballs.

Under him, the sheets and mattress caught fire. He convulsed on the Viking funeral pyre as she took his cock in her hand and rolled her hips over it, then in one great surge, took him inside her.

The bed frame cracked, the metal gone soft buckled and his hands came free. The bed fell to the floor and he clawed at the furniture crumbled into black ashes the walls the black disintegrated and underneath glowing white molten rock at the heart of the earth the beating rhythm her heartbeat. He came into her and was cremated and the walls fell in and they burned—

He came awake kicking and thrashing and shaking cursing wet all over and it was hot, God, fok, it was so hot... like trapped in a car parked in the desert, but not... He touched himself to make sure he was still there.

He lay on a queen-sized bed. A lattice of dull reddish sunlight filtered through blinds sketching out a blank, barely furnished bedroom. The same hula girl painting from his room at the Illikoi hung on the opposite wall.

He was handcuffed. He was naked. And she—

In the corner, on a chair, the husky Hawaiian cop sat with her gun in her hand, pointed at him like he wasn't naked and cuffed to a bed. Her face in the shadows was unreadable, but her eyes were wide and white and more terrified of him than he was of her—

He tried to sit up, to make his parched mouth ask for water, but she jumped up and made like she intended to feed him the gun.

"Stay back, fucker! You stay down!" She wore the same gray blazer and skirt from the ambulance, but her buttons were done up lopsided, a slit torn in her skirt almost up to her goods, hair a crooked mess like she'd slept on it. She backed up to the door and disappeared through it, turning in the hall to run, and what the fuck was her problem, he didn't know, but the last thing he saw before she was gone, a garter of discolored white cotton around one of her ankles. Panties.

Somewhere several empty rooms away, he heard a door slam.

He flipped over on the bed and stretched out his free arm to lift the blinds. Outside, beige walls and green heaving turf—condos around a golf course. He still had crumbs of asphalt embedded in his skin, but when he threw back the sheets, he jolted backward into the headboard.

His cock was a red, sticky mess. Moaning, "No," as a mantra. His balls, *Oh God, she'd taken his balls*—

Upon closer examination, he found his essential masculine equipment undamaged, but then he wiped his hands on the sheet and let out a disgusted shitstorm of Afrikaaner profanity. None of the blood was his, which meant it must be *hers*…

It took less than half an hour to detach the flimsy plywood headboard from the metal frame and get free of the bed. Lightheaded with hunger and increasingly agonized by road rash and miscellaneous contusions and the unthinkable defilement of his nether regions, he forced himself to stand up and make his way out of the bedroom.

He stopped in the bathroom and gulped water from the fancy Bosch sink fixture, washed the sticky red mess off his groin and his own dried blood off his face and chest. Bruises ringed his eyes, starbursts of scabs from glass and scratches ran down his arms, blisters and tender patches of hairless, scar-shiny pink skin. He wondered how much of it he'd gotten in the motorcycle wreck and how many came from… after.

This wasn't a dream. It was done, one way or the other. Time to go. Time to get the fuck out of here, off this island, back to America, Nevada, Las Vegas, and never, ever, *ever* come back. When he got back, he would no doubt have to answer some questions, like what happened to the item he was sent to collect.

Never. He never had ever totaled a repo. Never. And this one was worth… a lot more than his life, that was for sure.

In the next room, his phone rang. He turned too fast to go get it and crashed into the towel rack, ripped it out of the wall trying not to fall down. He smashed the mirror with the towel rod. He went to get his phone, picked it up and answered without looking and instantly regretted it.

"Enjoying your vacation, son?"

When Zef was a boy, he was so stubborn, he would refuse medicine even he knew would make him better. No reason he could remember, no hope or fear that motivated him. He'd be up screaming in agony all night with a toothache or an ear infection and still refuse any medicine. Almost died of fever a couple times, and diarrhea on a trip to Mexico.

His Dad would go right at him, threatening punishments of increasingly surreal brutality until he had his son in a sleeper hold with a teaspoonful of grape cough syrup in his other hand.

But his ma would pamper and humor him when he had a fever. She'd bring him his sippy cup of milk, and she'd apologize for pestering him until he fell asleep with the milk tipped over alongside his snoring face.

When he was old enough for real cups he noticed that the milk she brought him was purple. She just dumped the medicine into the milk and stirred it up with a wink at her own cleverness.

Not that he ever had a reason to trust his mallie. She collected candy. Dad said her ma never let her have sugar, so she was fixed on it, but she never ate the stuff, herself. Bought up retailers' display cases of candies at Costco and everywhere foreign they went and added them to her shrine in the sewing room. It was an irresistible candy panorama, but every last piece was poisoned, sprayed with a parethrum insecticide. One kid at the first sleepover he hosted got sick and almost died when he was seven, and nobody was allowed to stay over, ever again.

It wasn't that Mum was out to hurt anyone. She just hated confrontations, so she let the mark think he'd got his way and then came at him from behind, usually for his own good.

But now it was Dad, using the Purple Milk voice.

"Son, don't fret over the bike. It's just a thing. Everyone is simply grateful that you're alright. Just put it out of your mind and come home."

And that was the fucked thing about it... because up until just now, he wanted to do just that. But something in Dad's voice stank like the bait in a trap.

"Harv must be awful pissed, like..."

"Well, who wouldn't be? He's disappointed, surely, but he understands these things happen. Bikes get cracked up, they get fixed. It'll take a bit of money, but it can be fixed up good as new."

"Is his insurance gonna cover it then?"

"Of course not, you fool. But the damage estimate came to about sixty thousand dollars, y'see..."

Zef's ass puckered and sucked wind. He understood vividly. "But I still recovered the..."

"Less damages, son. You took the contract for forty thousand."

"Yo, he fokking tripled that shit."

"That was before you made a mess."

"So in his head I owe him twenty thousand dollars for finding his stupid bike for him, but he's just going to walk away?"

Dad didn't answer, but he heard a voice. Was his hand over the phone? Who else was there? Would he sell out his son to one of his old friends?

131

His voice cracked when he said, "But after all I went through…"

"You still got a nice vacation out of the deal, didn't you, boy?"

Zef thought he was in pretty solid shape until he tried to put his clothes on. His left arm was not broken, but it acted like it was. Likewise his ribs on that side. His back looked like bacon. He screamed when he slid into his shirt, gave up on tying his shoes. His pants had been scissored off him by the paramedics, so he just rocked his baggy boxers.

He was shuffling for the front door when the witch breezed in the back with an armload of groceries and a miniature TV.

Zef backed up towards the front door. "Yo, like, I was just leaving, so like…"

"Take the bag, stupid *haole*. You wen go, then go, but you better see this one paper first."

Mistrustful, he came over and took the string of canvas public television tote bags and dropped them on the counter. She held out a *Honolulu Advertiser*, shook it until he took it. At the bottom of the front page, under her stubby, tapping finger: LOCAL SURF HERO LOST IN TRAGIC NIGHT SURF ACCIDENT. The picture was of the local Donny Punani surfed against.

Zef took the paper, looking at the beaming grin in the oversaturated pic of the kid holding a huge surfing trophy. He shrugged. "Nothing to do with me. My job is—"

She didn't take the paper back. She held up a cheap little automatic pistol and let him taste the barrel.

"You had one job. You fuck up so big they tell stories about you. Your Hawaiian name Hewakeiki... You like that?"

The gun in his mouth nodded his head for him.

"Means 'Fuckup Boy.'"

Auntie Kalei said she never stayed in hotels, but she couldn't go near most houses, either. "Ghosts don't just come from people dying," she told him as she cooked some purple sludge that stank like manure on the stove. "They come from people living in a place. When you stay in one place it rubs off on you, but you rub off on it too, leave some of you behind."

She didn't like old houses where people had lived their whole lives, because ghosts soaked into the walls, a stink deeper than cigarettes and cooking and piss on the floor around the toilet. "That's how Marilyn Monroe can haunt like twelve different houses..."

Timeshares like this one were better. Only tiny but intense slices of people soaked into the walls, a hundred, a thousand of them in bite-sized pieces, all similar, shallow vacation ghosts. When she lay still on the couch, she could feel them, all the pent-up lust and hopes and expectations for the vacation, and all the frustration and rage when they didn't get what they wanted, all the guilt and denial when they did.

Zef sat on a barstool and listened attentively, or at least pretended to, as he had while she bandaged and stitched his impressive catalogue of wounds, because she jerked the thread in the wound or splashed alcohol into an open cut when he tuned her out. His eyes never left the gun on the counter, between her stirring spoon and the ashtray. She smoked a fat, swaybacked joint. She didn't offer him any.

He was looking at the gun so he didn't see the big wooden spoon until he felt it slap his face. "Hey, *haole* boy! You listen!"

She had a weird way of moving around the kitchen that made all the sounds around her into a constant, lilting rhythm. In the shower earlier, the water hit the floor in a slippery, musical cadence like she was doing the hula, or like she wasn't alone in there.

He'd tried more than once to tell the crazy old witch that his job was the motorcycle, and it was over, but she wasn't listening.

"Your motorcycle still here. Nothing ever leaves these islands. You don't know what you came for, what brought you, but it not done with you."

He watched her stir the purple shit. Big, lazy bubbles flopped and popped, exuding toxic gases. "Just like people leave mark on a place, places and their ghosts leave mark on the people, if they open or empty enough. Like when one lady on her period, or when man get one head full of bad drink and black out…" She smiled at him.

"None of this shit got nothing to do with me."

"You don't want to believe, you go ahead. But Donny… you don't need to believe in him. He's *kupua*. Ghost-god. Shapeshifter. Only a true *kanaka ma'oli* can take him down."

"Whatever, shit…"

"He eat you like spam, can and all. You need faith to beat him."

"I don't need faith to do nothing, baby. I'm a motherfokking ninja, an' shit. But anyway…"

"You stupid *haole* boy. You think you know everything but I bet you never read one book."

"Fok books. Books are stupid. Most of them come right out and tell you they're madeup bullshit. The rest, you can't even tell, but they always make shit up. They just push it at you, and you have to believe, because it's in a book. I'm a lie detector, baby. I can fokking *smell* bullshit."

She shook her head sadly. "You think what happening to you just happen, you got one more think coming."

"I don't believe in supernatural shit. Sonofabitch ain't no ghost. He's solid, he's alive and he's gonna die someday. But not from me…"

"He's not one ghost, I promise, he's *ghost-god*. You don't even know what one god is." She pointed at the row of plastic tikis arrayed behind the stove—squat dwarf bodies holding up huge totem pole heads that were not animal or mineral or vegetable, but somehow an abstract attempt to represent volcanoes and tidal waves and lightning bolts.

"The great gods—Ku and Lono, Kane and Kanaloa—came from Kahiki over the sea. Some say they were just men when they made the trip, but now they're worshipped all over, from the Marquesas to the Carolines."

Returning to stir the purple shit, she carefully spilled some into the fire, nodded at the hissing and redoubled stench.

"Anywhere nature still alive, some men can make her one slave, but nature, she make men to do her work."

She reached out and pinned his hand to the counter. "You were good to her, right? She take a lot out of a man."

For just a moment, Zef felt a blasting heat rise up inside him and bloom out of his face. "Who the fuck...?"

She touched a blister on his neck that wasn't there when he wrecked the bike. She whispered, "*Pele.*"

"Don't touch my fokking body." Zef backed up, trying not to feel like a little boy with his first stiffie. She suddenly didn't seem so old, the missing teeth didn't seem like such a liability. "I don't know nothing about no black soccer player."

"Don't matter if they real or not, or ever were. When they were *our* gods, they walked among us, and that power don't just go away. It finds its way into the people who need it, and it uses the people when it needs something done. And right now, it needs an end to Donny Nanaue."

She struck a thinking pose, hand on chin, eyes screwed up into a thousand yard stare, tongue slightly protruding from her wide mouth like she was posing for a portrait. It looked ridiculous, but it worked.

At least, for Zef, it did.

"What you need..." Auntie Kalei started to say, but then she saw the cheap Chinese automatic in his hand.

"Like I said, I'm not here to kill your ghost-god motherfokker. I got hired to take his bike. Mission accomplished. I'm going home to count my cash."

Tossing her head back, she cackled. "You one broke-ass lie detector, I promise." Snapping her towel at him, she snapped, "Go on! Go!"

He pointed the gun, then at the last minute dipped his hand and fired three rounds into the stewpot on the stove. The double-hulled pot slammed into the wall and danced on the burners. Scalding water splashed on Auntie Kalei's wrist and arm, making her yowl like a cat. Simmering poi mudslide gushed out and doused the blue gas flames in starchy swamp stench.

He backed up and ran for the door. She didn't chase him. Out in the yard, he dropped the gun in a birdbath and ran into the parking lot and saw her postal surplus Jeep with the door open and the keys in the ignition.

He was only a few miles from his motel room in Waianae, but he left nothing there he wanted to risk his life for. He stopped at a Purple Heart thrift store and walked out two minutes later in a red Marine Corps hoodie and Tapout sweatpants. He hit a McDonalds, where the McRib was apparently mandatory.

His return ticket was some kind of friends and family standby thing, so he only had to call the airline and check the flight load for the three evening flights to LAX and the one direct flight to Vegas. His chances of going straight home at eight o'clock looked excellent.

11

PLACE OF NOISE

He ditched the Jeep at a Tesoro station across the street from the rental car return and ran through the long-term lots all the way to the American terminal.

He had only met Kjirste, Harv's stewardess niece, once, when they flew to Atlantic City for vacation once. She flicked his ear when he tried to touch her ass, which was ridiculously huge and perfectly heart-shaped, like the fucking Hottentot Venus. His earlobe bled so fucking much they almost detoured the flight. That was when Zef was fourteen.

He had no idea what she looked like now, but he talked her up to the ticket counter staff. The lady was really nice. Tipping a glance at his hoodie, she thanked him for his service, jumped Zef to top of the wait list and chatted him up while she made a copy of his driver's license and went back behind the wall where the luggage went on the conveyor belts.

With no bags, he should get to skip most of the security line, too. They had customs here, but they were looking for people smuggling plants and animals and shit. An Asian woman with two pairs of thick glasses lined up on her nose collected forms and fed carry-ons into some kind of pollen scanner. He stuck his hands in his belly pouch pocket, fingering his wallet until he was next in line.

They weren't in there a second before, he'd bet on it, but just as he said he had nothing to declare, his hands touched the fibrous shell of some kind of big seed in his pocket. More of them fell out when he took out his wallet. The inspector blinked and bent over to pick one up as he flipped up his hood and walked away fast.

He nearly bumped into a uniformed cop who was watching the passing tourists and holding up a sheet of paper with a crummy composite sketch of a skinny, ferret-faced kid with a wispy joke of a mustache. He backed up and walked by with his hand up over his face. When he was a good distance away, he turned and looked back and the cop was looking right at him and picking his teeth.

Zef ducked into a gift shop and used his last cash to buy sunglasses and a hideous pink ballcap that said ALOHA! He put them on and walked out and looked back at the checkpoint. Three inspectors were out in front of it picking up those seeds, but there was another station at the far end of the terminal. He walked fast, trying to stay close enough to one big family or another to pass for part of their group. Exhausted kids towing wheeled suitcases and dragging bodyboards kept tripping him up. He fought the urge to dropkick them.

A nervous eighth-mile hike later, he reached the next customs station and flashed his license. The ancient

Japanese gentleman barely looked at it as he shrugged him through.

Fok. They didn't seem to have his name, but they were legging the sketch around. So he wasn't officially wanted, but the cops were looking for him on the down-low. If they combed the flight reservations, they would find nothing. The wait lists were not publically available, but they flashed on the screens at the gates every few minutes. He had a better than even chance of making it, so long as nobody recognized him.

Waiting next to the TSA guy at the security checkpoint, with his elbows resting on the amnesty box. Detective Bongwater yawned and dug around in his ear. He had a black eye and a splint on his nose. His wrinkled linen blazer bulged around the lines of a shoulder rig and a fat holster. He said something to the TSA agent as she vigorously frisked an elderly passenger, and she laughed and high-fived him. He took a butterfly knife and some prescription meds out of the amnesty box. Zef could read lips pretty well; the cop was saying what Zef was thinking: *Nothing leaves these islands.*

Backing up with the slowly creeping line between him and the cop, he went to a newsstand and picked up a magazine and pretended to read it. He saw two more uniformed cops by the doors.

All the blood drained from his head so quick he nearly fainted. His dick swelled painfully and swung like a dowsing rod to point across the terminal and down by the last Starbucks before the security checkpoint, where Pele stood naked and proud and defiant, jets of smoke curling up from her full, fiercely scowling lips…

No point in telling his dick that it was only Detective Doris, a premenopausal Polynesian woman pushing 230, currently sucking down a venti frapuccino like the antidote to a poison she'd been forced to take and rolling her eyes at her partner.

Amazing she'd even be here. Whatever happened the other night, she'd assaulted her partner and helped Zef escape and then knocked boots with him... because she was on her period and maybe possessed... But try and tell that to a jury.

There'd be no jury. He'd get double-tapped in a cane field and fed to the sharks, if they caught him. But she was here, and it was like he could smell the rich, overripe floral perfume of her bloody sex and he wanted to go to her so fucking bad, wanted to rub her like a magic lamp until the goddess came out to play. He tried to focus on her sweat-stained, flabby body and drab, indifferently styled hair, to picture her as a man, an old man with mutton chops, but it was no good. He still burned to ride her face like a bicycle.

Detective Bongwater started walking down the line, pausing to pop the lid on some confiscated medication. Tilting his head back, he cracked a capsule under his broken nose and snorted it.

Zef was almost to the door with a magazine over his face, learning about how a new patented bacteria promised to convert solid waste into edible and delicious meals for the homeless, and he crossed the concourse reading about the benefits of a $600 pair of noise-cancelling earphones that didn't play music. He reached the doors and the sidewalk and the waiting row of taxis and courtesy shuttles without having to learn anything else. The uniformed cops and the skycaps were trying to get a stretch limo out of the taxi line.

A big ex-cop in a nice suit stepped in his path and took his arm. "Mr. DeGroot, we've been looking for you."

"Well, here I am," he said as calmly as he could manage. He could scream and they would drag him away, or he could just go with them and get killed. "Where we going?"

The ex-cop opened a hole under his mustache to answer. Zef kicked him in the balls as hard as he could. The much bigger man's shiny black wingtips lifted a good three or four inches off the gum-streaked concrete.

Zef feinted back into the terminal, then juked around a passing luggage cart and made for the street.

A hand caught his flapping hoodie. Yanked him backwards off his feet. An arm like a python encircled his neck and lifted him miles above the ground. Breathing hard in his ear, blinking back tears, the ex-cop pulled him into the cowl of a payphone bank beside the doors. "My employer has an offer which will be of particular interest to you in your present situation. You can come with me to entertain his proposal with no obligation, or I can turn you over to the Honolulu police, who are under the misapprehension that you kidnapped and raped one of their detectives. What'll it be, sir?"

As soon as Zef could breathe, he said, "Let's go."

12

CITY OF REFUGE

The meal on the private jet was fucking excellent. Somewhere in the back of the plane, apparently, was a kickass sushi chef. Zef had hit the bathroom to puke up the McDonald's and kept him busy the whole flight. He ate alone and watched extreme cage fighting from the Philippines on the satellite.

They landed at a tiny private airstrip on a bluff overlooking a rainforest. The stewardess and the sushi chef bowed to him as he disembarked. An even more formidable ex-cop escorted him to a helicopter that dusted off as soon as he got in.

Zef goggled out the window as the earth spun away and the airstrip vanished. He'd never seen so much green in his life. He couldn't believe how undeveloped it seemed, after the jumble and stench of Honolulu. But then they passed over a terminator and the green was suddenly gone. Striated bands of naked metamorphic rock replaced the lush rainforests. Further south, the pilot told him over headphones that probably cost a lot more than $600 that the funnel of silver smoke on the horizon like a giant spliff blazing away in a crater was Mauna Loa. They circled over the volcano so Zef could marvel at fountains of lava spewing the raw, glowing stuff of creation out onto a landscape more desolate than the Mojave. This place wasn't just new; it wasn't even fucking finished, yet.

On a green, grassy plateau high above the nearest signs of human habitation, they touched down on a lava gravel pad behind a rambling McMansion that looked like the world's biggest steakhouse.

An old smiling Hawaiian woman kissed his cheek and put a necklace of black kukui nuts around his neck. She led him inside via a service door to a weird locker room where a valet approached him dubiously and held out a shiny gray suit.

"Yo, like, no thanks, like what, I'm like, already dressed…"

"He won't see you like that," the valet said. Attached to the coathanger, in separate plastic bags, were a new pale blue button shirt, a green and blue striped tie, a new pair of black loafers, dark green nylon socks and a spotless pair of white jockey shorts, all carefully stripped of tags or labels.

Suit in hand, Zef bitched, "I don't need new shorts, shit, yo."

"Put it on," the valet said, cool steel threats hidden in his words like pins in a new dress shirt, "all of it. He is superhumanly perceptive, and very, very easily offended."

"Who the fuck is *he*, anyway? Like…"

"Do not fuck with us. Put on the jockey shorts." Now, he took out a tackle box and a little flashlight. "Smile," he said.

"What the fok for?"

"Just do it."

Zef grimaced and bared his teeth. While the guy looked into his mouth, he said, "He has an intense and irrational dislike of bad breath and tooth decay. Exhale."

Zef blew in the guy's face.

"Christ," he said. He gave Zef a tooth brush, toothpaste, floss, a disclosing tablet and a mint. "Smile but don't grin, and finish or swallow the mint before he comes in. You won't want to be sucking or chewing anything when he sees you."

Zef started to ask more questions, but stopped asking when he saw the contents of the tackle box. In little drawers and compartments like a well-organized fly-fisherman's case, he saw assortments of individual false teeth and tubes of Super Glue.

The room was huge and furnished almost entirely in echoes. It felt like a museum. Tile floors, columns, floor to ceiling windows looking out on a pasture dotted with horses and cattle. A few things under glass set into the walls or in free-standing cases. Crowns and fans of feathers and beads from all over the world accompanied trophies and plaques and godawful works of "art" presented as gifts from grateful world leaders, celebrities, scientists, inspirational speakers and self-help gurus.

He immediately gravitated across the room to the largest, newest display. His heart dropped into his guts and hid behind his balls, which had crawled up into him at the sight of the exhibit under the fancy halogen pinlights.

Inside it stood the Captain America bike. The twisted front wheel, almost curled around the bent fork; the stars & stripes, gouged and crosshatched with dull silver, the shredded ruin of the leather seat. There was even a bit of blood on the grips and streaking down the crooked handlebars, right where he'd spilled it, only a couple nights ago.

The door behind him glided open and someone in heavy cowboy boots ambled in and belched loudly enough to produce an echo. "Shitfire, Hawaiians don't know fuckall about good barbecue."

Zef whirled around and backed up against the glass case, making the ruined Harley rock on its mounts. *Sweet Jesus, not again…*

The man was big, tall and barrel-chested, his big grin smeared with barbecue sauce he wiped off on the pearl-button cuffs of an impossibly elaborate embroidered cowboy shirt. Zef never watched TV in the daytime, but he recognized the man instantly from commercials, billboards, bus benches, tabloids at checkout stands. It seemed wrong to see him walk into a room without hearing a wave of canned studio applause.

"Shit, boy, why're you dressed like you just knocked up one of my daughters?"

Zef floundered for about ten seconds without making anything like a word.

"Like, yo, dawg…"

"Call me 'dog' or any of your ghetto honorifics again, and a man will come in here and break your jaw."

"Uh…"

"D'you know how to ride?"

"Wha—what, like a motorcycle?"

"No, damn it. I'm the proud owner of proof you can't ride a motorcycle worth a shit. Horses. Do you know how to ride them?"

"N-no… sir…"

"Fine," he grouched, going over to the window to wave away a trail guide and a couple saddled horses waiting outside. "Go ahead and wear that, then. Thought I heard you were from Nevada…"

Even on the edge of losing his temper, he had that kind of warm, sunny Southern accent that somehow sounded like both a dimwitted hick and a fruity snob at the same time, like that loser vice president who went crazy telling everybody we were all gonna melt if we didn't stop cows farting.

"You like the house?" Without waiting for Zef to answer, he brought over two glasses of wine from an old Hawaiian man who bowed and turned back into furniture. "I had all the rock taken from the Waipio Valley, where the last of the old cities of refuge on the Big Island was, before Kamehameha leveled them all. Used to be, no matter what you did, they had to grant you sanctuary. It kind of still works, I guess… My wife hates it up here because of the cold. Kids, too, because *everybody* works on my ranch. So this is where I come when I want to forget what I have to do for a living, and just be a man." He wrinkled his nose like something smelled. "You know who I am? What I do?"

"I think so... I mean, I don't watch your show... I hate that talk show shit." He didn't say how his mom had all his books and watched his show every afternoon as she rearranged her poisoned candy.

"Not half as much as I do, boy, I tell you what... But who I am ain't so important. What I am, is a member by marriage of the clan of King Kamehameha. Get your feet off my fuckin' couch."

Zef obeyed, head buzzing. This was the whitest Hawaiian ever.

His host went over to stand beside the Harley, set his empty wine glass on its case. "I was gonna have it repaired, but this is more authentic, more... real, you know? Like how the movie ended. You crashed it real good, real good indeed. Looking at this, I would've figured the fella who was riding it never walked again, yet here you sit." He raised his glass to be refilled. "Tough hombre."

Zef nodded shyly. The wine tasted like vinegary cough syrup.

"Yes, you're resilient, alright. Not a goal-oriented person, though, yes? More of a subsistence gleaner. Not a strategic person. You get by on whatever thrills and pussy you can scrounge up, and you kind of figure as long as you keep thinking small, you'll just live forever, pretty much the way you are now." He toasted Zef again, smile even bigger. He probably had a sweatshop somewhere in Europe where people grew hair matched to his for annual follicle transplants. It looked both ridiculously expensive and expensively ridiculous.

"See, just by looking at your cheap tattoos and your expensive sunglasses, I can tell you have no head for managing money, to say nothing for your raging impulse control issues. You have to fix something in your mind that you want, and work towards it, or people will always take advantage of you, son."

He refilled their glasses and set the empty bottle on a pedestal beside a bronze bust of himself. "I don't ride motorcycles, myself. Hate the fucking things. Hate the people who ride them even more. But it's an iconic item, one of a kind. Its value is almost entirely because so many other people would throw away good money just to have it. I make so much more than I need, that the only thing that makes me want anything anymore, is that somebody else wants it. I know it's a barrier to my spiritual development, but damn, it sure is funny to hear some maggot spit and cuss and cry as he accepts a direct credit transfer of seven hundred thousand dollars.

"If I fixed it, I would've just fetished on it until my son stole it to punish me for neglecting him, unaware that I'd had it rigged so it'd crash on him. Then I'd lord it over him and make him earn off the fair market value for a couple years, at least. But this... it's *inspiring*. So anyway... to business." He slammed his glass into Zef's, crushing it to shards.

"Whatever, man, fok..." Dropping the broken stem, he said, "So what the fok d'you want, man?"

"I gather your visit to our fair islands hasn't been the vacation of a lifetime."

"I'm not knocking it, but, like..."

"You hate it here."

Zef shrugged.

"Well said. Well, then you'll like this. You want to avenge yourself on this whole place, you do what I'll pay you half a million dollars to do, and kill Donny Punani."

"No fucking way."

Unhearing, the big man went over to a glass table and emptied a vial out on it. "You want some coke? This shit is pure Colombian product from a DEA interdiction in Juarez last month." Smiling absently, rolling a hundred-dollar bill into a tight tube, he passed it to Zef without touching any himself. "You look more like a tweaker, but you've never had coke this pure, I tell you what."

It smelled like a trap, but for two cardinal points. To wit: Zef didn't give a fuck what this fruitcake thought of him, and didn't want to work for him, so if it was a test, he'd fail with flying colors.

Furthermore, if he just wanted to drug or otherwise incapacitate Zef, he could've done the wine. But as Zef took the bill, some spark of a glint of something in the big man's eye made him ask for more wine as he bent over the lines.

When his back was turned, Zef blew into the straw and erased the line.

When he came back with another glass, the big man stared at him like he was trying to ascertain if Zef was, in fact, wearing the jockey shorts he'd been issued. "Yes sir, one tough motherfucker."

Zef snorted and rolled his eyes and grinned, knocked back the whole glass of wine. Overcome by curiosity, he took a tiny dab of the white stuff under his fingernail and rubbed it on his gums.

His heart went triple-time. The left side of his face went slack and numb as a eunuch's ball-sac.

"What kind of porn do you favor, Zephyrus? I'm guessing you like girl-girl stuff, strictly. Sure, it flatters your manhood that two women would make themselves available to you sexually, right? But you're really just intimidated by the sight of another man's erect penis. Probably some homosexual panic at work there, too."

"I'm not a ho—I'm not, like, an assassin, man. I'm just a repo ninja."

"Of course not. That's why I want you. See, the stone killer thing in action movies, it's a myth. They never pull one last job and turn into good guys and retire on an island somewhere. The window between becoming a competent assassin and burning out and either offing himself or getting offed by his employers is so short as to not be worth it.

"No, a competent operator in a specialized profession such as automotive repossession, gifted in stealth and blessed with initiative and good old-fashioned gumption, it's a short jump to contract murder, if he's properly motivated by hate and fear. Play the hand you've been dealt, kid."

"But I don't hate him, and I'm not afraid of him..." That image of Donny holding up the king of Hawaii's severed head swam up in his mind's eye.

Fuck it. Zef did a polite bump.

"You *should* hate him. He sure as hell hates *you*. And you needn't fear him, but you damn sure better be afraid of me."

Zef grinned until he realized it wasn't a joke. The tiny taste of coke made the defibrillator shock feel like a mild static zap from a shag carpet. Everything was blacklit with intrigue and drama. The big man kept talking.

"Y'see, most of the locals pay lip service to Christian doctrine, but in their hearts, they're still a very superstitious, spiritually backward people. Indulging in sorcery, animism—"

"Aw, sick! Like, what, like bestiality…?"

"It's even worse. Shut up now." Putting a hand over Zef's quivering lips, he went on, "So some people are trapped in this cycle of ignorance, and some other people take advantage of it. Your friend Donny Punani has gotten a free pass all his life from the Hawaiian community because they think he's some kind of a demigod—"

"Like Hercules? Or like Thor, like in that…"

"Right, exactly, very astute, gold star, Zephyrus. So anyway, this sack of entitlement passes himself off as some kind of god just because his mom didn't know who his dad was. The legend goes that he's one of Don Ho's bastards, from when he used to sing at Honey's, back when it was still in Kaneohe. You know, 'Tiny Bubbles,' all that shit?"

Zef, nodding the whole time, nodded faster. "If you say so."

"Fine. So that shit might even be true… I hear the sonfoabitch can sing the panties off a nun. But then his mom went batshit crazy and was going around saying her Donny was a ghost-god and that her real baby-daddy was a shark, can you believe that shit? And not just a shark, but King of the sharks, who could change into a man but was really a dragon or some such shit, and she was looking for someone to kill him…"

Omigod. "What's her name?"

"What? Who?"

"The old wi—the mother."

"Goddamn, I don't know. That shit's not gonna snort itself, ya know."

Zef noticed the sweat-rivets popping on the big man's forehead. The coke made him nervous. Dicks like this got off on their own self-control, like it was just another drug. Zef took his time with the next line.

Smooth as a tomahawk to the face. He wished that pussy Punani was here, right now. "So, like, how come you hate this fokker so much?"

Knocking off the bottle without dirtying a glass, the big man said, "So all along, this shitbird's been talking up this line of nativist supremacy bullshit. Hawaii for Hawaiians, bring back the King, all that shit. But when it finally comes time to walk the walk and do something about all the terrible hotels and ocean liners and tourism ruining his homeland, he goes on vacation in Las Vegas."

Zef looked up from the mirror, dust spilling out of his nose. The big man pointed a remote at a big portrait of himself by Thomas Kinkade. The ghastly painting vanished, replaced by a video loop of Zef's Dad's boss, Doug Zweibel, escorting two astronomically expensive whores down a hotel hallway to his penthouse suite. When the doors closed on the empty hall, the image jumped and crackled with static.

"That's the security camera feed from the night ol' Doug killed himself. None of those girls remember a fucking thing." Looking significantly at Zef, he finally said, "Anything with a pussy, he can turn on or off like a lightswitch… but I guess you already discovered that."

"I get it, fok. Go on…"

"So, here's the thing… The wizard-science shit you see on *CSI* notwithstanding, LVPD is a bunch of dipshits who couldn't find coke in Paris Hilton's purse without a TV crew to help plant it, so when the coroner came up short about half a head, nobody figured on foul play, but they got this bit of something they withheld from the media… It's amazing what you can find out when you have fifteen-hundred-dollar-an-hour lawyers at your beck and call…

"What they found in what was left of ol' Doug's head was a tooth, Zephyrus. A shark's tooth."

Zef's heart skipped a beat.

"How to explain such a thing? Fucked if I can, but it sounds like somebody trying to send a message. But I'm not praising myself too highly when I say I'm a hell of a lot smarter than the Vegas detectives, so instead of following Punani here, they've been leaning real hard on your poor old father."

"What's this got to do with my Dad?"

The big man poured out more coke but guarded it with an arm, plowing it around with a security card. "I hear jail and interrogation is hardest on ex-cops, boy… They know what to expect, but the helplessness eats them up inside. And if they've got half a brain over there, the Vegas dicks've got some big black bastard on his case.

"So anyway, they've got no leads except for this tooth and the security system on the top three floors going sideways and sticking on a loop right before Zweibel got offed. Now, Zweibel had the whole top floor, but that same night, a high-roller's suite was rented to a party on a card backed by a stolen ID. They were supposedly in their room after ten, but the cameras, like I said… Any of these pieces of smegma look familiar to you?"

Zef looked at the big flat screen and nearly ruined the fine Corinthian leather couch. Of course. Prowling the same abominably carpeted hotel: Punani, Kewalo and Peapea.

"So this piece of shit is partying in the building when Doug Zweibel gets his head smashed in and goes off the top of his own hotel, and then he takes your client's property and bangs his wife, too…

"Actually, apropos of nothing, this is just too sad not to share…" He got up and ambled back over to the wreck, leaving Zef and the coke alone together. "He tells me all this when I'm trying to close the deal. He put her in the hospital, this fellow you were working for, but she insisted the Hawaiian never touched her. She wanted him to, she told him—and at the extremities to which he'd taken her, she was in no position to lie—but he wouldn't do the deed. Said it would kill her. But she was trying to go find him when he caught her." He ran his hands over the ruined motorcycle. "Love, American style."

Zef wasn't doing well, being in the same room with the coke. Another molecule of it and he would agree to anything. "So, you were saying…"

The big man hit a button on his remote. Nothing happened. "So these bad motherfuckers come back to Hawaii…" Again. The Kinkade portrait came back.

"God damn it, what the fuck good is this piece of shit?" He threw the remote at a huge Lalique glass sculpture and shattered it, which seemed to calm him down.

"I don't need to tell ya, folks're shittin' kittens. Now, you may be wondering why I give a shit about your Dad, or some dickscrape Jew casino owner... Well, Zweibel is my partner, in the same sense that you're my employee. I bought him out of a huge hole he'd dug for himself in Atlantic City, so I'm using his muscle to expand his hotel chain into the islands and the Caribbean. Cuba is just a dead dictator away, and we're going to be first in on it... or we were, anyway. With Doug dead and his holdings tied up in court, a bunch of massive projects are dying on the vine, and the source of all our troubles is that fat poi-eating, blue-balled motherfucker."

"And you want me to dead him for half a million..."

"I don't expect you to do it yourself; we'll help you with support and cover all expenses."

"But he's some kind of ganglord..."

"A small-time pot dealer with delusions of grandeur. His fucking posse doesn't even carry guns. He thinks he's untouchable. He took this motorcycle because it was a totem of American power. He thought riding it would be like teabagging Uncle Sam, like it'd make him bulletproof. That's how his mind works. You and a couple cutouts show up at his door with heavy artillery, his own people will turn a blind eye and let you waste him. They're afraid of him, the dumb fuckin' sea-hicks."

"But I still don't see, like... why me? You're like the richest motherfucker on TV, you could hire like ex-

CIA killers or have the Navy drop a missile on him, or whatever…"

"I probably could, but you've got something I can't buy. You've got a motive. You came over here to repossess a motorcycle, and he gave you the full Wile E. Coyote treatment. You're down to your last inch of skin, boy. If they catch you—and we'll move heaven and earth to insure they don't—then they'll know the why and the what, case closed.

"So, you have no better friend than me, Zephyrus. But if you decide not to accept this commission, or if you duck out on your responsibility or attempt to implicate me in the unlikely event of your arrest, then your father will suddenly become the prime suspect in the murder of Doug Zweibel."

"Whatthefok—"

"Secret Cayman Islands accounts stuffed with embezzled funds will suddenly materialize in Joorgen DeGroot's name, and his security business will be embroiled in a web of shady dealings. The Feds love criminal enterprises, it means they get to take your house and your car and all your material possessions and sell them at auction. By the time anyone even gets around to asking your father what he knows about Zweibel's death in a court of law, he'll be a ghost."

Blowing the last of the coke into Zef's face, the big man laughed ominously. "But none of that needs to happen, does it?"

"Fok, man, this isn't the way to…"

"Make friends? Influence people? Don't try to lay that trip on me, baby. A wise man once said, 'I never ask a man for a favor unless I have his pecker in my pocket.'"

Zef ran a finger over the glass and rubbed it against his gums. Already, the shit was wearing off. He felt cold and feeble.

"So, do we have a deal, or do you want to hear a bit more about what's behind Door Number Two?"

13
CRUEL SUN

Everyone said Maui was different, and they nodded like this was some sage fucking shit. Oahu was a big tourist trap, but on Maui the peaceful and sedate pace of the islands held sway. Zef didn't need to turn off his new iPod or close his eyes and listen to his breathing to discover for himself how different it was, because there was nothing fucking here.

Maui—the guy the island was named for—supposedly pulled the place up from the ocean floor while fishing. He should've thrown it back. Two dead volcanoes made up the island, and in between, a field of sugarcane with low, cheap houses camouflaged on the sere grassy plain, built to minimize losses when they were washed away. He saw plenty of green on the north and eastern faces of the island from the chopper, but the rest of it looked like South Africa again.

Maui's western flank was surrounded by lesser islands that looked unfinished and empty, or scoured clean of any signs of life, any color but brown. Lanai was a hump of barren rock with some stubble of development at its summit—where rich people went skiing in winter, the pilot told him. The island was once owned by Standard Fruit Company, aka Dole, but now some Microsoft billionaire owned it.

Kaho'Olawe, an even smaller rock to the south, used to be holy ground, denied to living feet. The US Navy continued the native tradition by making it an artillery test firing range. A tiny atoll called Molakini, a horseshoe nub of rock, served as a snorkeling destination.

Molokai loomed like a storm on the northern horizon. Steeper and more forbidding than its naked neighbors, Molokai was swathed in tortured gray clouds, like an island of the dead. It was easy to see them for what they were, from the air. The ocean wasn't the desert; it was fucking outer space.

The islands were worlds unto themselves, fixed with the same face always into the trade winds and the rains, so the windward sides looked like the Amazon, while the leeward landscapes looked like the Transvaal. The black-red sands of southern Maui were like mounds of rust, washed across the central two-lane highway loops like dried mineral blood.

They dropped him off with his luggage on the Kapalua Plantation golf course on the northwest corner of the island. He jogged across the putting green to take keys to a red rental Mustang from a tubby Hawaiian kid. "You need anything, bruddah, you call Yolo. You got one fat credit line, I hear." He gave Zef a little tourist guide with numbers handwritten all over it. On the cover, a scribbled shaggy stick figure with a huge dick jizzing out the word "YOLO" and a phone number.

"This a real small island, yeah? They not too many bad men left, but he know guys who work clean, you wanna get hooked up or beef out a crew."

Zef had thought about very little else. If he could hire a reliable assassin and split the fee, it was all good. And hiring a professional killer should be easy. People had to do it every day. Murders went unsolved all over the place, and Hawaii was no different. You only heard about the ones who fucked up or tried to welsh out on paying.

Lahaina was like Dodge City or Deadwood, the main drag a tourist trap with the neon and plastic wrapped around a core of old gray wood and brick and whalebone. The buildings along the waterfront had balconies like New Orleans, and wood sidewalks leading to posh art galleries, jewelers and T-shirt places and shaved ice huts. There were only three streets running through downtown and they were all blocked up like Black Friday. Zef pulled into a pay lot across from a dive shop and strolled down Front Street.

Hawaiian shaved ice was pretty good, but the fat fuck put weird beans and condensed milk on it, and it melted so fast his hand was purple and he had a brain-freeze trying to keep up, so he tossed the shit in the ocean. He sat on the wall overlooking the harbor. They used to hunt whales out here when there were still too many, and bring the oil and blubber and ambergris here to sell. Now, a ferry took rich people—a few carrying fucking skis and poles, no shit—across the strait to Lanai, and speedboats went by towing tourists attached to parachutes, like they were fishing for giant birds with fat white bait.

Wasn't so bad… A G could get used to life here, if he was old and had nothing else to look forward to.

It was nice and quiet, and then a slammed pickup truck jerked out of traffic and jumped the curb and a Hawaiian giant with a Mohawk jumped out and came running at him.

Zef looked around, thinking this couldn't be about him. An old ex-Navy guy with a little Japanese wife was crossing the street on a walker and cussing out the hostess out front of Bubba Gump Shrimp Company, but otherwise the sidewalk was empty. The guy was maybe ten yards away when Zef jumped off the wall and ran, still looking at the fucker over his shoulder.

Ripped like a weightlifter, mid-twenties, huge, juiced pecs chewing up his Da Hui tanktop as he came pumping after Zef, not so much running as kicking the whole world in the face at incredible velocity. Before Zef got ten paces, he was almost close enough for Zef to smell the protein shake and Spam he had for lunch.

Zef jumped off the curb and onto the sloping hood of a minivan, sprang off it onto the roof of a station wagon, and stage-dived into a thick crowd of totally unprepared pedestrians. A fat guy and his wife in matching aloha shirts took his weight. With their half dozen kids and grandkids in matching shirts and muumuus tumbling on top of them, Zef popped up and ran into Old Lahaina Center's parking lot.

Zef rounded a corner and crashed into a fat lady and knocked over a grandpa in an OLD GUYS RULE T-shirt. Screams and curses echoing behind him, he sprinted through the drifting shoppers like a tight end threading a slow-motion defense. But high and tight on his ass, he heard the fucking Mohawk plowing everyone he'd missed. Somebody tried to tackle Mohawk and whatever happened to the fool set his wife screaming like a Greek funeral.

Zef's lungs were on fire. Sweat ran into his eyes, blinding him and making him slap at his face. This guy would run him down like a cheetah taking a chain-smoking gazelle in an open sprint, but his muscles would turn to dead weight on him fast in an endurance run. His fucking buddies were circling around the block in their truck, and he didn't even know what the fuck this was all about.

Zef passed close to a kiosk called Sarongs & Thongs and threw the bikini display down in his wake. He heard Mohawk grunt and a satisfyingly prolonged crash of metal and glass. A tubby security guard shouted at Zef to slow down, but he gave him the finger and ran in the back entrance of Banzai Blacklite Indoor Minigolf.

Day glo-inflected darkness and dank AC were like a moldy bag over his head triggering an acid flashback. Banzai flags, barbed wire, dayglo camouflage and a gaggle of little kids throwing tantrums all over eighteen jungle boobytraps.

An ancient Asian man in a beige forage cap and baggy fatigues stood by the door under yellow newsclippings: *LAST TO SURRENDER—Japanese Officer Lived 32 Years As Castaway, Fighting WW2 Alone*. Zef snatched a putter out of the old Jap's hand and blundered into brats that screeched like dry ice on steel underfoot. The screechers' father started in on him just as Mohawk came in the door.

Zef teed off on Mohawk like a samurai bisecting an uppity peasant. The putter's head buried in the weightlifter's taut belly, folding him over as he stampeded past. Zef took an unopened Coke from the brat's dad and kicked him in the junk. He ran back out to the parking lot and looked around to find no slammed pickup, no Mohawk. Maybe he lost the fucker—

Someone screamed long and high in Banzai Blacklite. Mohawk bounded out the door with a bent putter in each fist. Zef threw the uncracked Coke and hit him in the arm. A putter sailed over Zef's shoulder and speared a Honda's windshield.

Across the minigolf lot, Zef jumped a guardrail and went through the Chevron station. He intercepted an older woman as she was about to put the hose in the tank of her Mercedes. "Sorry, Ma," he said, and he yanked it out of her hands just as Mohawk came around the corner of the gas station.

Zef pulled back the rubber safety sleeve and squeezed the trigger. A thick jet of 96 octane premium unleaded sluiced Mohawk's mouth and eyes just when he would appreciate it most.

Zef kept spraying the big motherfucker after he collapsed on the pavement, then rapped him on the skull with the hose gun.

Taking out a Bic lighter, he knelt in front of Mohawk. "Fancy a smoke, fok?"

The Hawaiian couldn't see or hear Zef. His eyes were swollen shut and streaming like runny poached eggs. He vomited a thick paste filled with vitamins and supplements and nothing remotely like food.

"Who the fok you working for? Why you wanna fok with me, cheese?"

"You," Mohawk gasped, still dry-heaving, "killed... Primo..."

Holy fucking shit. Fucking Hawaii Five-Oh... "No way, bitch. I was way tight with Primo. Some local fok ate his face..."

The TV on the gas pump said something that made Zef's head snap around so fast something tore in his neck. They said something about Mexico's drug wars coming home. "Bodies of suspected members of Mexico's notorious Iglesias cartel were found in the Shadow Rock Park area just outside Las Vegas..."

Zef swallowed hard. He recognized the terrain behind the cops escorting plastic bags out of a shallow ravine. It was ten minutes from his parents' house in Sunrise Manor.

"Sheriff's spokesman Donald Luna declined to provide details, but confirmed that FBI agents have stepped into the case, which bears all the hallmarks of the brutal executions committed in Mexico, but anonymous department insiders said the forensic evidence was contaminated by animal attacks—"

The slammed pickup roared into the Chevron lot. Zef kicked Mohawk in the face and ran, vaulting over a wooden stake fence and through a thorny wall of bougainvillea.

He was in a pay lot. The pickup went through the fence and clipped two parked cars coming after him.

He ran for the little booth with a tired Samoan woman who just pulled down her shade as he passed.

The pickup was right on his ass and anybody at the wheel under those circumstances probably would've missed all the signs and driven over the tire spikes, just like he did.

The truck screamed and hissed and face-planted on its front bumper. Zef ran looking over his shoulder, bent double and coughing laughter until a surf school van ran into him and honked. He shoved off the grill and ran through the McDonald's lot and across Papalua Street.

He could hear them coming after him on foot, one of them shouting, "Stop or I'll cap your ass." Another weightlifter, but shorter than most middle school kids, and a big tubby amateur who ran with his hand down his baggy board shorts to keep his concealed gat from falling in the street.

Traffic fell off to a few bicyclists telling him to *Mellow out* as they passed before he could knock them down, the only sounds the syrupy songs of birds in the trees and his fierce, whipsaw breathing. His legs burned, his shoes felt like they were full of hornets and broken glass. Over his shoulder, the weightlifter was sixty yards back and fading. The tubby bitch was grabbing his chest and leaning against a parked car.

He could get off the street and catch his breath somewhere, then circle back to his car and find this Yolo clown...

The gunshot was not loud at all, just a flat clap, but it startled the birds from the trees. Zef heard it smack the trunk of a tree just ten feet off to his right. The last of the starch in Zef's shorts went out and he fell down hard on his ass.

He rolled in the street. Crawled between two parked cars. Jumped a ditch and ran across Honoapiilani Highway. Four lanes of screeching, fishtailing tourist traffic. Bum-rushed the entrance of a surf and dive shop. Through the store and out the back behind a Pizza Hut fused with a Taco Bell. Behind him, the midget and the tubby bitch humped across the highway amid the mess made by his crossing. Gun concealed again. Purple fury faces.

Zef felt like he was falling, not running. Falling forward, crazy legs scrambling to catch up, and if his brain was too freaked out to form words, it still felt good for just this moment, to be a skinny little fucker. A bigger man would've had to stop for breath and gotten his ass clipped. These fuckers had no idea who they were fucking with. This shitty place almost made him forget who and what he was. Every last one of them would regret their mistake—

Zef was climbing over a fence to hide in a condo pool area when they shot at him again. He heard one of those whining ricochet noises like bullets only make in movies. He jumped the fence and landed bad on one ankle, limped through chaise lounges and sunbathers like meat on a grill. He staggered into a table and knocked over a big umbrella. The midget weightlifter vaulted over the fence. The tubby bitch was circling around. Zef couldn't remember how many shots he had left.

Through a shaded palm tree arbor and across another lot, and he ran out of land. Beyond a high chainlink fence, there was a canal about twenty feet deep and almost ninety across: steep concrete flood channel walls just like back home, with a little ribbon of scummy green water down below. Nothing but open space in both directions along the canal. And beyond the canal, Walgreens, dive shop, Foot Locker and an Inaminnit Urgent Care Clinic.

"Where he go?" he heard one of them, so close he almost jumped into the canal on reflex.

Just down the canal a hundred feet or so, a thin, rusty corrugated tin drainpipe crossed the canal like a bridge. The fence with barbed wire around it had a sign that said NOT A BRIDGE PLEASE.

He scaled it easily and started to run across when a gunshot went off and he felt the hot ballistic wind just over his shoulder.

Zef dove and flattened, hugging the blistering sheetmetal pipe. Halfway across. Rust crumbs flew up in his face. The pipe settled. Without stopping, he ran on all fours across the pipe like a spider monkey, whooping breathless and shitting hot brown spray down one leg until he leapt over the barbed wire on the far end and it caught on his shirt and tore it clean off.

He hit the ground rolling and came up with a rock in his hand and the midget was stumbling along the pipe with his hands out like a circus tightrope walker while the tubby bitch covered him with the gun.

Zef took aim and hurled the rock in a perfect spiral longbomb pass. The midget raised his hands up like to catch it, but the sun was in his eyes, and then so was the rock. It clocked him solidly in the forehead, sent him flying backwards to land straddling the pipe, then he rolled off backwards and landed headfirst in the slimy channel.

The tubby bitch screamed and fired once more into the air in his frustration. Zef threw a few more rocks at him, taunting him to come get some, but the goon ignored him to get down to save his friend.

Doubled over coughing, Zef lay until he could breathe and then called the number from the matchbook.

It rang. He heard it ring in his ear. And also down in the shallow canal. Sitting up, he saw the tubby bitch picking his way down the embankment to rescue his friend, who was maybe or maybe not breathing.

Yolo. "Fokking hell!"

Maybe he should call the big man's people right away and order another gangster.

A huge old Ford Bronco full of surfboards cut him off and three local guys with long, fierce hair got out.

"You wanna ride," the littlest one said. He was big enough that Zef would get a nosebleed climbing him.

"Yeah, sure. You know where the Hilton is, right?"

They thought that was funny.

No way were they cops, and yet they felt like cops, the way a fucker took hold of his head to push him down as he got in the back seat, and yet they couldn't seem to get him in without steering him into the doorpost twice.

The marina was on the south side, at the bottom of the valley between the two dead volcanoes, next to an aquarium and a minigolf and a Carl's Jr. A fat guy in Titleist golfwear splattered with fish blood came storming up the dock with a squealing grade-schooler under each arm and an older boy in tow silently crying and staring daggers at his dad, and a flushed, drunken wife who berated him up the dock to the parking lot. "Why didn't you *do something*? Your son will be telling this to a therapist, and how do you think you're gonna come off, *Papa*? I'll tell you why you didn't do anything, and why you never will. He's twice the man you ever were…"

Zef followed the local posse down the pier to a big grotty fishing boat with a shark hanging by its tail over the stern.

A huge old Hawaiian with white hair down to his elbows leaned against the gunwale of the boat, watching the family flee. He burped and cut the rope so the shark fell to the pier and flopped almost onto Zef's shoes. "Don't forget your trophy, fuckers," he growled.

Zef looked at the shark. Pretty decent-sized fish— seven feet long, maybe a hundred pounds and change. Its mouth was torn and streaming blood onto the white plastic, and its pectoral fins had been chopped off.

"Try to show *haoles* something about nature," the giant said, "you wasting your time."

Zef stood on the dock, wondering what the fuck to do. He wanted to get on this boat about as much as he wanted to fuck that shark. Two of the big longhaired fuckers who brought him there crowded him up the gangplank.

"Yo, why you got such a hard-on for sharks?"

The plank bobbed under him as the two big guys backed the fuck away from the boat.

The old kanaka grinned. "They got a hard-on for me. Permission to come aboard granted, motherfucker."

Zef stepped over the gunwale, averting his eyes from the big old local's wide, flushed face. Bad idea.

Looking at his shoes, looking for his shoes… He had no feet. Or calves. Or knees. Or thighs. His huge torso terminated in a slightly abbreviated pelvis, but both legs had apparently been amputated at the hip joint. Amputated, or eaten.

He dropped off the gunwale and padded across the deck on catcher's mitt hands. His arms were thicker than Zef's thighs, gnarly worker's muscles under a deceptive layer of fat. He closed in on Zef and offered a hand to shake. He stood perfectly balanced on the other hand. He still came up to Zef's shoulder. When he had legs, he must've stood almost seven feet tall.

"Maui Isaiah Waiwaiole. People call me Yeti." Turning to roll up the ropes the thugs tossed him from the dock, he gently shoved Zef into a fishing chair at the stern and padded to the bridge. A little old geek standing at the wheel gave him a thumbs up.

The boat snarled and threw up a roostertail twenty feet high as it blasted out of the marina. The two big thugs watched until they were out on open water, like they were expecting Zef to jump and try to swim for it. He had been thinking about it.

They turned west, doubling back up the wild, barren coast that Zef had just seen on the ride from Lahaina. The scenery looked like a drawing by a hyperactive child with only two crayons. He didn't see anyone else on the boat besides Yeti and the geek. Was this a burial at sea? Zef figured he could take an old motherfucker with no legs, even if he did still outweigh him…

A powerful hand on his shoulder twisted his arm half out of its socket. He followed it, trying not to whine. The half-giant shoved him against the stern, bent him backwards until the spray doused his neck. The mighty inboard motor roared underneath him, making his ass go numb.

The sun was falling fast behind a miraculous wall of clouds over Lanai, like an oil painting in a church. The nearest boat was a toy on the horizon.

"You that motherfucker the cops want on Oahu, yeah? Tied up with Primo." He said it casually, like it was no big shit at all.

"Yo, I barely knew that dude, man. I'm just here on vaycay, looked him up to party with, y'know, and…"

"And you touch down on Maui in a private chopper and with a quickness get into a running gunfight through Lahaina with Primo's fucking cousin."

"Yo, I wasn't even strapped! And I didn't know that fokker, either… All I know, like… Yo, where we going, man?"

"Depends." Yeti smiled and let him go, trotted on his palms to check three big angling poles rested in scabbards off the stern. Their lines dragged in the wake, reminding Zef of getting clotheslined in Pearl City. Zef came up after him, looking for something to use as a weapon.

Yeti threw a balled-up rag at him. Zef shook it out and grudgingly put it on. A tattered, oil-stained T-shirt, it said KEEP THE COUNTRY COUNTRY.

Yeti laughed. "I gave it to you to wipe that shit off your leg."

"Lemme borrow yours," Zef said.

One of the poles bowed almost double. Yeti climbed up into the chair and snatched the pole out of the scabbard. "You know, a shark can taste blood on the water a hundred miles away. Follow the trail for days across open ocean to get at it. Course, by then, the open water is pretty full of other sharks, and they have a feeding frenzy. Tear each other up, turn the water to red shark soup. They don't even like human flesh. They'd rather eat each other."

Zef's eyes involuntarily darted downwards. "Listen, it's all just a big misunderstanding, y'know wha'm sayin'?"

"Yeah, I hear. You just on vacation." Yeti laughed, winding the reel in. "You havin' one shitty vacation, brother."

"Hawaii hates me. But, like, you don't have to…"

"Bullshit, brother. I think Hawaii trying to save you. I don't have to do shit, except find out who you workin' for."

"I'm not working for… well, I'm like freelance…"

A big callused hand came up and caught his jaw. The other hand whipped the pole back into its scabbard. "Truth, or I take you fishing. You just the right bait for what I'm looking to catch."

Zef looked back over his shoulder. The wake of the boat was a white carpet of foam paved over the jagged, dancing peaks of the deep blue sea. Something lurched up out of the wake, obscured by spray, impaled on Yeti's hook.

"I'm working for, like some people in Vegas, y'know what I mean? Heavy hitters, yo. And, like, if I go missing…"

Wiping a tear from his eye, Yeti said, "You too dumb to be with the cartels, *haole* boy. So how come my cousins say you got picked up by that TV Doctor fucker?"

Zef's poker face sucked.

Draining a beer in one mighty pull, Yeti dropped the flattened can in a recycling bin, belched, and took up the pole. "They treat us like furniture, so we hear everything, *haole* boy. Shit, that motherfucker owns almost as much of these islands as his fat hogbitch boss. Think he's gonna be one motherfucking chief, and shit. What he want so bad, he gotta hire a repo ninja?"

Zef choked down the insult and tried to think about this. Every one of these fuckers was somebody's cousin. He couldn't think of a good lie, so he just said it. "Donny Punani."

He expected the big amputee to blanch and change the subject like everyone else had, but Yeti took his hand off Zef and let him sit down. He stared into the sunset as he fought the big fish dragging in their wake. The wind lifted his white hair and made it look like fog around a mountain. "You know why fuckers call me Yeti?"

He didn't wait for an answer. "Five-O did it to piss me off, but it stuck. I was the Abominable Snowman, no joke. One bad fucker, never convicted. I ran with the gangs because there wasn't nothing else to do, like what a warrior would do in the way back. If you don't want to join the Navy or play football, you can work in the hotels. Only reason we remember our culture at all is for shows for the tourists. So I connected these islands to the cartels and made it snow.

"We tried to flip it and sell only to the tourists and the squids and grunts. But the gangs over here were like everything else, just a franchise, bringing poison in and pumping all the money back to the mainland. One gang fronts for the Mexicans, another for the Japanese, now the Chinese want a piece. So fuck that shit. I walked away, and now I fight the real fight, against the real enemy."

"Who's that?"

"Ha! Against *you* people," he said, with a smile. "I fight for *kanaka maoli*, the true people, to have our islands back."

"That's crazy, man," he said, but something in his gut felt way past its expiration date, all of a sudden. Something the big man said… "So you fighting a revolution, like, or what?"

"Oh, we never gonna drive you out in a straight fight, but someday, the shit you sow gonna come to harvest, and America gonna be too busy keeping her own head above it to keep her thumb on the old bloods anymore. Queen Lilioukalani's people gonna be free."

"That's cool, yo, like I'm with that, like fight the power, shit—"

"When the white missionaries came, they outlawed our culture, our sports, our magic and our gods. They made us believe we were savages, cannibals, because of what happened to Captain Cook."

Zef nodded, didn't ask who Captain Cook was.

"We cooked him," Yeti winked, "but we didn't eat him. We had stories about monsters who ate human flesh that we told to remind us, when the missionaries or the plantation overseers weren't around, of what it really meant to lose your soul. Donny Punani is the kind of monster they thought they were saving us from."

The boat had turned north. The sun went down behind the shoulder of Lanai and the sky turned purple. The coast flattened out and sported clusters of lanais and walled estates, a few stand-up paddlers working the lazy waves like raking the rows of a garden. The fear that he was going to get killed out here started to recede behind a cloud of utter incomprehension. What the fuck did this old geezer want?

Trimming the line, Yeti said, "Fucker's getting tired. You look down there and you see all kinds of fish and the sharks just swimming among them, they seem to have no strife. But when you catch a fish, everything else in the sea come in to take a bite. If you not fast, all you get is the head."

"So, like… It's cool if I, uh…"

Yeti scowled. "Help me land him."

"Who?"

With a growling roar, Yeti hauled on the pole and dragged a six foot blacktip reef shark halfway out of the water. Zef gasped, looking into its empty eyes, its gasping, blood-rimmed mouth. Holding it where Yeti showed him, he grappled its weight out of the water while Yeti got something out of a smelly bucket. "I can lift him in," Zef said, but Yeti shook his head. "No, this one's too small. I put him back. But first…"

Yeti held up something so the shark could see it, then dropped the big black pincushion—a sea urchin—into its mouth.

The shark thrashed against the boat like a hanging man. Though it made no sound, Zef could feel its agony.

Chuckling, Yeti cut the line and let the mutilated shark fall into the foam.

"If you think you can catch him, then I'm cool."

Zef stared into the water, waiting for the thrashing shark to leap back into the boat. "Well, like, I was supposed to have, like, a whole crew to back me up. That fok Yolo was supposed to hook me up with some fokking artillery…"

"Yolo runs—or ran, who knows—the ice kitchens on Maui, and his cousin Primo was the Mexicans' favorite errand boy. He probably could've got you some guns. I'm not the Mafia. I'm more like the IRA or the Klan." Yeti signaled to the old geek, who aimed them at the Lahaina waterfront. All the sunset booze cruises were coming back into port, blaring Iz and Don Ho.

Zef saw the parking lot across from the dive shop where he'd parked his car, about two hours ago. He probably had a fucking ticket…

Like half a gorilla, Yeti sprang up onto the gunwale and threw a rope to a kid onshore, who lashed it round a cleat and caught the next one as they eased up against the dock.

Night was falling fast and Lahaina had its lights on. Loud bionic dub rhythms blasted out of an open terrace nightclub across the street, making him feel halfway high.

Zef stood up, but Yeti perched on the gunwale, blocking his way. "You really wanna get him?"

He almost screamed, *Hell no*, but by now, he could kind of tell this wasn't a trap. *Everything* was a trap. "It's what I'm getting paid for. But like…"

Yeti steadied the gangplank for him, gave him a card. "Call tomorrow early, before eight. I gotta full-day charter. I'll set you up."

"Thanks, yo, I… thanks."

Looking down at the swirling water, he saw shapes circling, bumping against the boat. *They got a hard-on for me…*

"You don't know this place," Yeti said, "and you got no friends, so you better loosen up and look out, because this a small island."

"Where should I start looking?"

"Try right behind you, *haole* boy."

Zef jumped. He saw no looming, grizzled homicidal Hawaiians among the thinning crowd of tourists looking to recover shit they lost on a cruise or submarine ride.

Yeti laughed. Zef flipped him the finger and walked up the steps to the sidewalk. And that's when he heard it.

The techno dub had abruptly cut out at the terrace club on the second floor of the snooty restaurant across the street, and a plodding, colorless instrumental rendition of "No Woman No Cry" started to play.

Zef preemptively gagged. Fucking Hawaiians were worse than the Japs with their fucking sloppy, sentimental karaoke.

The singing started…

And this cavernous, gravelly, world-weary sound came floating out over the boulevard, and somehow, it was like nobody else had ever sung the fucking song before.

Zef crossed the street thinking, *It can't be*, but he fucking well knew that it was. He may not remember anything else about that awful night, but he remembered the stony steel breeze of that voice, and the way the room immediately reeked of pussy juice.

He looked at the stairs in the restaurant—a too-white Italian seafood bistro—and he thought about going up there and he was off the curb and cutting between two honking cars under the soft lanternlight of the night and that voice, he wanted to fuck it, he wanted it to eat him—

A gaggle of women and girls jostled him running through the restaurant and up the stairs. He remembered what happened last time. He wasn't strapped… as if he could even use a gun. He'd never shot anything bigger than a ground squirrel.

Just keep walking. He passed the restaurant and crossed back to the other side. An old woman running the shaved ice place swayed and cried.

He turned back and looked over his shoulder at the sound of a man shouting. A sweaty, drunk white guy dragged his wife down the stairs and onto the sidewalk, swinging and swatting at everything that ruined his date. His wife was crying, but Zef stopped to watch her turn her back to her husband as he tried to hail a cab, and masturbate sobbingly, leaning against a lamppost.

14
ROCK FACE

The woman next to Zef at the bar wouldn't shut up. Something about this new self-help book, something else about Aspen this time of year. She was pushing sixty, but holding up better than his mum. Said she was on her honeymoon, like it was supposed to make him want to nail her.

"You pretty rich, then," he said, unable to think of any way out of this conversation.

"I suppose some would say that," she said, "but you know, it's all about how you see yourself. Visualize, I mean. Like, the more houses and cars and things come into my life, the less it all means. I'm above it. You know, like homeless people, they're clinging to their shopping cart of junk, or whatever, they're—"

"Like Gandhi."

"What?"

"The dirty Indian diaper-guy, like... Gandhi, but like, with a Lexus."

"No, not quite. I'm like Gandhi *because* I have a Lexus. It's not getting what you want, it's wanting what you get. So, are you holding?" Her hand ran up his thigh to cup his package like testing grapefruit.

Zef squirmed. "I'm, uh, sitting on something if you…"

"My husband likes me to smoke up, because when I get relaxed, he gets anal. Of course, with *you* around, he probably won't even notice *my* brown eye."

"OK, listen…"

"Fine, he'll just watch. But you're only getting three hundred."

He didn't want to, but he forced himself to look her in the eye. Like in one of those old cartoons with the castaways on the desert island, when they look at each other and suddenly they turn into a hot dog or a hamburger; she was a stack of shrink-wrapped titties and ass cutlets.

When he opened his mouth, he might have drooled a little. "No, listen…" Wiping his mouth, "You can't talk to men like that."

"Like what?"

"Like they're, like, things. Just because we like to fok doesn't mean we can be bought, and if we can't whistle and check out your shit, you should pay us the same respect. Shit like this is why people get raped, and read those fokking 50 Shades Of Twilight books, yo…"

Horrified like she'd been insulted by her horse or her dog, the lucky bride poured her drink in his lap and stormed out of the bar. A couple people laughed, but Zef took it in stride.

He could've taken her up on her offer. He had the room and car rental and about fifty bucks in cash after replacing his lost clothes and luggage. The big man's people hadn't returned his calls. He could've at least gone with her and stolen her purse, but something had gone bent inside him, or maybe it was just gone.

He thought of the yellow crap that came out with the drugs when Kalei "massaged" him. He didn't feel any better or happier for having his "poison" extracted, he just felt empty.

The Hilton Kaanapali was like a Bond villain lair, modernist glass bubbles stacked against the forbidding black lava cliff at the north end of a too-perfect beach. His room looked out over a golf course. The room was reserved under Marlon Pussybone. He usually registered as Robert O. Saber or Roberto Sabor, both of which he could back with fake Nevada IDs.

He tried to relax with a little autofellation yoga, but something didn't feel right. Usually, it felt as natural as jacking off or picking his nose. His penis ramming the back of his throat felt as natural as his own tongue; the taste of his semen was as familiar as his own saliva. But tonight, his dick felt like a stranger's dick, which his dick liked very much, but which repulsed his mouth so that he threw up in a dry cleaning bag, then ordered a bottle of vodka and a pitcher of pineapple juice and drank until he passed out.

That night, he swam in the ocean, but he was not cold and he could see quite well, gliding through the water like a bird on the wing, short powerful strokes, and he could follow the burning trail that glowed for him like fire in the water.

Follow it into the shallows and the thin pair of legs like a crane's, scaly and stringy and alone out in the moonlit breakers, and the tide rolling back tugged his prey off balance.

The wave recoiled and reared and the wave lifted him high above his prey who turned to look at him and dropped his joint and drink and he saw his own stupefied face, broken nose askew like a bony comma, eyes bugging out in disbelief and Zef opened his mouth wide and multiple rows of jagged teeth extruded out of his lipless grimace as he tore himself in half.

Yeti's message told him to look for an old hippie who looked like Tommy Smothers, whoever that was. Zef wandered around the farmers' market and crafts fair at Banyan Park in Lahaina. The park itself was little more than a village square with benches in circles around a grove of creepy trees like melted candles. The canopy of their shade turned the morning sunlight deep green but seemed to magnify the heat.

"It's all one tree," said someone behind him.

Zef turned and stepped back with his hands up. He'd gotten pretty good at reacting to fuckers sneaking up on him, this trip.

The geezer had chamois leather for skin and shaggy gray-blonde hair down to his shoulders and a scruffy, lopsided beard. He wore a threadbare aloha shirt with a luau scene on it, a lurid green sarong and cracked old OP sandals. There had to be some mistake. He was the least deadly looking motherfucker Zef had ever seen.

"The banyan tree starts there," he said, pointing at the forking tower of gray trunks at the park's center, "and it throws out root bodies that pop up as satellite trees." He spun around to encompass the whole arbor, then leaned in close and winked. "It's all one tree, man."

Zef scratched his head and tried not to sound as stupid as he felt. "Kind of like... Like it's all one ocean, or whatever."

The old hippie put out his hand. "Right on, man. My name's Paul, but everybody on the islands calls me the Hodad." He shook Zef's hand, grinned and gripped harder when Zef ripped out, "Fok!" and tried to jerk away.

"The locals call me Unauna," he said, displaying a scaly, grayish claw with only a thumb and pinky on it. "Means 'hermit crab.'"

Zef wiped his hand on his shirt, looking for a snack bar with wet wipes. "What happened to you, man? Shark bite?"

"No way, man. Sharks *love* me. I'm a vegan, so they know I don't play their games. What's the matter, you never shook hands with a leper before?"

Zef choked on his spit trying to scream. He held his hand away from his body like he wanted a trash can to toss it in. "You fokkin' touched me with leprosy, you motherfokker..." His unclean fist shot out at Hodad's smiling face, but the guy wasn't there when the fist showed up. Looking like he got tired of waiting, he was standing on Zef's left now, until about a tenth of a second before he threw an elbow at his gut.

"Relax, man. It's not nearly as contagious as they make you think. Nobody wants to look at it, is all."

"How did *you* get it, then?"

As he walked, the little old surf geezer did a quick routine, passing both hands in front of his face, inspecting them, then down his neck. "Traded a guy for it."

"The fok you get in trade?"

Hodad just smiled. "You need help locating a guy."

"Need a lot more than that. I don't think you can lift the weight, frankly."

Hodad continued the inspection, running his hands down his legs, then holding them up and deliberately looking them over. Rolling his eyes, he explained, "No nerve endings. I have to do a visual exam every few minutes just to make sure nothing's on fire or bleeding."

Zef blinked. Motherfucker couldn't feel pain? It was less like a disease, and more like a superpower.

"You'd be right, brother. I'm not a violent man, but I'm good to have around. Nobody knows their way around here like I do, and that's a fact. And I don't know what you believe…"

"Pretty much nothing…"

"Right, but you don't got to believe to see how things work out here. So much mana floating in the air, but hardly anybody knows how to take hold of it and make it work." He snapped his two fingers in Zef's face, making him flinch. "So, who're you looking for?"

Zef studied the spaced-out watercolor seascapes laid out in rows on the ground at his feet. The woman who did them, presumably, snored in a hammock chair. "Native Hawaiian…"

"Ethnic or just legal? I'm third generation Hawaiian on my mother's…"

"He's like Polynesian or whatever, yeah, dickhead? Long hair, lotta scars, he's a karaoke killer…"

"That's half the island, brother."

188

"He and his friends like eating people's faces… Fok off! Fok off!"

A short guy in a wifebeater and a pimp hat strolled up with a big scarlet macaw on his shoulder. Zef went into a pugilist's stance and batted his hands at the bird. The parrot fanned its wings and squawked. The little guy backed up after passing a tinfoil bindle to Hodad.

Hodad puffed up his cheeks, then exhaled like he was blowing a pig's house down. "Dude, say no more. I can help you track him down, no problem. This time of year, he's holed up in Hana. Kinda hairy to go in and get him, though… But if you don't, you could be waiting for weeks."

Hodad stopped at a craft booth. "You're very talented… how much?"

The woodcutter looked up from the tiki he was chopping with a hatchet. "Fo what? What one you want?" The sullen dullness in his voice was a warning wrapped around a plea for help. But his carvings *were* pretty badass…

"For the talent, brother. How much do you figure it's worth to you?"

"Not much… Hardly nobody buy tikis no mo."

"So how much? I'll give you two thousand."

The carver looked up at last. His red-rimmed eyes were choked in wrinkles from a lifetime of squinting at tiny imperfections in koa wood. He looked at the tiki in the old haole's hands, and at the money.

As they walked away, Zef said, "Yo, what you need money for, if you can afford to blow it on tikis?"

"Oh, this?" he held up the little shrieking totem pole thing he'd paid as much as Zef just offered him to do the job. "This is junk. I'm sure I can do much better, now."

A scream came from behind them, almost before the other sound. The axe bit into concrete with a tuning fork tone so sharp and pure, it hurt Zef's ears like the axe itself biting into his head. The tiki carver dropped to his knees, weak from blood loss. The split between his middle and ring fingers extended down to his wrist.

"You should get a massage," Hodad said.

"What the fok…?"

"If we're going to do this, we've got to be pure, you know?"

"No, I don't know, and I don't—"

"No man should know his wife before we do the deed."

"What about, like, if it's not your wife?"

"I'm not a marriage counselor. But keep hold of your seed, if you want to succeed." Chuckling, he added, "I just made that up."

"Great, whatever... so, yo, like…"

"And don't step in dog shit, or any kind of shit, for that matter."

"Why?"

"It's *kapu*, man. Taboo. Also, it's, like, *shit*, man."

The next guy on Yeti's list was dead.

The guy after that was a tweaker who showed up late for the interview at a shrimp truck at a crossroads in the middle of sugarcane country. Chewing his tongue and interjecting pointless motorhead chatter whenever Zef let him talk. Dishonorably bounced from the Navy. Said he knew "Indian Country" real well because his ex-wife was "one of them." Never heard of Donny but would go anywhere and do what he was told. Threatened to shiv Zef when he told him to fuck off. Begged for a second chance even after Zef got up and left. Ran after Zef's car then dropped in his empty parking space to do pushups until he passed out of sight.

The next guy on the list was supposed to be the easy one.

Zef had to drive out to the little house near the end of Kulike Road on the North Shore, near a funky hippie town called Haiku. He drove past it the first time and had to turn around amid a jumble of trucks and surf wagons at the end of the road.

Jaws was what they called the place. Surf spot, but the waves he saw, three, four stories tall, rising up like skyscraper mouths and crashing down chewing up the earth under their feet, they were scarier than any fucking shark.

Turned around, he saw the sign for the Nectar House, obscured by shaggy walls of bougainvillea and pampas grass. Behind the hedge walls, an overgrown lawn and a couple halfpipes, a drained swimming pool partially filled with stagnant black water.

The rambling 70's modernist beach house had all its windows smashed in. The driveway out front was paved in crushed green beer bottle glass and cigarette butts. A burnt-out car chassis lay in the deep end of the pool. A naked chick came out on the porch with an unlit cigarette, but bolted back inside when Zef parked out front.

A shirtless kid a few years younger than Zef answered the door. His nose looked freshly broken. A joint like a Cuban cigar hung from his free hand. He nodded and let Zef in when he said who he was looking for. "Just take him with you, alright?"

The house looked like it had hosted a continuous kegger for a couple years, and like most bad parties, it had gone seriously south when the assholes nobody wanted to take home were left alone together. Dank rooms reeked of beer and bongwater and smoke residue. The brown deep pile shag carpet was rigid with gum, puke, surf wax, semen, pizza grease and worse; the walls scabbed with posters and stickers and psychotic graffiti; holes punched in the drywall stuffed with empty bottles and cans, rotten food and condoms.

Nektor Surfware went out of business a couple years prior, but a few successful pro surfers kept the lights on until the last Red Bull Jaws Invitational ended early, only last month. Their big booster got washing-machined and broke his neck just down the road. Zef didn't exactly give a shit about the trials and tribulations of extreme athletes or the surfwear industry, but Hodad had been quite effusive on the subject. Apparently, the guy he was here for had been quite the shit for a few minutes, a while back.

At the end of a long hallway lined with doors locked or knocked off their hinges, he found a dude on a waterbed under two bleach-blonde beach bunny burnout chicks who looked like a mother and daughter.

He yanked on the guy's big toe and said, "Bagby?"

The guy was too tall and built like he was raised on a planet with next to no gravity. He blinked at Zef and levered up on one elbow. "Fuck no," he said. His toes pointed the way to the bathroom. "Try in there."

The toilet was filled with syringes. There was a body in the bathtub. A lanky, weirdly overmuscled redhead with a face like if Gary Busey banged a horse lay in the tub up to his chin in cold, soap-scummy water with ratty old Walkman earphones on running to a boombox on the corner of the tub.

Don't take any shit from him, Hodad said.

Zef hit Pause on the boombox.

He's like any tool, Hodad said. *Don't let him get rusty. Point him in the right direction when you use him.*

Bagby came out of the water like a dolphin, on his feet and slamming an open palm into Zef's solar plexus. Zef tumbled backwards. Air wouldn't come into his lungs. He was drowning in his own chest. His head hit the wall hard enough to divot the plaster. He was charging back at the asshole before the cranial trauma could even make its presence known, but the boombox hit him in the crotch and when he tripped and fell down, the earphone cord was wrapped around his neck and he was being garroted and pressed facedown in the filthy bathwater.

In his ear, Bagby whispered, "Uncle?"

Zef blew bubbles and tapped out and eventually was allowed to sit up and cough up the water in his lungs. Then he puked in the tub. "Fokking cocksuck…"

"You shouldn't interrupt somebody when they're meditating. You're not a surfer. How the fuck did you get in here, man?"

If he'd had a gun, Zef would've shot the freak, but he found his gut was cool and pragmatic about Bagby as a draft prospect. He needed at least one guy on his team who could actually kill people. "I heard you needed work, and you're down for... well, shit like... you know." Still coughing, he took out a joint and sparked it, hit it just enough to burn off the twisted endpaper, passed it to Bagby.

Bagby scratched his arms and shook water out of his coppery red dreadlocks. With a sigh of relief, Zef noticed the freak was wearing swimtrunks. Laughing bitterly, he took the joint and puffed it. "Yeah, I'm looking for work. I don't care what you want, I'll do it. When I came out here, I had a Volcom sponsorship... sick gear... trophy hoes... Nectar, bro."

"Then what happened?"

"I... I'd rather not talk about it. You don't want to know, literally." Bagby puffed a good inch off the joint and didn't exhale. He was splattered with almost purple freckles, as if he'd been pelted by berries. Passing back the joint, his mouth leaking smoke thick as shaving cream, he growled, "I'll do just about any fucking thing for the money to get the fuck off this fucking island," he said.

"Are you a junkie?"

"Fuck no."

"Can you shoot? Can you drive?" Zef hit the joint but not so hard that he'd lose his ability to speak and remember. This was the same deadly purple shit Peapea and Kewalo had bushwhacked him with... fuck, was it only last fucking week?

Again, that nasty laugh. "I can shoot good enough. At the end of the day, it's not who can shoot straight, it's who can keep their asshole watertight when the shit goes down. Lotta guys don't even know they're yellow until the first time. You face a wave, fifty, seventy feet tall and make it your bitch, you learn how to act faster than most people can think." Sucking the joint down to a stub and swallowing the roach, he forked out his fingers for another. "How much are we talking about?"

"Three grand, if you're worth it."

"Oh, I'll give you your money's worth. Thirty-three eighty-nine."

"What? OK whatever, that's cool." Lighting up another joint, he passed it to Bagby.

"When?"

"Starting today. A third now, the rest…"

"Half now."

"No, I can't…"

"Fine, fuck off."

"Alright, shit, what difference does it make?"

"I need to settle some shit." Bagby hotboxed the joint, got a good inch-long orange-red cherry glowing on the end. "Can I get a ride with you?"

"Sure, that's cool…"

"Ok, let's go."

"What about your sh—your stuff?"

"I don't have anything left, man. I'm free! Lemme go tell the boss!"

Women screamed. A loud crash and a thud. Bagby came out with a black eye, drywall dust in his hair and a bindle made from a Nektor T-shirt wrapped around some stuff.

"Let's go, before I get a better offer."

* * *

This is going to work, he told his hands for the ninety-fourth time. *It has to...*

They had more or less stopped shaking by the time he got through his third piña colada. The cheap rum floated on the top and hit his stomach like weed killer, but he sucked it down and savored the cold turning his brain to a freezer-burned leftover in the back of the icebox. Slowing thought, stopping the second-guessing in its tracks.

He left Bagby in Haiku with a cash retainer and a disposable phone and fled with all due dispatch, stopping at a dive bar in Kihei that seemed to cater to abusive local men of early middle age determined not to reach fifty. The walls were covered in posters for Italian cannibal movies and nekkid snapshots of ex-wives, ex-girlfriends, lewdly and viciously defaced. It smelled like they pissed on the floor. They called him something that probably meant "queer" in their tropical jibber jabber when he ordered a drink from one of the hypnotic Slurpie machines behind the counter.

Driving back from the bar. The dark had closed in and the stars were unbearably bright, nothing in sight beyond the glow of his headlamps. There were lots of observatories out here, Hodad told him, because no light pollution. One more thing he didn't need to know crammed into his head like a flu virus, weakening him when he had to be stronger than he knew he was.

The logic was so simple, he followed it over and over, right off the same cliff. He had to kill this guy. One guy. But he was not a killer. But he had an expense account. Sure, the subcontractors were flakes, but how many reliable professional hitmen would sign on for a murder safari like this? So instead of being an assassin, he had to be a ringleader, a master of men, a bandit chief...

Freefall.

It felt like he was falling whenever he closed his eyes. Was this what all those pussies complained about on TV? Was this a *panic attack*? They had drugs for this shit, didn't they? The big man said drugs were for weaklings, especially the prescription kind. *Take you for example*, that bullying Dixie voice drawled in his head. Slapping himself didn't shut it up.

He followed the road along the seaside and stomped on the brake, cursing the red and blue sunrise.

A couple police cars sat on the uphill side of the road with their lights turning. A dozen or so ordinary cars and trucks lined both sides of the road. Off to the right, a few widely separated pools of klieg light described the rough outlines of a construction site. In the center, under a light that made it look like a misplaced tourist attraction, a bunch of natives in grass skirts and togas and diapers were doing some sort of pagan ritual shit.

Zef rolled up, trying to drive the speed limit and think sober, legal thoughts. A cop stepped out in front of his car, waving a flashlight. Zef stopped and held his breath.

The cop was a cherubic local. Smiling awkwardly at Zef, he said, "OK, you must be lost. This isn't for tourists."

Zef suddenly felt sloshed. Talking out the side of his mouth, he said, "I'm going back to Kaanapali, sir..."

"Oh, please don't *sir* me, sir, I work for a living." The cop scowled at him for a second longer, then cracked a smile. "Just kidding, relax, brah. Anyway, this road dead ends about fifty yards up, where they were going to put the golf course, so what you need to do…"

"What're they doing, over there?"

"What? Oh, them? It's harmless, really. It's a traditional purification ceremony."

"Looks like a funeral…"

A group of men in feathered capes gathered around a hole, and began to dig. Under the earth lay a bed of glowing coals, and underneath that…

Zef's mouth watered. He could smell it from here. They were roasting a pig.

"They were gonna put up a big new resort right here, yeah? Would'a been a lot of jobs, too, but the guy who runs the parent company or whatever? He jumped off some casino in Las Vegas, for real, though. My brother-in-law was over there when it happened, only at Circus Circus, 'cos he got kids…"

Zef tuned him out and stared at the ritual. As the men unearthed the pig, a man in a bright red robe held up short stone axes and descended upon the carcass to carve it up. Another in priest's robes and a *ti* leaf headdress moved stiffly around the group, sprinkling water from a calabash gourd on the people and then on the construction equipment.

"So, like," Zef interrupted, "are they gonna share that pork?"

The cop laughed. "Oh, no, but that's funny!"

"How come?"

"It's like a protest, kinda...? The pig is like a stand-in for the casino guy, I think, or white people in general, no offense... They're gonna offer the meat to the gods by burning it or chucking it in the sea, something like that, and keep the bones for some magic stuff... I don't know this stuff too well, you know? My parents raised me Lutheran... But like, it's supposed to take his curse off the land and then the hotel won't happen. But that's crazy, it'll get built sooner or later and all these same people are gonna be working there..."

Zef wished the cop a wonderful evening and turned around, driving slowly past the construction site and the weird ritual again.

The priest carving up the pig was not kneeling.

He had no legs.

15
WATER OF DESTRUCTION

All the computers were tied up in the business center, but Zef stood behind one asshole with his hand tucked halfway down the front of his sweatpants until he logged off, cursing under his breath about how fucking golf reservations weren't worth this.

He quickly found a *Las Vegas Sentinel* feature on the dead Mexicans. It was a big deal because one of them was Raul De La Iglesias, the don who unified the Sinaloa cartels and brought order to the drug trade. Since the bodies were discovered, Culiacan had descended again into internecine warfare, while American authorities were trying to explain how he got into the United States in the first place. According to the decidedly less-awesome-than-on-TV Vegas CSI, the Mexicans were killed almost two weeks ago, and found two days ago. Someone might have reburied them after animals had been at them, which made identification difficult.

Yeti said Primo and Yolo worked for the Iglesias mob. Drugs and labor smuggling, weapons, contract murder, kidnapping, the whole thing, and their footprint spread from Central Mexico to the Philippines.

Zef was all but certain that Kewalo killed Primo. And all three of those fucking freaks were in Las Vegas when these Mexican guys got killed. Something ate their faces, but it wasn't coyotes.

The same fucking weekend that Doug Zweibel jumped or was thrown from the penthouse of his own hotel… which threw a huge development deal on Maui into the shitter. The same fucking weekend, Donny Punani took the Harley from the dealership, but he didn't crate it up and have it shipped out of McCarran. He and his two henchmen drove from Vegas to LA on motorcycles.

They didn't stay in Hollywood or Beverly Hills; they stayed in Long Beach. Which is, unless you have a hard-on for shipping terminals, oil refineries and street crime, a godforsaken shithole.

That narrowed things down considerably. They were only in LA for two days, and…

Xan Hong, a former Communist provincial middle-manager who became an overnight billionaire in real estate and construction and counterfeit goods and drugs. Retired from the business to play with his American real estate empire from a yacht in Long Beach Harbor across from the Queen Mary. And that's where they found what was left of him.

Another Chinese executive "allegedly" connected to the human smuggling and drug problems in Honolulu turned up dead a couple nights ago in Chinatown.

Donny Punani's gang got away clean with at least five murders on the mainland, and nobody was even talking about it.

Zef needed more killers.

* * *

The food court at the luxurious Whaling Village mall smelled like the world's biggest garbage disposal trap, and also a locker room. Hotter than outside and everything felt like it'd been dipped in fry grease.

Hodad told him about these two Filipino guys who worked as a team. "They'll punch any ticket for five grand, man. And they do it *clean*."

Not even Hodad knew how they got hooked up, but clients found them steadily, and abusive husbands, unfaithful wives and ungrateful heirs died of unusual but totally plausible accidental circumstances. Zef didn't believe they could make Donny Punani slip and break his neck in the shower, but it was worth checking out. At this point, anything was.

He ordered a McNugget meal at the McDonald's from an ancient Asian lady bent almost double under her hat and headset. As she pushed the buttons with pictures of food on them, she looked at Zef oddly, waggling her crayon eyebrows like she was also selling primo Maui Wowie...

"Whatever, sea-hag." Zef went to sit with the little plastic number that he got instead of food. The tables and chairs were bolted to the floor, and bright orange, like what highway workers and deer hunters wore. Rubbing his eyes, he sipped his soda—flat and warmer than the sweat streaming down his face—and studied the food court denizens. If these guys were truly invisible, they wouldn't carry on and dress like gangsters. There just wasn't anywhere to hide, on this fucking island.

A little Asian guy with rubber gloves and mustard stains on his uniform palmed the number placard and reverently set a tray with a paper plate of deep fried lumpia down in its place.

Without looking up, Zef said, "Wrong, I got McDonalds," but he left it there and Zef was fucking hungry. Still scanning the room, he dipped one in runny pink sauce and damn, what did they put in this shit? Shit was off the hook.

He looked around, realizing he'd made a loud complimentary noise.

The Asian guy hovered over him. His apron said *Teri's Yaki Bowl*.

"Isn't it rude to tip Asians?" Zef said.

"I think we are to meet," the little guy said. Quiet, so you leaned in without realizing it.

Zef looked through him, scanning the crowd. "Naw, I'm waiting for somebody…" He looked at the guy again. Soft brown eyes and a face you'd never find a word to describe. He looked like a Filipino, somewhere between thirty and sixty, with no distinguishing marks except for clusters of ringworm scars that dappled his arm.

"I need—"

"We know what you need. You pay us what we ask. We make arrangement."

Hodad said these guys were worth it, but they would run up the expense account and cut into Zef's end. "Well, like, I'm a little, like unconvinced…You got any references? Like…"

A hand passed over the table and left a small newspaper clipping. *Billionaire Suffers Bizarre*

Accident—Brain Injury Was Accidental, Self-Inflicted.
Zef skimmed the article, something about some prick
billionaire financier who was jogging on Kauai. Tripped
while picking his nose and landed on his elbow, driving
his index finger up through his sinus and into the front
of his brain. Vegetative, not expected to revive, but well
cared for by his third wife, ten years younger than her
brain-dead husband's youngest son.

"She didn't want dead," the little Filipino said. "His
family want estate, but she keep everything. She pay
some extra."

Zef laughed like clearing his throat. "You did this?
Fok you…"

"We work quiet. Get to anybody."

"But this… I don't know, show me something real,
like…"

The Filipino made a sound like a flower wilting. Zef
saw him nod at a woman behind the counter at the
teriyaki place. She came around pushing a mop bucket
into the dining area.

Zef looked around and put his hand over his face.
The rich bitch from last night sat a few tables away.
She wore a suede bikini that would've embarrassed
a prettier woman half her age. A big go-cup had
slopped strawberry daiquiri across the table and she
was complaining to someone on the phone. The old
woman at the McDonald's called out her number, but
the honeymooner stood up and shouted for someone
to bring it to her.

The moment she stood, the Filipino man went
behind her and for just a moment, his hand brushed
across the back of her chair. Then he took the mop

bucket from the woman and got busy. The yaki bowl lady brought the woman her McDonald's.

She sat down and started to feed her still complaining mouth when she went rigid in the chair. Her back arched so violently that her belly banged the table and flung her Quarter Pounder and strawberry daiquiri all over her piled shopping bags. A breathless, keening death-shriek came corkscrewing out of her, along with a torrent of blood-flecked foam.

The whole food court sprang into action. People at all the adjacent tables got out their phones to take pictures. The Filipino man knelt beside the rich bitch and lifted her head off the table.

The Filipino woman was next to Zef. "Sea wasp," she whispered. "Very poison."

"You're fokking crazy, yo… You gonna get us all caught…"

"Do you believe?"

Zef looked into her eyes, or tried to. Her hair was too thick under the net, like a doll's hair, and one of her ears looked like melted plastic. Otherwise, she looked exactly like her male partner.

"Okay, fok, you fokking crazy…"

A man shouting that he was a doctor shoved through the press of spectators. The Filipino man took one of the dying woman's shopping bags and laid her head gently on it. Before the doctor could get to her, the woman was coughing and crying, but she had recovered from her seizure. "The food… it made me sick."

"She had McDonald's," the Filipino woman said.

"Someone call an ambulance," the doctor said. He was also wearing only a swimsuit. Kneeling and checking her eyes, he looked around in disgust. "Doesn't anyone here know the number for 911?"

"I thought I was dead," the woman kept saying, "I was having a stroke…"

Zef pushed his tray away. The Filipino guy came over to the chair. In one hand, he had something wrapped up in saran wrap. In the other, he had a syringe. Poison and antidote.

"I'm not paying for that…"

"Just demonstration," the little guy said. "You believe now."

Zef's key card wouldn't open his room. When he went down to the front counter to get a fresh one, the desk clerk blandly informed him that Marlon Pussybone had checked out. She made it sound classy and French, then paged the concierge to bring out his baggage.

He was storming around the lobby when a blast of tepid sax flatulence came sharting out of his hoodie's pouch pocket. He whipped his phone out and was about to crush it like a bug when he realized what it was.

Oh shit. Suddenly, he felt strung out again.

"I'd like a progress report." Sigh of relief. It was only the amateur dentist dick who gave him the underwear.

"I'd like to know what the fok is going on with my hotel…"

"You're being moved. You're attracting too much attention."

"What the fok?"

"A man matching your description was involved in a foot chase and gunfight in Lahaina."

"I don't what the fok you're talking about, man…"

"You don't watch the local news…?"

"Why should I?"

"You should. This is a small pond. Sudden, violent actions make ripples…"

"I'm not here to watch birds, am I? Yo, tell your boss…"

"There is no 'boss.' You work for *me*."

Deep breath. "So tell *yourself* that shit is getting done. You can relax, I always deliver."

"Yes, I'm looking at your last 'delivery' right now. Try not to make such a mess of this one."

Swallow it. Here came the concierge with his duffel bag, holding it like it had just been fumigated for vermin. "Where am I staying, now?"

The condo was in the midst of Wailea Estates, a gated "secure community" surrounded by a golf course, on the south side of the island. Armed security guard in a pillbox out front might've been a mannequin or a cardboard cutout. He didn't so much as nod when Zef cruised into the lot.

The lap pool on the back lanai was filled ankle-deep with lost golf balls. Dreary tan stucco exterior. Furnished with Ikea showroom leftovers, off-brand kitchen appliances in muted colors that gave the unmistakable impression of punishment. Like this was where the big man kept mistresses who had annoyed or disappointed him. The bookshelves were filled with his self-help books in ten different languages. *Pull Your*

Pants Up, Dawg! Dr. Bill Raps With America's Youth was left on the bedside nightstand. DVD's of his best shows and special self-improvement videos were stacked everywhere else.

He turned on the TV and dumped his duffel bag out on the bed. Everything from his room at the Hilton was there, plus a manila envelope too heavy to contain mail. He thumbed it open, giving himself a nasty paper cut that he sucked, cursing, as he let the contents hit the counter.

Five thousand dollars in grubby twenties and hundreds. And in a smaller, white envelope labeled MOTIVATION, three separate sandwich baggies. One contained a bunch of pills; the second a couple dozen thin, machine-rolled joints; the third had almost an ounce of white, crystalline powder.

He stashed it all in his suitcase. Shit would be useful for steering Bagby, maybe, but he would have to keep away from it, himself. He needed to strategize, but his brain was just so much cotton wadding stuffed in his aching head.

The news anchor said a young lady named Mariko who'd come from Osaka to be married was struck in the head by a tumbling bullet and killed instantly on Kaanapali Beach yesterday afternoon while posing for pictures. Authorities were hoping someone would come forward, but while witnesses reported hearing gunshots in nearby Lahaina, the terrible tragedy was unlikely to be solved.

Zef turned off the TV and went to get his iPod and the MOTIVATION bag.

This shit was nothing like the coke Dr. Bill plied him with. Crystalline granules like sea salt that burned his sinuses like sulfuric acid and left his mind doing Tasmanian devil tornadoes around his skull. He figured it had to be ice, or even glass—highly refined, pure, clean crystal meth.

He'd only tapped out a brief bump to take the edge off the unwelcome feeling that he'd had something to do with killing some random Jap chick on her wedding day, but when he realized he wasn't going to sleep for at least twenty-four hours, he chopped up a fat S-O-S and snorted it and got dressed to go walkabout until he figured out what he was going to do. He rushed into the living room and practically charged into her arms.

"Fok!" He jumped back and knocked over a vase, which he caught, dead ready to beat someone's head in.

She stood in the open sliding glass door off the lanai. "The front door was locked," she said with a smile.

It smelled like her, that musty, flowers and spice smell, but this one was younger, maybe half the hag's age, maybe another of her nieces. Her hair was long, thick and unruly with flowers lost in it, but it was black, not gray.

"Auntie Kalei said you'd need to finish your massage." Her voice was higher, less husky, but every bit as lascivious.

"I don't need a massage…"

"You still jacked up from crashing that bike. Auntie made you to heal quick, but you need to finish your cleanse, I promise."

Now that he thought about it, he probably still should be in a hospital bed. And yet, the bruises all over his body were already yellowing and faded, the countless cuts, contusions and road-rash scabbed over. His nose was still tender and his voice sounded like he had a kazoo shoved up his sinuses, but it seemed to have healed. But was that anything to do with the old witch?

She was gentle, at first almost tickling, like mice running up and down his arms, but it still hurt. In the middle of her work on his back, he cried out with shooting gas pains like corkscrews winding into his belly. He rolled off the bed and barely made it to the bathroom.

It erupted out of his mouth onto the bathmat and the toilet seat. He slipped in it and dropped in the bathtub just when it really got going.

It was runny and nothing like anything he'd ever eaten. He knew without poking around in it that his drugs weren't in there. It smelled worse than shit or vomit had any right to. It was black. Not like he'd eaten a lot of fungus or even like digested blood, but *black*, like crankcase oil.

The smell and the taste in his mouth almost made him puke again before he flushed. He felt a surge of endorphins, much more than the brief euphoria of puking up a lot of alcohol, but like he'd purged everything bad, down to his cells. He felt new.

He looked through a crack in the door at her. She looked like Auntie Kalei just enough, and she made him feel the way he felt on Oahu, like his balls were full of lead shot. Only worse. He'd thought he was losing his shit when he felt that way about an old witch, like a weird response to panic and maybe responding sexually to someone he recognized and hoped might help him.

He tried all his sexual defense tricks against her. He tried to picture her as a man. Couldn't.

Sweat gleamed on the ripeness of her body as she disrobed, stripping down to a camisole and panties and pouring scented oil onto her hands.

He pictured his mother, but it didn't help, even when he imagined her in the throes of a herpes outbreak. *Your father's little dividend from his last boy's holiday*, she called it. Sores so bad she sometimes had to wear a veil.

It didn't help a bit.

"Come back and lay down," she said, rubbing her hands together. He noticed a bandage around one hand.

He came over with the towel tented in front of him and dove onto the bed on his belly.

"No," she said, giggling. "Turn over."

"You've been cleansed," she said, when he was falling asleep, "but still not purified. You should pray."

Irritable, he said, "Pray to who?"

"Whoever you believe in."

Sitting up too fast, he hit the headboard and a Chinese edition of *Pull Your Pants Up, Dawg!* fell in his lap. "I don't believe in shit that don't exist."

"You don't need faith in shit that *do* exist. Faith in something, or he eat you up."

"If I can't do it myself, then maybe I'll try praying."

16
THE WINNING

Hodad showed up early with a bag of fresh scallops and a hibachi, and had Zef grilling on the lanai before the other guests arrived for lunch.

"Pissing down rain out there, man!" He came close enough that Zef wanted to cover his mouth. He was soaked, but it was sunny outside.

"Hey," Hodad whispered, "who's that smoking hot wahine, with, like, only flowers for a bikini?"

"What the fok? What the fok you mean, man?"

"In the kitchen, making poi! She yours, man?"

"Get out of here, fok..."

Zef went into the kitchen. Auntie Kalei was cooking that starchy purple shit again. She blew him a big toothless kiss.

Zef remembered falling asleep next to the girl just before dawn, thinking he should be up for twenty-four hours off the ice he snorted, but content, clean and strong.

She was gone when he woke up, of course. He'd done a tiny bump in the bathroom to fortify his wits and chemically reaffirm his confidence in the Plan that he'd figured out between fucking and crashing. Now, his brain felt like a stainless steel paperweight and his hands wanted to feed somebody some teeth. Now, he was jerky and prone to babble and worst of all, he was starting to feel warmly towards these psycho pieces of shit.

"Get out," he said.

She was gone.

Beer was chilling in the fridge and he'd made one fine batch of margaritas before he burnt out the motor on the blender. Chips and pineapple salsa and whatever that purple shit was took up the dining room table, and a mellow Gasoline Monk mix oozed from the intact speaker of the dope alarm clock with iPod dock that he'd lifted from the Hilton. It already felt like a party.

"Where'd she go, man?" Hodad wanted to know.

"You don't know her?" Zef threw a beer can in the trash. "Thought you knew everybody. You've never heard of Auntie Kalei?"

Hodad frowned. "She's a kahuna. One of the few who claim they can do the old death songs. Steal your soul away, you let her get her claws on you. But not that hottie…"

Zef shivered. "No shit?" He took a joint from his pocket and lit it. "How's that work?"

Hodad smiled affably and took the joint in his claw. "Everybody's spirit—your soul, like your ghost before you die, you know, it goes wandering while they're asleep, you know? They go out looking to *party*, man, you know, do whatever their body can't.

Hodad passed the joint but found no takers. "A kahuna will put a few coconut cups of *awa* out at night, and when the right ghost comes up to take a drink, he just grabs it and eats it. Then he tells the victim his soul's gone, and within a day or two, *he's* just gone."

Zef choked on smoke, coughed until his eyes ran with tears. "No... way..."

"But that ain't the worst, brother. A Hawaiian witch can take a ghost and trap it and pray a lot of *mana* into it, and bind it into a familiar spirit to do her bidding. Fierce and ferocious, and they can't be killed. Even dying, an *unihipilii* can't get free."

Zef tried to think how he met Auntie Kalei. He couldn't. She had just eaten with him when he came out of the blackout at the pancake house. "Yeah, whatever, man... I'm pretty sure that didn't happen to me."

"Oh, it can happen to *anybody*, brother. They trick the victim into giving up his soul when it goes wandering, or like, they'll lure it astray and trap it in something, like a coconut or maybe a bird..."

Zef's head snapped around on his neck. His heart stopped. "Or a chicken?"

"Sure," Hodad cracked up. "But don't sweat it, dude. That shit only works on you if you believe in it."

Ringworm and Earwig showed up exactly on time, dappled with raindrops and reeking of deep fry grease but dressed in what they probably wore to church. They came in shyly and quietly, eyeing the mess in the kitchen ruefully as they passed into the living room. Hodad offered them a beer, which they politely declined. Ringworm gave him a big pot of sticky rice. Earwig gave Zef a tray of her *lumpia*, which set him to drooling.

Bagby came last. He brought three growlers of microbrew and a plastic grocery bag that reeked like filthy laundry. A fetid, gangrenous stench filled up the room. Zef ordered him out on the lanai. Ringworm and Earwig followed him, licking their lips.

"Fucking barbarians, all of you," Bagby shouted. "This here's the King of all Fruit."

Hodad covered the hibachi and moved all the other food away. "Man, it's not even legal to carry that shit on a bus in Singapore, never mind eat it in public."

Bagby took out a couple spiky green balls. The smell raped Zef's nose. "Gimme a steak knife, man."

"Get it yourself," Zef said.

Earwig went to get one, but Hodad seized the durian fruits and flung them out onto the golf course. First the two exposed ones, and then the whole bag.

Bagby came at him drunken-uncle style with a pocketknife. Hodad sidestepped it, trapped Bagby's arm and tripped him. The taller, younger, stronger man fell into the lap pool. Hodad was on top of him, holding his head under.

"Yo, man, let him up…" Zef pried Bagby out of Hodad's iron crab-grip.

Bagby got out smirking like he'd just been the butt of a bad bar joke, and not just almost drowned over some stinky fruit. But his eyes never left Hodad.

"Sorry, man. Bad memories associated with that shit." Hodad did one of his quick visual checks and stopped, frowning.

"Hey," Bagby said, "where's my knife?"

"So this belongs to you?" Hodad pulled Bagby's pocketknife out of his skinny asscheek, wiped the blade off on his sarong and dropped it in his breast pocket. "Mine now." He didn't wince or evince any more discomfort than if Bagby had ripped his shirt.

Shrugging off help, Hodad took a first aid kit out of his medicine bag.

"Fuck it." Bagby shook green pool water out of his hair, walking inside. "Where's the tequila?"

"So like, how many of you know who Donny Punani is?"

Hodad shrugged and nodded like he'd been asked if he was familiar with the Pacific Ocean. Ringworm pursed his lips. Earwig cracked a shy smile.

"So everybody…"

"Kill a local," Ringworm said, emptying a Sprite can into a plastic cup of ice, "it's a lot complicated. Cost extra."

"What the fok, you said you'd do anybody…"

"We live here after you go home," Ringworm said. "Nobody who live on Maui care about tourists."

"Nobody will touch you for this," Zef said. "Not the law, not the pineapple mafia, nobody. Everybody wants him deaded."

"Everybody but him and his friends…"

"Fuck the nips, man," Bagby slurred. Tequila covered up something worse on his breath. "I'll do it for their

217

share. All you fags stay here, I'll go do it myself. Where the fuck is he?"

Zef looked to Hodad, who stood up holding a pint of IPA in his claw. "So nobody gets confused, I'm not a shooter, I'm just the native guide on this safari.

"Pauwalu Don Nanaue, a.k.a. Donny or Johnny Punani, has never been arrested or prosecuted, but everybody on these islands knows he's a drug smuggler, a mainland mob sellout and a killer. There are even stories that he was a…"

"Fuck stories," Zef said. "Facts."

Hodad grinned. "Whatever, man. So the grapevine says he's holed up in Hana. He's got all the action he can handle out there, and nobody will ever rat him out. They're afraid of him, mostly, but they hate him because all their women want to fuck him."

Zef pictured the view of Donny's room—the girls grinding each other while he sat fuming. He wasn't in it for the pussy. "So let's go over there," he said.

"Not a good plan. It's Indian Country, brother. The locals who don't want to play Tonto shows for the tourists are dug in on the coast and up in the cloud forests. Folks who spit on the flag and see all white men as a hostile occupying force. And since their Queen was overthrown…"

"Get to the fucking point, professor!" Bagby threw a beer can.

Hodad caught the can and threw it back, drained his pint and wiped his mouth with a claw. "Sorry, I actually used to be a professor."

He beckoned them all around the dining room table and unfolded a Triple-A roadmap. "Anyway, we're here."

He pointed to their spot at six o'clock on the island. Hana was at two o'clock, but getting there was not easy. The road to Hana was in the Guinness Book for most waterfalls and bridges on a single road, but that didn't begin to do it justice. Cleaving to the coastal cliffs that thrust out into the sea and then retreat into countless narrow, rain-carved canyons, the skinny, mostly two-lane road often became a one-way track over antique bridges clogged with day-tripping tourist idiots in rental minivans. Wildlife preserves, botanical gardens, lava tube tours and zip lines dotted the coast, but the village at the end was an anticlimax. No resorts, no franchises, no fast food, no tourist amenities. Roadside stands had flowers and fruit laid out for sale, but no one was there to take your money. Just a box for the cash and the sense that people who couldn't stand to deal with you were somewhere nearby, watching...

Hodad said Donny was somewhere along the road, probably not in Hana proper. "They harvest a couple times a season, so he could be anywhere up in the mountains, if he's around at all. They say he goes out on the ocean for days at a time..."

Zef looked at the map with his brow furrowed. "Why don't we go round the other way?" It was a straight shot around the bottom of the island to Hana, with not a damned thing between them but dirt.

"Well, there's nothing out there, and it doesn't get much rain. The road is fucked up... Parts of it are closed during the winter to get worked on, but there's no real reason you couldn't just come in on a boat..."

"They see us coming," Ringworm said.

Tracing a route from the development in Wailea, Zef figured it'd be a cinch to go that way, but there seemed to be no road connecting the whole southwest portion of Maui with the southeastern coast road. You had to go to Kahului on the north shore, then double back on a parallel road. "What the fok, yo?"

"There is a shortcut, but it's private," Hodad said.

"That fucking TV shrink has a ranch up there," Bagby said. "He's never even there, but his people have it fenced off."

Impatiently, Zef said, "So going to get him is a waste of time."

"We'd probably never find him," Hodad said.

"No fucking way we'd get out alive," Bagby said.

"I thought so. That's why we're going to get him to come to us."

Zef rooted around in a pile of Dr. Bill books and found a notepad he'd jotted some things down on. "What do we know about this Punani fucker? He likes to take motorcycles that don't belong to him, and he likes to sing. So we set up a karaoke contest, and make the prize a motorcycle."

He sat back and wished he had a mic to throw to the floor. *Peace out, bitches!*

"And then what?" Hodad said.

"Then we kill him! Fok, why did I hire you punkass fakers?"

Hodad said, "It offers a lot of advantages, but how much time and money can you afford to throw away…"

"I like it," Ringworm said. "We can work better if we bring him in."

"Kill him many times," Earwig put in.

Bagby said, "Assuming you can get all this shit together, how do you want it done?"

"We take no chances. He's got to be dead *for real*. If you have to check for a pulse, he's not dead."

"What you got, man?"

Zef pushed back from the table. This was the sweet part. Moving expansively, keeping all eyes on him, he went to the living room and pulled an Army footlocker out from under the coffee table. One of Yeti's longhaired thugs delivered it first thing in the morning.

He opened it and let them marvel.

Two shotguns, four automatics and an authentic AK-47 that looked like a battlefield trophy. Guy told him these were lifted from a safe in a vacation home in Haiku. If they were caught, it was an added burglary beef.

"Gnarly," Bagby said. "Dibs on the AK."

Zef and Ringworm each took a neat Italian semiauto shotgun; Earwig took a .25 Beretta and hummed the James Bond theme under her breath. Bagby grabbed the assault rifle and stuffed the pockets of his cargo shorts with banana clips.

Watching him poke and prod the gun, Zef asked, "You ever shoot one?"

"A Hawaiian? Not yet, why?" A wubbing dubstep ringtone sounded from his pocket. He went in the kitchen.

Hodad asked, "So when do we spring your plan?"

"Shit's already on," Zef said. "Gonna see about renting a bike tomorrow, and go to a Kinko's or whatever and make flyers. We set it up with a club in Lahaina…"

"OK, wait…" Bagby came back in. "So we could do all that gay shit with the karaoke and the flyers and shit. OR," pointing to his phone, "we could grab our guns and go to where he is right… fucking… *now*."

17
JAWS

Clouds tossed and roiled in the sky like laundry in a giant washing machine. The wipers screeched, flinging buckets of water off the windshield about half as fast as it was coming down.

Racing north on 311 through a sugarcane wasteland of black, harvested stalks, Zef tried to come across like he was in charge of what was happening, like he understood it.

Last week, he would've said he didn't believe there was such thing as a soul. Now, he tried to convince himself that his soul wasn't trapped in a chicken or a coconut.

This was him striking back. This was his fist coming down. This wasn't a drug using him for a sock puppet. Wasn't some TV asshole or a witch making him do their bidding. Wasn't some burnout surfer hijacked his hit squad to strongarm his frienemies' stash.

It sounded stupid, on the face of it.

And the more Bagby had talked, the worse it got. "No time to explain, he's gonna be there in an hour…"

"Where?"

"North Shore. Tick tock, bitches."

Ringworm and Earwig were against it. Hodad reluctantly agreed it was worth trying. Before casting the tie-breaking vote, Zef adjourned to the bathroom and did a blast of ice.

Fucking aye.

He offered Ringworm and Earwig a grand each to walk away, but they stood pat.

Bagby explained in the fuckpad's fancy new minivan while he drove. Hodad studied a map and Zef tried to look like he knew how to handle a Glock 9mm.

So these "friends" of Lowell Bagby's—a couple of whom were total kooks, but overall brothers of the board and bud... Anyway, they were all flat broke and facing eviction from paradise. Backs to the wall, they had used uncharacteristic ingenuity in stealing a couple clones from an outdoor grow in a canyon up above Hanehoi Stream in the hills. Instead of smoking them, they planted them out back of the house, and before you know it, the shit had taken off.

It yielded indoor quality and bud density when left alone outside. So naturally, they started selling the shit. This had been Bagby's pet project, but the ingrates had usurped his fledgling empire and taken all the profits for themselves. Which had turned out to be not the brightest idea, because the plants they stole were Donny Punani's property.

The unique purple strain was pretty hard to mistake for someone else's. So they returned from surfing this morning to find a very polite handwritten note on the dashboard of the Nektorsled, thanking them for caring for his plants and informing them of his intention to come collect them at low tide at 5PM, which he assumed would find them at home.

Bagby's bros had contacted him not so much to plead for help as to curse him for ratting them out, which was ridiculous, because Bagby wasn't some kind of punk who rolled over on people, and anyway, this shit was like bionic Kula Crippler... And it was this spooky, radioactive blacklight purple, so sooner or later there was going to be a reckoning, which was why this was all so perfect.

"It's like when you're out past the breakwater and a storm is coming in. You surf, little man?"

Zef said yes and didn't even register the slight until Bagby was talking again. It looked like they were doing seventy through a car wash.

Bagby finally passed the joint he'd been bogarting. Smoke poured out of him with his words, on and on. "It's like we're right in position and the swell is building and we're about to drop into tube city. You know my man Shane?"

Zef said no he didn't, and thank god he didn't give Bagby any of the ice. His plan was a good one, like inspired by those crafty Fed sting operations where they'd send out these notices to all these fugitives and crooks with outstanding warrants that they won a boat, and they always showed up and said, *Where's my boat?*

Face it, the plan was brilliant, but it would have taken a week of setup and another couple grand out of pocket to stage a karaoke contest and find a bunch of clowns to fill it out and rent a bike, and the outcome would be as sure as one of those Roadrunner cartoons.

And when it was over and Donny Punani got away again and took the rental bike and fucked off to the next island, Zef would truly and finally snap, and he would be just like the psychotic burnout in the driver's seat who was still talking…

"…Fags said it was my fault, what happened, but they got it all backwards, man. Shane *lived* in the Tube. There's only one wave, and when you catch up to it, it's that one forever moment, right? Shane came to me the night before, man, and we'd partied before all the time, no big, but he said to me, 'Lowell, I need to dose up and vision-quest, brother, because I'm going to die tomorrow, and I really want to know if I have to.'"

The joint came round to him again. Bagby hit it, staring into the rain. "He saw it coming, man. He figured it out. Paddled out and never came back. That's the way to go, man, when *I'm* through with this shit… Just paddle out."

"I'm only paying for Donny," Zef said, in a weak voice he hated. "Whatever shit you got going with your friends, chill it 'till our deal is closed, or…"

"Or what?" Bagby laughed. "Relax, man. All things are working to produce the highest good." Fishing a CD out of his pocket, he said, "Hey, how about some mood music?"

Zef braced himself for speed metal, dub reggae or even techno, but this… it was so much worse. It was like Muzak on bad acid… Freaky birdcalls, hissing rain and croaking frogs came from every corner of the van. Fruity xylophone and marimba runs made like malaria shivers.

"Martin Denny was a fucking genius, man. That pansy Baxter may've wrote most of his hits, but Denny fucking *invented* the whole exotica movement right there, man, as a live lounge act. Ruled Don the Beachcomber's in the Sixties, back when Waikiki still had a decent split peak. I would've killed to see that shit, back in the day. Y'know, nobody in Waikiki even remembers Don's, let alone Denny. Fucking disgraceful, don't you agree?"

Zef agreed, hoping that would end it.

It didn't.

If anything, it was raining twice as hard on the north shore. The slope of Kulike Road became a sluice. As they got close, Bagby doused their headlights. The apron of gray rain in front of them vanished.

"Shut up!" Bagby hissed, turned around and snapped shut the pulldown monitor on which Ringworm and Earwig were watching cartoons.

They slowed to a crawl as they passed the bougainvillea hedge walls of Nektorhaus. No cars parked on the road. A couple VW microbuses and an old Mazda pickup with a camper shell, but nothing that set Bagby off. No motorcycles, but who would be out on a bike in this weather?

Bagby hit the lights after they passed, swung into a driveway ending in a gate.

"He's not here," Zef said.

"Island time, dummy," Bagby said. "We set up the flips as lookouts and we go inside and lie in wait. He comes in, we take his picture. Everybody gets paid."

Hard to argue with that. "He better show up."

Bagby looked wounded. "Would I lie to you?"

Ringworm and Earwig stayed in the minivan. Bagby and Zef went up the road to the opening in the hedges. Even over the black noise of the deluge, Zef could hear the booming artillery barrage of the waves.

He snagged a poncho from the van, but the wind blew tepid rain up under it and plastered his hood to his face so he tore it off. He cradled the fancy Italian shotgun—Benelli M4 with a collapsible stock—and touched the Glock tucked in his waistband, two extra clips in the pouch of his hoodie. He followed the gun like he was walking a big dog.

He didn't doubt that he could shoot whoever and whenever he had to. What he feared was shooting the wrong person, or a lampshade instead of the guy about to shoot *him*. It didn't take guts to start a gunfight. It took nerve to *function* in one. Shit didn't slow down like in the movies; it happened and you were in it and ninety-and-some people out of a hundred didn't even realize the shit hit the fan until it was over. Zef had always fancied himself one of those people.

The floor-to-ceiling windows were blacked out by curtains, but weak yellow light seeped out through the cracks. Straining through the sound of the rain, the faint throb and wobble of dub reggae. And cutting through the rain like the spoor of a skunk orgy, the bittersweet perfume of weed in industrial quantities.

"Cover me." Bagby shook water off the AK and ran across the yard to the porch. Zef watched him give some of those stupid hand signals commandos did in movies. Was he supposed to watch him, or follow him?

"Over here, fuckhead!" Bagby shouted. Zef ran up to the porch and hit the doorframe opposite him.

Bagby set the AK against the wall and dug into his knapsack, came out with the tequila and a short pistol with a fat barrel.

"A flare gun?" Zef asked. "The fok—"

"Shock and awe, dude." Bagby unscrewed the lid on the tequila bottle. It wasn't tequila. Probably gas siphoned from the minivan. "Shock and—"

Raising his leg to kick the door, he did an awkward two-step when the door opened on its own.

Dim inside. A purple curtain blocked most of the view, but Zef saw three young dumb surf punks with the obligatory sunkissed, shaggy blonde manes and stoned, expressionless faces. Their vacancy was taxed to its limit at the moment, perhaps because of Bagby's unexpected appearance, or perhaps because of the pound or two of freshly trimmed and bagged purple buds in front of them. Their eyes were cast not on the open door, but on whatever lay behind the purple curtain, which, upon second glance, proved not to be a curtain at all, but a bedspread draped over a gigantic Hawaiian whose face, way up there in the smoky shadows of the cavernous living room, became more than half teeth at the sight of Zef and Bagby.

"*Haole* boy," said Peapea.

Whatever plan Bagby may have had for storming Nektorhaus and setting up an ambush for Donny Punani's gang, he improvised brilliantly for someone with no functioning brain.

The four hundred pound giant at the door reached out to palm Bagby's head, but Bagby smashed the tequila bottle in his face and shot him in the mouth with the flare gun.

Peapea came storming out onto the porch, his head a blazing torch. Bagby went around him, shouting, "Shock and awe!"

Zef jumped left, but there was no dodging the fucker.

What to do? *You* are *holding a shotgun…*

This timely realization caused Zef to pull the trigger with the big semiauto shotgun pointed at the floor.

The point-blank buckshot storm took Peapea's left foot off at the ankle. The giant collapsed on top of him, pinning him to the wood porch. Peapea screamed but no sound came out. Head engulfed in crackling flame, green phosphorus dragon breath jetting out of his mouth.

Zef screamed too, inhaling barbecue fumes and mouthfuls of ash from Peapea's blazing face. Shotgun somewhere out of reach, dropped in panic. Glock trapped between them, a lethal hard-on he was sure would go off on its own. Twisting away from the sparks Peapea tried to pour down his throat. Breathless, buried alive, Zef bit into the heel of a hand that closed over his face, squeezing his head fit to pop it. Teeth meeting in muscle, screams bubbling through blood.

He heard a wild spree of shots like two-by-fours clapping together, teenage screams going up and cutting out and Bagby laughing and screaming, "HOW YOU LIKE ME NOW, BAXTER?"

Zef thrashed in earnest, trying to get out from under when hot droplets of melted fat dripped on his face. The flare had burned through Peapea's cheeks and made a brittle black ruin of everything below his nose. The stench of pot and body odor and cordite were extinguished by the palpable miasma of charbroiled flesh.

At last, Peapea fell still and died on top of him. Zef tried to make a bridge of his legs and roll Peapea off, but straining until his colon nearly popped out, he only managed to adjust the corpse so its guttering flames didn't drip shit in his face.

When a hand finally took Peapea by his muumuu and rolled him off Zef and helped him up, he didn't even flinch when he felt the two-fingered claw.

"Hey man," Hodad said, "I don't want to neg your pos, you know, but…"

Throwing up and crawling away from the corpse, Zef thought, *Get up, he's HERE, it's almost over…*

"Dude, get your checkbook out," Bagby shouted from the back of the house. "I got your boy back here."

Zef had to climb the wall to get upright. Could it be? After all this shit, could it really be over? "Yo, wait up," he called, voice cracking.

Hodad tried to help, but Zef shook him off. Two surfers on the couch lay splayed backwards with their lungs hanging out their backs like popped water wings. Down the hall, stepping over a third surfer swimming the filthy shag carpet. Passing a half-open door when the cheap laminate flew apart as three separate starbursts came through it where Zef was supposed to be.

Dropping on his ass, he pointed the gun at the door and shot four, five times. A big local guy with long hair on the toilet tipped over and sprawled into the whirlpool bath. Bagby seemed to really want a bonus,

231

because he'd completely shot off his face. Zef's heart skipped a beat. He wanted it to be Donny so fucking bad he couldn't look at it.

So he scoped the dead local girl leaning against the shattered mirror with her bare ass in the sink and a gun on the counter beside her still smoking. Bagby must've executed her boyfriend while she was giving him a blumpkin or something, but even he had balked at killing a girl.

Another notch in your belt, ninja. Scope my new merit badge. Ladykiller!

Bagby stood over him. "You OK, bro?"

Zef got up. "Said you had him…"

"That's not him?" Cackling, Bagby ran into the master bedroom and fired the AK into the ceiling. Zef heard a woman screaming. Naked jailbait ran shrieking from the waterbed. The alpha surfer sat up and knuckled one dreamy blue eye and tossed his sun-bleached hair and said, "Bagby, you… fucking fag… just take your fucking kine…"

Bagby leapt onto the waterbed and kicked the alpha dog in the chin, then pinned his head to the wall with his knee. Labored giggles, not so funny now, but still, you had to laugh as Bagby stubbed his fat joint into the blonde guy's eye.

He screamed louder and higher than the women. Bagby took a huge hit off the joint. The room filled up with a pungent smell like scorched egg whites. "Dude, you gotta taste this!"

18
LOW SKY LAND

The smart thing to do, what a boss would do, would be to put a bullet in Bagby's brain the next time his back was turned.

But Zef just watched him punch the one surviving surfer in the face over and over, and couldn't pick up the gun.

"Jesus man," Hodad said, "he doesn't know shit. What're you punishing him for?"

"Not punishing *him*," Bagby grunted between blows. "I'm *rewarding* me."

"He's not here, yo... what the fuck, he's not here, and..."

"Relax, bro," Bagby said, popping his knuckles. "You on Island time."

"FOK YOU!" Zef grabbed a fistful of dreads and yanked Bagby backwards, swept his feet out from under him so he landed flat on his back. Sticking the Glock in Bagby's face, he snarled, "I'm not paying for this."

Bagby looked like he'd just swam a hundred laps in a pool of blood. Everything red but his grin. "I'm sorry, bro, it's just... I always hated these fucking guys."

"What the fok is really going on? You fokked up my whole operation…"

"Relax, man, nothing is fucked. They thought they were gonna take my pot and bail. They were cleaning the shit all afternoon when that fat fucker out front showed up early and caught them. He was sitting on them waiting for Donny, who could still show up any minute, so instead of getting on my case, maybe you wanna get ready to paddle out…"

Zef dropped Bagby and turned on Hodad. "Where're, um, the others…?"

"Isidro and Maja? Outside, waiting for your man."

My man. Fok! "Who?"

"The nice Filipino couple you hired. Those're their names, man."

Pull it together. This can still work. Nobody called the cops, and in this storm, nobody saw or heard anything. He's still coming…

Zef's phone played smooth jazz. *Please, not now…*

"Yo, get that fat dead fok off the porch, yeah?" He hit the button. "Yo."

He heard the deep, angry nasal breathing and thought, *Fok me.* "Hi, boss. Yo, like…this is a really bad time…"

"Oh, it's a bad time? I'm sorry. Are you and your friends tripping on LSD?"

"Uh… no…"

"Well, you better tuck into that bag I gave you and hook up a few doses of GSD."

"Some what?"

"Getting Shit Done, son."

"Yo, I really don't need this right now…"

"Tell you what…" Deep, deep breath. "When *you* pay *me* to do a job and *I* royally shit the bed, then you can feel free to call me at whatever hour you like and put a foot up my ass at your own discretion."

Zef backed up the hall, looking in doorways for a room without corpses in it. "OK, fok, I'm sorry, it's just… we're making mad progress."

"Son, I'm beyond losing my religion with you. You're actually making me start to doubt the power of money. Why is the good money I've spent not yielding the result I've quite reasonably requested?"

Finally, a room with a futon, a hookah, a couple broken surfboards and no dead surfers. He closed the door. "If it's so fokking cake, yo, whyn't you get your *rooinek* homeboys on it?"

"I don't even understand your ghetto jibber jabber, and I'm not impressed by it. You are fast approaching the point where, for me to do the thing myself would've been easier and cheaper. You've done nothing but fuck up since you were hired, leaving me to suspect that even my limited, conditional trust in you was totally misplaced."

How did he know? "Yo, nothing is fokked, OK? Just relax… you're on island time…"

"No, *you* listen. I just had to send a sizable contribution to the Maui Sheriff's Toy Drive Charity, and I've written a whole book about how bad for society charity is. And all so they would sit on a shitbird drug dealer in the ICU at Wailuku Catholic with everything below his mouth broken, who says you killed his cousin in Honolulu, and then tried to kill him. They like him for manslaughter for the dead Jap, but they're threatening to go for Murder Two if he doesn't shut up about you.

"This is what it's come to, and it'd be simpler at this point to just crimp his breathing tube and let the beeping sing him to sleep, but then *I'd* be hiring killers to clean up *your* mess… You see why I'm at my wit's end, here?"

"Sure, boss." Zef thinking, *Heh, joke's on you, I'm like three royal fuckups ahead of that one. Try to keep up, cheese…* "You said you'd cover expenses. Well… those are, like, expenses."

"Thing is, I know where you're at. Right about now, you're probably in the very trough of the doubting phase. You're thinking you're not up to this. This is how people like you sabotage themselves. You know damn well what I'm talking about."

Zef couldn't think of anything to say in his defense. Dr. Bill's voice had gone all soft and warm, and he wanted to nod and agree and thank him for letting it out, the yellow poison and the black, stored up inside him.

"You've been in love with a whole pack of lies about yourself, and now that you've seen those lies utterly discredited, you don't know who, or even what, you are. And that… is… perfect."

"Dr. Bill, I'm afraid, yo… I'm not a…" *I'm not a killer,* he tried to say. *I mean, sure, I can kill people, just not on purpose.*

"You're trying to convince yourself you're not right for this job. Well, let me tell you something. Jesus Christ wasn't taken down by a bigger messiah, was he?"

What? "No, it was like the whole Roman Empire."

"No, it was a conspiracy of weaselly little shits, Jewish Pharisees and Roman thugs had it in for him, but nothing could've happened without Judas. JFK wasn't killed by a bigger, better man. Bobby was a bigger hero, so they got an even bigger loser to bag him. Jesse James, Gandhi, Che Guevara, Crazy Horse, the list goes on. To snuff out light, you need darkness. To take down a hero, you need a loser to shoot them in the back. And you're the loser for the job. Which you're going to do."

Wanting to argue that Gandhi never ripped anyone's head off with his bare hands, he stuttered, "You can't talk to me like this… You got nothing on me that I don't got on you…"

"OK, I'll bite. What do you got?"

Think, think… "Well, I'm sure someone would be interested in the drugs you supplied…"

"Which drugs would those be?"

"The coke you gave me… The ice I've got in my pocket right now."

"Oh, you stupid kid. Go ahead and get that shit tested. It's a very potent but widely prescribed ADHD medication. Face it, boy. You've got the attention span of a gnat. I know I publicly argue against using drugs as a crutch, but drugs work. As for the grass, I'm pretty sure you stole it. It's medical, anyway. Legal in Hawaii, if you've got a card. As for the rest of it, it's your word against mine. But if you want to renege…"

"Yo, whatever, I'm on the motherfokking case, shit. But we gonna have to talk about the bottom line…"

"That's what I like to hear, I think. Call my people if you need anything. And Zephyrus…"

"What?"

"Don't leave me any more messes."

Bagby was standing in the hall outside the door. "What *is* the bottom line, dude?"

"Go cover the front door, dog." Zef moved to push past Bagby, who blocked the whole hallway.

"A rising tide lifts all boats, right, wigger?"

"Yo, don't even trip, bitch," Zef said. His hand went to the gun in his waistband.

"Boys, put your dicks away." They both looked at Hodad. "Van outside."

Zef went right through Bagby to get to the windows.

An old Ford Econoline was indeed stopped in the driveway. Headlights jabbed the house. Haloes blocked the driver's face. Maja came out of the bougainvilleas like a ghost with two automatics and put them both in the driver's face. She was looking back at the house. *She's looking for you, stupid.*

Hodad sat cross-legged on the floor with his eyes closed and his claws resting on his knees. "Om," he said.

"My bitch better have my money," Bagby said in a taunting, falsetto voice. He went for the door.

Zef stiff-armed him out of the way. "Cover me."

"What?"

"Lowell, you've done nothing but fuck up since you were hired, leaving me to suspect that even my limited, conditional trust in you was totally misplaced. So stay back and don't pop a cap, unless you want to find out what getting fired from a job like this entails."

Pushing past the baffled burnout, Zef went down the steps, picking up his shotgun and holding it like he knew how to use it.

He walked around the microbuses and up to the van, the lights still blinding, making the rain a forest of glowing chains. Where the fuck was Ring… Isidro?

He came up alongside Maja, who looked at him eagerly from under her sopping wet wig.

"Aloha, brotha," said Kewalo. "I'm picking up my cousin."

Zef shook his head. "Not him." Wiping water out of his eyes, rubbing sensation back into his numb face. Nudging Maja aside, he stuck the shotgun barrel in the window. "You can't come in. We're busy."

"Yeah, I figured." Kewalo smiled. His teeth were fishhooks. His grayish skin glistened in the reflected headlights, like it was covered in tiny, tiny beads. Or teeth. "I can wait."

Just do him. Just shoot him in his fucking face. Kill him like he killed Primo, in cold blood while he sat in his fucking car.

Maja called for Isidro, moving down the road into the dark. Zef told her to stay close, but she disappeared. *What am I in charge of?*

Just shoot him. He almost did. And then everything happened at once, and it was way too late.

In the house, Bagby shrieked, "NO WAY, FUCKER! NONONONONO!"

The front windows blew out on tongues of fire. Bagby came running out the front door with the AK high against his chest and a burning trash bag flopping against his leg.

The windows on the passenger side of the van shattered before he heard the barrage of shots. Kewalo dropped behind the dashboard, popped the van in Drive. The Econoline jumped forward to smash into a microbus. Zef flew backwards into the thorny embrace of the bougainvillea hedge. Who was fucking shooting?

Bagby was on his ass in the front yard, shooting at the front of the house, now engulfed in fire. Nothing else was coming out that door alive.

The van jumped into Reverse and sprayed a curtain of red mud going backwards into Kulike Road. Maja came running up the road with both guns up and pouring lead into the van, screaming like an air raid siren. The van slewed across the road, pointed at Maja, then jumped into Drive and started rolling downhill. The engine screamed and the radiator dumped. Maja dropped the dead mags out of the guns and loaded one with the other under her arm, standing in the road like a gunslinger.

Zef ran up alongside the van and stuck the shotgun in the window, pulled the trigger and shot nothing. The seat was empty. The back doors flew open and Kewalo jumped out into the road and joined the dark before Zef could get turned around.

Maja jumped out of the way of the empty van, which hurtled down the road, headed for the ocean.

Bagby ran out into the road. "Where'd those motherfuckers go?"

Zef pointed up the road. "Find him!" Then he turned to the house. *Think like a boss.* What the fuck just happened? Kewalo dropped someone—*Donny*—who went around back into the house and started the fire. Bagby was inside, skull-fucking his friends' corpses or something, and almost got caught. But Hodad...

"They're somewhere around, right now! Big bonus on whoever brings me his fokking head."

"He was right *there*, man!" Bagby shouted, voice hoarse from smoke. "I double-tapped his fucking ass, *clack clack*! Fucking came out of nowhere and everything was on fire..."

Zef stalked back out into the road. "You got him...?"

"I shot him, sure," Bagby said, "but I didn't stop him."

"Where the fok is he now?"

"Dude..." Bagby said, with all the gravitas he could muster, "he's fucking everywhere."

Dr. Bill's gonna be shittin' kittens.

Maja was kneeling over something in the shrubbery across the road. Looking sideways, holding the gun up like a shield, Zef ran over to her. Cops and fire trucks would be here soon. What they would make of this, he had no idea, but fire was probably the best answer.

It had Isidro's poncho on, but no face, no jaw. The whole front of his skull was gone. His right hand had only a thumb and index finger on it. His other arm was a ghastly red stick from elbow to wrist. He'd thrown up an arm to hold it back, to stop it...

What the fuck was it?

"I'm sorry," Zef said.

Maja said something in Tagalog. She reached out and her tiny hand was like a pit bull's jaws on Zef's biceps. "We kill him many times."

"Fok yeah," he said.

The dark was peeled back by headlights. Zef ran to the minivan, thinking he should've shot Bagby when he had the chance but it was never too late, when he saw Bagby running for the same van. It backed up out of the driveway, sliding almost sideways in the road. Zef, Bagby and Maja shot at it as it rolled away into the dark.

Zef screamed and waved the shotgun in the air. He almost pulled the trigger, but you couldn't fire into the sky without killing someone, here.

"Let's go," he shouted at Bagby. "Get in the fokking bus!" Screamed, really, his voice cracking.

Someone came out the front door. Zef raised the shotgun, but then lowered it, shaking his head.

Smoking and sizzling in the rain, Hodad walked down the porch with a bale of weed under each arm. "What'd I miss?"

Beyond Kulike Road, the 36 turned into the 360, the infamous Hana Highway. There was no substantive debate about which way to go, whether to chase or give up. They had nowhere else to go.

"He'll go back to Hana," Hodad said. "But he could stop anywhere on the road, and you'd never see him."

"Then you drive," Zef said.

"Sorry, brother, but I'm legally blind. Also," holding up a claw, seared and blistered up to his shoulder, "doesn't hurt, but it plays hell with my reflexes."

"I'll drive," Bagby said. Zef stared at him. He didn't trust the burnout not to wreck them, but he trusted him in the backseat even less.

"Then move," Hodad said, getting into the backseat directly behind Bagby. Maja got in the shotgun seat and curled up facing the window.

Zef and Bagby zipped Isidro's corpse up in a neoprene surfboard sheath and put him on the roof. Hodad threw the bales of weed in the back. Bagby said, "Thanks for saving my crops," which made Hodad laugh.

"Sorry, man, I didn't see *your* weed for all the smoke of that fire you left me in. This here's *mine*." And he held up the other shotgun, resting his pinky on the trigger.

"Whatever, granddad."

The microbus grumbled, but its indestructible German engine caught and snored amiably on the first try. They rolled out onto Kulike and lurched and bucked while Bagby got acquainted with the clutch.

Zef tensed up around the shotgun. Did he hear sirens, or were his ears ringing from all the gunfire? "Jesus Christ, step on it!"

"I'm fucking doing it, but this shitbox is even worse than that minivan. Which has my fucking Denny CD in it..." He flipped on the hi-beams, which made the visibility worse.

The rain came down in leaden sheets, the jungle stacked up high and tight against the road, which swerved and switched back on itself like a drunken snail's trail, trying to find its way around the coastal cliff. All of them stared into the dark, eyes peeled for any sign, but there was hardly a shoulder, let alone a turnout. Still, every once in a while, he spotted a cabin or a lanai tucked in the trees, and every once in a while, the turn of the road afforded them a view of the empty, ultimate blackness that must be the ocean far, far below.

The road went on and on and the silence stretched on impossibly. Bagby had turned on the stereo, but the radio was broken and he ejected the Lord Kitchener CD halfway through "Dr. Kitch's Needle" and chucked it out the window.

Zef tried to stay ahead of shock. He knew it was coming, knew the enormity of what had happened was creeping up on him. When it hit, he was going to be good for nothing at all. And they weren't done fucking up, tonight. They were in hot pursuit of a badass motherfucker into Indian Country, leaving a flaming crime scene and a busload of bodies that would have to be identified by dental records.

"You've done this before, I suppose," Hodad said.

Zef didn't look away from the window. "I got a lot on my mind right now, man."

"Sure you do. I expect you must feel pretty bad about all those kids."

"They were big enough to steal from gangsters." Zef tried to sound cold. "Would've got deaded tonight, anyway."

"Exactly my point," Hodad said. "But this job was way hairier than you told us it was going to be."

"None of that was my doing," Zef said.

"But you subcontracted us out of your nut," Bagby said, "and these guys are fucking monsters, man. I think, given everything we've been through together, that we're entitled to a bigger piece of the pie."

"Not gonna discuss it now," Zef said. "Kill somebody I want killed for a change, and we'll talk about the bonus situation."

"Bet your boss would be more reasonable."

"You have no fokking idea, yo."

"Hey," Bagby said, "I see them."

They slowed down, passing a dirt turnout for Papaaea Reservoir. A van was parked just off the shoulder, but it looked like an ice cream truck. But far off ahead, they saw a flash of red. Taillights.

"Speed up, fok," Zef growled. "He fokking lives here. You think *he's* driving like a fokking bitch?"

Bagby let the wheel go and held his hands up in surrender. The bus veered towards a flooded ditch. "You wanna drive, cocksucker? Climb over the seat and drive."

"Everybody can the negativity for a minute, please?" Hodad stood up in the bus, hanging by a strap from the ceiling. "Our chances of finding him out here on a night like this are abysmal, even if he wanted us to. And he does want us to find him. Just keep driving, but don't be looking for the minivan."

"Sit down and shut up, old man," Bagby said. "You can keep the fucking weed, but I don't see you getting a dime of a payout on this motherfucker's scalp."

Hodad sat down.

"Don't worry," Zef said. "He's not in charge."

"Nobody is, brother," Hodad laughed. "Nobody is."

"You want us to drop you off, we'll pull over anywhere."

"Relax, I didn't mean anything by it. 'Events are in the saddle, and ride mankind.' That's Emerson...

Anyway, don't beat yourself up. You were doomed from the start."

"I don't want to hear it."

"Who hooked you up with this crew?"

"That's on a need-to-know basis…"

"*I* don't need to know, but whoever it was, he was taking out the island's trash."

"He gave me your name first."

"My point exactly. A leper, a psychotic burnout and a gay Filipino couple who kill tourists for money. You expected a smooth outcome?"

The road seemed to level off and straighten out for a while, which was a relief. They passed the Garden of Eden Arboretum, and then they turned towards the sea and down a narrow ledge alongside a sheer cliff face.

"They must've told you all kinds of crazy bullshit to get you out here." Hodad sounded tired, rubbing disinfectant into his burns. "Big money, maybe even threats. Lot of people out here still think they can do business like that. They're used to getting their way, and out here, they get to thinking like the old *ali'i*, the chiefs. Make up a law somebody can't help but break, and sacrifice your troubles away." Hodad yawned expansively. His breath smelled sweet, like he'd been chewing herbs, a welcome respite from the scorched hot dog smell of his body. "I don't reckon I'd trade places with you, right now."

"I don't know, man. I've seen worse."

"The hell you have. What would you give, to trade places with someone else, right now?"

"I don't know… I'd give up a lot. Name it, I'd do it, to get out from under this shit…"

Incongruously, Hodad stuck out his claw. "Whatever happens, it's been a pleasure working with you."

Zef looked at the hand with naked distaste.

"Come on, don't leave me hanging. You can't get it from a handshake…"

If it would shut him up, Zef shook the creepy claw, and turned to face the window.

Shut Hodad up? Perish the thought. "Hawaii used to love to bathe itself in blood, but those days are long gone. This isn't Africa or Jamaica or Haiti. Shit like this doesn't *want* to happen here. Somebody went to a lot of trouble to bring the old stories to life again. You're fucking up the story, but that's the real reason they sent somebody like you."

Zef leaned against the window, staring and pretending to fall asleep. "I got no time for your stories, old man."

"You got time now, *haole*, and this time, you better listen."

Hodad started talking, telling some kind of story Zef barely heard for studying the road and spacing out. The sound of his voice was like the rain, soothing but maddening at the same time.

When he finally stopped talking, Zef couldn't say, but when he looked over, he found Hodad gone and the loading door open to the storm.

Bagby laughed. "Motherfucker just jumped out in the middle of the road! Fucking coward…"

Zef turned to look back and he saw nothing. The road ran down to the teeth of the jagged coast, then vanished around a hairpin turn.

Bagby screamed that he saw taillights. They came around the turn and suddenly the taillights were just ahead of them.

Bagby whooped and stomped the gas. The minivan seemed to vanish, and the microbus felt different because the road was gone, and they were flying.

19
KING OF SHARKS

In the beginning, the sky raped the earth and made gods, and the gods raped women and beasts and made monsters.

So taken was he with their beauty and the excitement of their human games, that Ka-moho-alii, king of sharks and brother of Pele, put on a human disguise to visit the people of the Waipio Valley on the island of Hawaii. After he had given them the gift of surfing, he seduced the most beautiful girl in the village and gave her a son. He warned her that she must never allow her son to swim with the other islanders, and never let him eat meat. Then Ka-moho-alii returned to the sea.

Nanaue was a handsome and strong child. Only Kalei, his mother, knew why he always swam alone in a lagoon far from the village, and why he must always wear a mantle of tapa cloth over his shoulders. This was to hide the gaping, razor-toothed mouth that split the skin of his back, always snapping and ravening for flesh.

Kalei kept Nanaue safe and his secret secure until he reached manhood and was taken by his grandfather to eat supper with the other men. Nanaue's appetite for meat proved bottomless. Nothing could stop the strange new craving the taste of meat had ignited in him.

As a child, Nanaue always swam alone with his mother, but now, he followed the other villagers down to the sea, and one by one, people began to disappear in the surf, eaten alive by a ferocious and freakishly cunning shark.

Though many in the village suspected Nanaue was not quite right, no one could imagine he was behind the attacks. But when the villagers gathered to plant their communal taro patches, a nosy neighbor ripped Nanaue's cape off his back, revealing his hideous hidden mouth, and got his arm bitten off for his trouble.

The whole village fell upon Nanaue and bound him up with ropes, and made ready an oven to incinerate him, for such a misbegotten offspring of a shark-god must be utterly destroyed. But Nanaue transformed and slipped out of captivity, swimming down a stream to gain the ocean, ahead of the rocks and spears thrown by the people of Waipio.

Driven from the land but unable to survive for long in the open ocean, Nanaue turned up next at Hana on Maui's north shore, where he soon won the hand of a chiefess and a place of honor in the kingdom. Before long, he challenged others to swimming contests, only to disappear while, in his place, a rogue shark appeared to devour Nanaue's opponent. Others simply vanished without a trace, always when Nanaue was absent.

Nanaue chafed at having to hide, and eventually gave up all pretense of a double life. Dragging a beautiful girl into the waves in full view of the village, he transformed and ate her. The people of Hana tried to catch him, but he escaped again, this time to the neighboring island of Molokai.

When swimmers and fishermen again began to disappear, the people of Molokai consulted their kahunas, who maintained an inter-island gossip conduit that soon brought news of the shark-man's rampage on Maui. The fishermen of Molokai cast their nets and captured Nanaue, dragged him onto the beach, dismembered him and stuck the monstrous fillets into an oven to be cremated. Nanaue's corpse was so massive that blood and fluids gushing out of it doused the flames, forcing them to cut his body into strips to dry, and to cut down a whole bamboo grove as kindling, to finally rid the world of him.

20

MANY DESTROYED

You know what it was like? It was like one of those annoying old *Twilight Zone* episodes, where some guy goes back in time to kill Hitler or save Tupac or whatever, and through his attempts to change history, he instead ends up *saving* Hitler and *killing* Tupac...?

It was like that.

Engine racing, higher and higher like an airplane prop, the bus floated for a long, fat second. Long enough for Bagby to say, "That ain't right," and Zef to stand up between the seats and scream, "Fokking hippie!"

The moon hung dead center in their view through a ragged hole in the clouds, etching the rain and the heaving sea with silver filigree. Beautiful—

They fell for a few seconds, at least, long enough for Zef to see the minivan's taillights gutter out beneath the waves below them, for Bagby to throw open his door, saying, "Ain't that a bitch," and for Maja to brace her feet against the dashboard, and Zef to keep screaming.

The face of the waves hit them like a black brick wall. The flat front end of the microbus smashed into it and passed every cubic ounce of impact onto its contents. Zef somersaulted into the windshield like a bug, landing on his tailbone just as the safety glass pulverized and gave way to a piledriver of frigid seawater. Bagby seemed to have pulled one of those ingenious cartoon maneuvers where the droopy dog or the woodpecker jumps off the falling elevator at exactly the right moment, and emerges unscathed from a devastating wreck.

Zef had the wind knocked out of him by the fall and then was flung back up through the descending microbus, now the world's shittiest submarine. Water slammed into him from the open loading door, crushing him against the far wall and up into a bubble of air trapped in the back of the compartment. Awash in burrito wrappers and flipflops, Zef gasped for air. Something brushed and slithered by his legs. He squawked and kicked out. Something shaggy bobbed up to cling to his arm. Maja's wig.

OK, this isn't a Bug and it's not floating, so you have to go. It was so fucking cold, he could barely think, let alone move.

Move!

Numb, fumbling, he ducked underwater, found the doorway and was swept out into the ocean. He could see only blackness shot through with strings of bright silver bubbles that told him which way was up. The sky was bright, shining down into the sea. Picking out hordes of long, sleek torpedo shapes between him and the surface.

A newborn wave lifted him up from the inky deep so fast his ears popped and his gut surged, but before he could break through, the tide receded and sucked him back down. His lungs swelled up with nothing.

Clawing his way to the surface, he felt something else brush his leg. This time, he was pretty sure it wasn't a Filipino transvestite hitman's wig.

Then it bumped him.

Every bubble of air he let out of his mouth left him heavier, weaker, sinking... He kicked and paddled and crawled, feeling like he was trying to squirm out of a fist of black ice closing around him, crushing him—

Slim, razor-finned bodies slipped past him, converging on something behind and below him, something he fervently hoped was Lowell Bagby.

Finally, his head broke the surface. He gulped air and hacked up briny snot and knuckled his eyes, but there was nothing to see.

There was no land. Before and behind him were rolling black swells and a bunch of unoccupied surfboards. When he looked in the direction the waves were headed, he saw a sight to make him cry. The black cliffs of Maui were maybe a quarter mile away. And the tide was pulling him out...

Something brushed his leg hard enough to shred his track pants and break the skin. "Fok!"

Surfboards.

Zef flailed over to the nearest floating object, a longboard in a travel sack, and dragged himself halfway onto it. The wind was colder than the water, but it was a wet cold, and it didn't feel good enough he could fall asleep and die. He shivered and spastically ate his own lips, but he willed himself to put his arms in the water and start paddling.

Was he doing it? He couldn't feel his arms. Maybe they were paddling right now. The board was moving, at least.

It wasn't just moving, it was jerking around.

He dipped a hand in the water and something tugged on him. He kicked out and shouted, "Fok you!" but inside, he almost welcomed being eaten.

But there were worse things than sharks in the ocean.

"Hey bro," Bagby gasped. He dog-paddled over. "Dude, how sick was that shit?"

Zef's head weighed a thousand pounds. His body was one big cramp. But he reached out for Bagby and took hold of his dreadlocks and held him under.

The hands came clawing at him, but they were too weak, and with no leverage, they just batted at him. Bubbles kept coming. How could someone who smoked so much *dagga* have so much air in his lungs? They kept coming, and Zef kept fighting until something snatched Bagby out of his grip and the water got about ten degrees warmer, for a while.

Peace at last. He curled up on the board just as the nose went under and water sloshed up his nose.

Something was tugging on it, pulling it down. A wavelet slopped over the nose of the board into his face.

He was on the neoprene surfboard bag with Isidro's mangled corpse in it. Something was tearing the bag apart to get at Isidro, who was probably leaking a blood slick sharks could taste from here to Easter Island.

The board tilted almost vertical and Zef rolled off. A sleek snout butted against his chest. He punched it, elbowed another, but they pushed right past him to get at Isidro.

Another longboard came slicing down the next swell and Zef threw an arm over it, thinking, *If you're a shark, fine, just eat me, I don't care—*

The board tugged Zef along after it and bore his weight graciously, dragged him until he flopped out of the water onto it.

He'd surfaced between sets, mercifully, but now, the ocean drew itself up into a mountain to dwarf the coastal cliffs. Zef clung to the board and steered as best he could with his hands. As it gathered mass and force, the swell became a wall that Zef sledded down on a toothpick.

He raced to the bottom and pivoted desperately out of the pit when the wall began to bow under its own weight to form a tube. He felt weightless. The board was as big as a battleship, the wave moved as fast as ice cream melting. Eyes closed, navigating entirely by his inner ear, he rose up onto his knees, and then his feet.

The highest cliff was crowned with a broken guardrail. Maybe two hundred yards off and the distance was shrinking fast and there was a break in the cliffs, way off to the left. Maybe an inlet from one of the hundreds of fucking waterfalls, or maybe a nice, soft sandy beach...

The tube was eating up the ocean like a jet turbine, collapsing at his back and gaining on him. He kept cutting back and down and away from the gnawing mouth of the wave and he was *surfing*, he was fucking surfing a winter wave on the north shore of Maui at a spot that made Pipeline look like a fucking kiddie pool, and where were the crowds?

His legs buckled, muscles seizing up with cramps. Zef nearly went down on one knee but he would wipe out and get swept onto the rocks he could see now, black teeth as tall as the board was long, lava rock fangs that would rip him wide open for the fish to nibble.

There was no getting around the point. The cliff face loomed up to block out the driving rain and it was the blackest black he'd ever seen. The cliff seemed to rise up like a mighty hand to clap the rushing slapping hand of the wave and he'd be crushed in between them, crushed and burst open and aerosolized in a burst of red spray.

He backed up on the board until the nose tipped up perilously, shimmying under him and he was going to wipe out, and before him the wave breaking on the rocks—

It didn't break. It flowed right into that black cliff face's gaping maw like a tongue into a mouth, so black so dark he never saw what swallowed him.

Falling down to hug the board, deafened by the booming artillery roar of the wave pounding up the narrowing tunnel, he put his head down and closed his eyes. It would happen any moment now…

He lay in still shallows and felt the wave's gentle tickling kiss as it rolled back down the smooth bore of the lava tube, leaving him facedown on sand like black kitty litter, crawling up to where it was dry and soft and melting and soaking into the sand.

* * *

Down in the tube, in perfect blackness, he felt cut off from everything, even himself. His thoughts wouldn't come in words. His emotions wouldn't come at all. It was most disturbing, like how your radio goes dead when you go through a tunnel. Like his ideas and feelings, his essential personality, was coming from somewhere else, and his body only a radio playing a program that, he suddenly realized, was almost constantly an unbearable asshole of the lowest caliber.

The TV doctor was right about him. He was a hole filled with bullshit. He'd wasted his whole life to become something he'd hoped would simultaneously disgrace and impress his father. And for what?

He'd killed the fucker, hadn't he? Donny Nanaue had to be fucking dead. Zef saw the minivan go into the ocean, and he never came up. Just like he'd seen the motherfucker take a bullet to the chest and wreck a truck and come back crooning. For him to still be alive now, the crazy bullshit Hodad and Auntie Kalei said would have to be true, which was funny as hell.

So why wasn't he laughing?

He thought of that chicken the old witch had buried, and now he knew it wasn't any kind of magic trick. They were just stupid, so dumb you could make them look at something and forget all else while you buried them alive. He knew exactly how it felt. He wondered if he went back, if the chicken was still alive down in the earth, still staring at that spot, waiting for a worm.

Maybe if you dig up the chicken and eat it, you could get your soul back.

That wasn't funny.

So why was he laughing?

Was he laughing? He heard laughter... but it sounded like an old woman, far away...

Too tired to move, too cold to sleep, he lay there until certainty that something was creeping up on him or would come out of the surf after him overpowered his fatigue.

Hot. Dripping not seawater, but sweat. Was he dreaming, or was this a fever? He felt the cold sea leaving his clothes as steam. He sank into lava rock that softened into yielding, perfumed ladyflesh that sighed when it closed over his head.

Crawling and moaning deliriously, he made his way up the lava tube. The dreamy softness trailed off and the floor became unyielding stone. The tunnel sloped more steeply, following the path that a vein of superheated magma had taken through the softer shale and sand to reach the coast. Too weak to stand yet, every few minutes he lay down to rest for a few hours, drifting in a semi-conscious fugue where Dr. Bill lectured him and Yeti cut chunks off his ass to bait fishhooks.

Somehow, he found himself crawling again. He thought he could see light, though he'd forgotten what light looked like, what seeing felt like... And then he bumped into a wooden railing, scabbed with paint and wobbly in its concrete foundation, but definitely manmade.

Something flew in his face. Hundreds of somethings. He choked back a scream, terrified they'd fly into his mouth. Did Hawaii have bats? Running for the light, he stumbled up a flight of stairs, pulling himself up into green undergrowth dripping with dew and rosy gray predawn light and *fuck you, stupid world, yet again you have failed to kill me.*

Lying on his back in the grass, he watched a swirling cloud of butterflies or moths come streaming out of the lava tube. His hands and face were feathered with shredded sapphire wings speckled with flecks of silver so pure he could see his reflection in them. Fok, you couldn't scratch your ass in Hawaii without killing something beautiful.

The tube looked like a retired tourist trap, with a rusty sheet-metal hut, picnic area and chainlink fence collapsed under the weight of the jungle. Past the hut, he saw why it wasn't still entertaining visitors.

The trees partially hid a short field with about a hundred purple marijuana plants taller than Zef. Punani probably had patches like this all over the North Shore. It was way too much for local consumption. The fucker was killing casino moguls and eating Mexican gangsters to stop them exploiting his people, while grooming a massive cash crop of shit more potent than opium.

Dirt road outside passed by little cabins cut into the mountainside. He crept past these, then crawled around flooded fields where they grew that purple shit Auntie Kalei cooked. He saw cars up on blocks, chickens and pigs roaming free, but no people.

He made it to the foot of the mountain without encountering anyone. The dirt road came out of a stand of banana trees that he raided, and he found himself on a paved road.

He had to figure anyone and everyone he encountered for an enemy. He was wearing a hoodie and boxer shorts and nothing else. Also, he was a fugitive from a crime scene with at least six dead bodies, and a drowned VW microbus with maybe three more.

He'd lost the gun and the phone. He had no idea where Donny was holed up and no way to do the job. He had to get the fuck out of here, get off this island, let Dr. Bill do his worst. There had to be a way to hang this around his neck, but right now, he wanted only to get out.

The road took him around a rocky bend and into the murky red-gray glow of a rising sun buried under storm clouds. A little shrine of neatly mortared lava bricks had a cross on it, but under its peaked roof, he found plates of fish, Spam, candy and coconut cups of inflammable booze set up in front of a row of tiki fetishes.

The biggest one was a black humanoid figurine with a mouth for a head, studded with shark teeth. Thinking, *fuck you, Hodad*, Zef drained the booze and took the shark tiki, hefting it like a club.

Something like a village, with a baseball field and a general store and a little chapel of rough-hewn blocks of rosy coral, but all the signs in Hawaiian and no people at all. After the church, the road just gave up, with thorny trees and spears of lava rock pointed at the waves like some kind of barrier.

He saw a white car coming and he dropped on his belly behind a rock, but then he jumped up and came running.

The postal Jeep was covered in bumper stickers and he could see flowers piled up in the back. He ran out in front of it and waved his arms and ran for the driver's side, remembering that there was no passenger door.

She didn't stop. He turned to jump out of the way when she hit him and threw him across the road. The tiki flew from his hands into the undergrowth.

He landed rolling. He couldn't see her, but he heard sandals slapping wet pavement, felt someone turn him over.

"Yo, Auntie Kalei, *wotthfok...* you gotta..."

"What do I gotta?" Kewalo asked.

"*Fok!* Help—"

Kewalo's hand covered his mouth. He felt thousands of tiny teeth bristle against his skin, ready to take his face off. "Tried to tell you, *haole* boy," the shark-man said. "We *love* trouble."

He woke up to kisses. Earnest, passionate kisses.

Dog kisses.

Tongue like a big man's hand slathered up the side of his face and forced in between his lips. He spit, cursed, tried to bite the tongue. Growl he could feel in his bowels.

His hands were tied behind his back with plastic zip-ties, and something tied his bonds to a wooden post in some kind of sheetmetal shed.

"I fucking knew it," someone said. "I knew I'd find you here. I knew your fucking wigger ass would be jungled up with these fucking savages."

Zef shook his head and strained to see past his crooked nose. Silver-blue pit bull with a head like a claw hammer sat at attention in front of him.

The livid, sunburned face hanging beside him in the dark sneered and spat in his eye.

Detective Bongwater.

"What the fok you doing here, Five-Oh?"

Bongwater shrugged. "I heard what happened to Yolo. I knew you and your party pals were fucking shit up out here. So I came over off the clock…"

Zef choked on a high, unbearable giggle. "Yeah," he said, looking at the chains the Honolulu cop was hanging from, "you one hell of a clever detective."

"I figured your shit out pretty quick."

"If you weren't the dirtiest cop in these islands, you could'a done something about it, too."

"You and your fucking pineapple-head friends cut off the whole pipeline. There's nothing coming in, and the fucking Mexicans and the Chinks are killing each other, because your fucking friends opened a new front in the drug war."

"I tried to fokking tell you before, I'm not with them. I just came out here for the fokking bike…"

Bongwater wasn't hearing him. Tossing his head and snapping his chains taut, he tried to rip down the wall. "Locals all hang together, even fucking Doris. These fucking native sovereignty nuts are just another gang. Think they're gonna take over and push us out of our own fucking country."

"This ain't your fucking country." Kewalo walked into the shed. A big, dull-witted guy followed him— Peapea's understudy. The pit bull cowered.

Kewalo came over to the cop and smiled at him.

Even hobbled and bound on his knees, the cop came up to his shoulder. He threw himself at Kewalo

264

like a junkyard dog on a short leash. "You pigfucking sonofabitch—"

Kewalo grinned and shrugged. "We didn't think repo ninja boy'd show up, but now we got him, we don't need you, no more."

"Cut me loose, you half-nigger island trash, and I'll snap your fucking neck like a twig."

"I not one fighter," Kewalo murmured, leaning in close. His skin rippled and broke out in goosebumps like tiny catclaw teeth. His bare, almost childish hand reached out to touch the cop on the crown of his skull.

Bongwater whipped his head around, trying to headbutt or bite. Under Kewalo's feather-light touch, his skin came unzipped and sloughed away bananapeel easy from his skull to fall over his eyes in a shiny pink blindfold.

The cop's screams went up so high only the pit bull could hear them. The dog whined and lunged, but the big guy caught his collar.

You had to have a heart of stone not to laugh.

"Look how he bunched up his cheeks," Zef said. "I bet he's smuggling drugs."

"We better find out," Kewalo said. "If he holding, it go bad when he get where he wen go."

The big guy untied the cop from the wall and dropped a knee like a telephone pole on his back to pin him to the dirt floor. Kewalo went up behind him.

"I'll talk, I'll tell you anything, you motherfucker, but please don't..."

"I don't want to know anything, but what you got up there," Kewalo said, patting himself down. "Shit, I ain't got no gloves. You ain't got no diseases or needles or other sharp objects up in there, right, Five-Oh?"

"Please, God, stop them, make them stop…"

"You must be crazy." Kewalo wiggled his fingers in the cop's face. His fingernails seemed to grow into claws like teeth. "Gods *love* this kind of shit."

Without preamble or benefit of lube, Kewalo fisted the cop, whose screams became so unreal, the pit bull latched itself onto his shoulder and shook him to shut him up.

"You lied to me," Kewalo said, pulling his fist out. A few feet gnarled gray intestine popped out of the ruined sphincter. "Ain't nothing up there nobody wants."

Zef stared in horror, relief and guilt, and he still wanted to laugh.

The big guy pulled the pit off Bongwater's arm. Kewalo came around to kneel in the cop's face. Weeping, mewling like a crushed kitten, Bongwater whined, "Please…"

The big guy made worried Hawaiian noises. Kewalo snapped at him, turned and sank his teeth into the cop's cheek. A long, gray tongue rasped up the cheek, flaying meat off bone like steel wool on whipped cream.

Still blinded, the cop struggled, but it was pathetic, like leaning into it, wanting only to end it. He tried to make words, but Kewalo licked his lips off. Biting away the flap of scalp covering his eyes, Kewalo sucked one and then the other out of its socket, popping them in his mouth with inhuman relish.

Kewalo stood up. His mouth split his whole face to his ears, but still couldn't contain all his teeth. "We gotta check you next," Kewalo said as he turned to leave, "but I be gentle this time, I promise."

The pit bull barked at the cop's ravaged rectum, then clamped onto the dangling length of bowel and entertained itself with a game of tug of war.

And the cop kept crying.

21
RED SAND

You deserve this.

None of this would have happened without you thinking you were the shit, trying to play fokking Scarface. Look what it got you. Look what it got a whole bunch of people who otherwise might have been alive.

Some nice Japanese lady came all the way over here to get married and fok only knows how much it costs over there, where a watermelon is like a hundred fucking dollars... And in the middle of getting her pictures taken, a bullet falls out of the sky and knocks her brains out in the groom's face.

Would the world be a better place without me?

The pit bull was throwing up its dinner of raw, unwashed human intestines. But getting sick only seemed to make it friskier, and now that Detective Bongwater had finally passed away, it was interested in him.

You deserve this, he reminded himself... forced himself to look once more at the faceless, disemboweled cop... *but you don't deserve* that.

But what're you gonna do? What would a ninja do? Your hands are tied and you have no weapons and you can't move without getting your throat torn out. Well, you'd better figure out something…

What Kewalo said… Something about how they didn't think he was going to show up… They were coming back, and they wouldn't do this to him, because they had something *worse* in store for him.

He thought of that ritual at the construction site… the body roasted in the ground…

Think

Faster

Something…

The dog looked up at him like it could smell his idea. Its surgically bobbed ears twitched and drool overflowed its shitty, bloody muzzle.

The dog was probably the only audience in all the world who would not think any the less of him for what he started doing next.

Tucking his body into a tight ball, relaxing his back vertebra by dislocated vertebra he stretched his neck until his chin rested upon his terror-shriveled package. Tugging off his brine-crusty boxers with his teeth, he closed his eyes and focused on his breathing until he could feel his pelvis dislocate. Then he curled his pelvis up even tighter under his chin, straining and squeezing and *oh fuck*, something snapped like a rubber band in his lower back, but fuck it, he had no choice, did he?

Push and flex, pull and *relax…* He stuck his tongue out until he felt like it would tear free of the floor of his mouth, he tickled his own asshole.

He had tried everything else. He got it out once, but when he shoved it back in, it must've lodged in the elbow of his colon, or something. In spite of his relaxed attitude towards auto-fellation, he had definite reservations about bad-touching his own sphincter. That his dumper was one-way exit only (except for emergency personal storage) was dogma etched in stone, not because it would mean he was gay, but because it was shit.

He tasted it now, and holy crap, was there ever a good reason for some taboos. The black stuff he'd vomited up had been awful, but *SHIT*. While he could smell the brown funk of his own backdoor well enough and could taste it all too well, he could only go through with it because his ass was strangely oblivious to all the attention.

Tucking even tighter, until a miasma of fetid methane and toxic chocolate erupted in his face, he forced the tip of his tongue past the puckered ring of tough, scowling muscle and into the surprisingly soft tunnel beyond, so oddly unlike a cunt. The warm, velvety softness was poop, but he gagged and pushed on, tongue like a prodding finger wriggling all the way up against the anterior wall of his colon, desperately massaging his prostate and trying to make a miracle…

The dog came over. Its huge, flat tongue laved his buttcrack like there were Snausages in there. He would have stopped, would have collapsed in a dry-heaving pile of self-hatred or seized up and sent a cracked rib through his lungs, if he gave himself an orgasm, but it still felt like he was rimming the ribeye bone in a steak.

Suddenly, a rolling spasm passed through him, a grand mal convulsion that made him bite his tongue and shit all over the pit bull.

But, he saw through tear-rimmed eyes… it *worked*.

The plastic bag drugs he'd expelled—twice, now—lay in a lake of chocolate syrup, hanging out of his asshole by the sharp corners of the Zip-Loc mouth. The dog barked at it, crouching on its forelegs like a puppy at play. Zef wiggled his ass a little, causing the dog to pounce on the plastic bag and scarf it down.

Some animals never learn. They're a lot like people, that way.

Its muzzle began to ooze foam almost immediately. It bounded around the shed, stopping only to frantically hump Detective Bongwater's corpse. Then it started howling and chasing its own boner—trying to imitate Zef, maybe—and wheezing and coughing up foam, and then it dropped dead happier than anything that ever lived or died on earth.

That wasn't an orgasm, Zef told himself. *Just a muscle spasm. Zero percent homo. The dog did it…*

So next, he had to hook a foot under the dead cop's arm and pull him close enough to sit on and go through his pockets. His slacks were down around his knees. His keys were everything Zef could hope for, with a tiny pepper spray can and all kinds of keys and a little utility knife.

It cut right through the zip-ties. The blood rushing to his hands made him want to cut them off, too. Screaming into the dirt, he made himself get up and go for the door. He didn't hear anyone outside. The light was watery gray, filtered through a canopy of jungle overgrowth. Through the cracked door, he saw another hut like this one, and red, bare dirt and then jungle and then sky.

He heard nothing outside but crazy bird noises. He opened the door and walked into the barrel of a gun.

It fit in his mouth like he was born to suck guns.

His hands should've gone up and he should've surrendered, but he spat out the gun and had his hands on the person behind it before they could react. Hugging them close with the gun hand trapped under his arm, he slammed them into the wall.

"Twenty thousand," said a little brown man with a shaven head and no ears.

"Holy fok, Earwi… Maja, right?"

"My rate go up. Need new partner. You still pay…?"

"Yeah, shit, I pay. And don't make it look like no fokking accident."

Maja tossed her head down the slope, towards the village and the sea. "Follow."

Down a trail that was little more than a rain-cut channel in the spongy red soil. The sun was somewhere in the west.

"Hurry," Maja said over her shoulder. Running, bare feet slapping earth, muffled gusts of desperate breath. Zef struggled to keep up. His left leg was sore from getting hit by the Jeep, this morning. "Sunset will be too late," she said.

What the fuck did *that* mean?

The trail cut across a road flanked by KAPU—KEEP OUT signs. Zef glanced up the road when he passed, saw the lights of a general store, a town. Their town, their store.

I don't want to kill anyone.
I just want to go home.
There is no home.
The world wants you dead.

The trail went through broken lava rock with tortured hala trees under canopy so dense the fading, failing light was deep, deep green. Maja disappeared into the curtain of leaves hanging down from the trees and Zef followed and when he came through the curtain, he stood on a black beach lit up by clusters of torches.

Girls in grass skirts danced to a languorous rhythm that echoed the waves crashing on the beach. It looked like a luau, except no tourists, no bar and nobody smiling.

A grandmotherly woman stepped forward and hung a lei round Zef's neck. She wore a grass skirt and no top to cover her drooping breasts. She leaned in to give him a big toothless kiss. Zef recoiled into the arms of another old crone who trapped one of his wrists in a pair of handcuffs. Zef jerked away from her. The first old woman zapped him with a taser so her friend could catch his other wrist.

"Twenty thousand," Maja said again, but not to Zef. Clad in a canary yellow robe, Yeti came out of the dark between the torches.

"You get it, Maja," Yeti said. "Mahalo."

You know that movie, everyone's seen it, where the guy goes to the island and he tries to save an innocent girl from being sacrificed by a bunch of pagan maniacs, only to find out that the girl's in on it, and the sacrificial victim on the block is *him*?

Zef DeGroot never saw that movie.

Kewalo came up behind him and shoved him to the ground. The bare hand slashed his back, flensing off his sweatshirt and laying bare his spine almost exactly where he'd done it before, ripping out Auntie Kalei's stitches.

Kalei—

They brought her out next, covered in flowers. She walked willingly with them and stood proud and naked on the sand, but the look on her face was sad. She searched the crowd until she saw him, and then she looked even sadder.

She looked younger than Zef now, and more beautiful than the volcano-bitch-goddess who raped him in his dream.

A procession of men in red and yellow robes came out of the dark to surround her. Kewalo made her kneel without quite touching her.

Yeti came up to him, smiling like he was doing Zef a huge favor. "This isn't exactly tradition, but I think we muddle through, I promise."

"I was trying to do what you wanted me to. What the fok are you doing?"

"What the hell does it look like? We're trying to call the gods back."

Baskets and trays of offerings were laid out around Auntie Kalei. It was a trick, it had to be...

"She's an old woman. Donny's mother and nobody knows who the father was, but my father did rituals around her and brought Ka-Moho-Alii into her body to awaken a ghost-god in her womb.

"We got a man, instead. But we've worked on the man. If he eats his last tie to his human face, he'll change and never go back."

"So he turns into a shark, so what?"

"Not a shark. The king of sharks. The *kanaka maoli* will know the gods are awake, and return to the old ways. The white man will never know peace in our ocean. The waves that fall on Waikiki will be red with his blood. This place will devour them and drive them out, and the kingdom of Hawai'i will be restored!"

Zef nodded along. It made sense. "Yo, you wanna do that shark-shit, go ahead. What the fok you need me for?"

Yeti balanced on one hand while the other took Zef's head in it like a softball, and squeezed. "When a chief passed away, a sacrifice was required by the gods. The *mu ai kanaka* was charged with finding that sacrifice, so whenever a ritual was called for, every able-bodied man in the village took to the mountains.

"Do you have any idea how hard it was to find sacrifices? Tabus of every kind were invented, just to feed the gods. All the tabus meant death by sacrifice, so the mu policed the people, but once you weed out the stupid and the arrogant and the unlucky, you have to start letting foreigners in."

A cold hand stroked his guts. If he had anything left in it, it would've come out now. "Yo, you can't just, fok, man you can't let him *eat me*…"

"Don't worry," Yeti said, "you're not for him, you're for us." Resting on his tailbone, he held up a massive obsidian knife. "We cook you, but I promise we won't eat you."

"He's not coming," Kewalo said.

"Give him a taste," Yeti said.

Kewalo came over to Zef and admired his the ink on his back. "That's a nice tattoo, brah. Can I have it?" His finger traced around the crown on Zef's shoulder, clipping it out like a coupon.

Zef bowed his head, but said nothing.

"I always wanted to get one, but I not like needles. Did it hurt?" Kewalo dragged his hand over the shoulder. Curls of skin backed with a thin sheen of fat sloughed off like sliced cheese.

Kewalo licked his hand, but his eyes were hooded, blank. "Scream, you fucker!"

Zef was aware of the damage and saw the blood arcing out from his bare muscles, but he felt nothing.

"Leave him alone!" Kalei screamed. Her voice sounded hard and haggard. She slashed at her young girl's nubile body with her nails, making runnels of red down her gently rounded belly.

"I thought you were butt-buddies with Donny," Zef said.

"*Fuck you,* brah." Kewalo peeled Zef's skin down to the waistband of his boxers.

"He can't fok girls without eating them, right? So I thought you and him must be like…"

The phrase *bit his ear off* gets thrown around so much these days, ever since Tyson bit Holyfield, but almost without exception it's a gross exaggeration. Tyson barely nipped a notch out of Holyfield's indigestible cauliflower ear.

Kewalo took off Zef's right ear and a good chunk of his scalp, and he didn't spit it out. He didn't gag. He just swallowed it.

It didn't hurt a bit.

It wasn't shock, and he wasn't one of *them*. He was definitely dying from blood loss, light-headed as his precious fluids gushed out of him. But it didn't hurt, and that clearly freaked them out.

It should've freaked *him* out, but the answer, right now, was almost a gift.

The fokking hippie…

Fokking leper…

The way he'd traded with that woodcutter in Lahaina… The shit he'd talked in the bus, right before he vanished.

He'd traded him for leprosy? That was a shitty deal. What did he give up?

No, it was bullshit. *Relax, dude*, Hodad said in his head. *This kind of shit only works if you believe in it…*

Just then, a massive shadow came out of the trees and into the channel of darkness that lay across the beach.

"Fuckin' cut it out," said Donny Nanaue.

The priests encircled Donny, pouring flowers onto the ground at his feet. He suffered them, but his eyes never left the lady on the sand.

"What's he going to do to her?"

Kewalo laughed. "He gotta do the big change, and he gonna eat her up."

As Zef talked to Kewalo, he finally succeeded in trapping Maja's eye. "So like, that's why you selling him out? Because you're like mad queer for him, and he's not into you?" To Maja, he mouthed, *thirty thousand*.

Kewalo raised a hand and hissed. His teeth had grown so long and thick that he could no longer speak. A spray of saliva was all the response he could muster.

Maja's eyes brimmed with tears, but she made no response.

Yeti dragged the knife across Kalei's breasts, sendng rivulets of blood cascading down her chest. Donny pounded his fists into the sand and came charging.

Staring into Maja's eye, Zef rolled his eyes to indicate the man standing over him, and said, "Isidro."

Donny roared and ripped off his clothes. He approached Kalei, panting, but then, pawing at his face like he'd drunk poison, he turned from the offerings and charged toward Zef.

A gun went off, then twice more before anyone hit the sand. Maja stood over Kewalo, straining to lift the big smoking automatic in both hands, then emptied the clip into his head as he tried to get up.

Yeti got in the way, chanting and holding a torch of smoking leaves, but Donny swept him aside, spoiling his canary robe with a splash of scarlet.

Three of Yeti's robed goons overwhelmed Maja. Zef got up and tried to save her, but his right arm wouldn't do what it was told. It dangled and flopped against his hip like a purse.

Donny waded into them, snapping limbs and biting throats until he freed the assassin. Lifting Maja up over his gaping mouth, he roared until his voice ripped. Blood gushed from his mute mouth.

Zef sat down hard on his left hand, dislocating his thumb. His left hand slid free of the cuffs and popped painlessly back into place. With his one working arm, he frantically searched the sand where he'd seen Maja drop the gun.

Yeti pranced around Kalei on his hands, leading a guttural chant that seemed to egg Donny on.

Donny twisted an arm and a leg out of their sockets, eliciting only a sigh of agony from the assassin. Jaws working like he was singing to himself, he flung Maja into the jungle and turned to look for someone else. His eyes were black, empty but for the reflected torchlight.

Yeti advanced on Donny and held up a cutlet of breast flesh at him. Donny turned, aroused by the familiar scent even in his blood-glutted state. He caught the gobbet of flesh and wolfed it down. His mouth seemed to eat his face until he was all snout and teeth. He looked round and saw Zef just as he found Maja's purse.

Donny came lurching at him, jaws snapping, but his legs stopped working all at once. He fell on his belly and thrashed in a frenzy to get at Zef. His hands pawed the black sand as if he'd forgotten how to use them. His forearms blackened and split open to slough off at the elbow, leaving his upper arm flat blades of muscle.

Zef turned the purse inside out, dumping ruined cosmetics and notebooks and bits of trash, and then finally a loaded clip for the Beretta.

A piglike grunting came from his twitching gill slits as Donny scooped up one of his discarded arms and then the other, gobbling them up as he came closer, crawling on fins and half-fused feet.

Zef stared into his abyssal eyes as he tried to work the unfamiliar automatic one-handed and he thought, *thank God for leprosy!*

But he wasn't just infected with it. He suddenly *had* it, but he hadn't given up anything that he knew of for the dubious gift.

He remembered what Hodad said when he asked him how he got the disease.

Traded a guy for it.

He wouldn't say what he got in return.

In the black, flat eyes on the mottled gray monstrosity humping towards him, he saw nothing like humanity, but he could see agony and rage and something else no one else could understand.

Donny Punani didn't want pain without the release of death, immortality as a ravening beast. He didn't want to be a ghost-god. The King of Sharks. He'd rather be nothing.

You're no fokking ninja, but what is a ninja, anyway? A killer, skillful, silent, utterly in control. To be all those things, you can't be full of yourself. To be so full of all that good shit, there's no room for a self, at all. So, to be a ninja was like trying to be a shark.

Zef reached out with his working hand to stall Donny for just a moment, long enough to meet his eye and say, "*Wanna trade?*"

Donny kept coming, his mouth wide enough to bite Zef in half.

Zef stuck his gun in Donny's face. Donny's massive jaws surged out of his gaping mouth and closed over Zef's left arm up to the elbow, then bit it off.

Zef fell on his ass, screaming and sobbing and hugging his stump, but once the shock of seeing it happen wore off, it was no more painful than a lost phone or a parking ticket.

Inside Donny, Zef's severed arm spasmodically twitched, pulling the Beretta's trigger until the clip was empty. A string of muffled pops, and Donny belched cordite fumes and vomited blood. Then another bang, and the flat gray top of his head bulged and split open. One of his eyes popped out.

He sighed and slumped to the sand and died less than a foot from the high tide line.

Yeti came bounding at him with the stone knife in his teeth cutting a wide smile into his red, apoplectic face.

Zef went down on one knee and torpedoed himself at Yeti, a man with no arms grappling a man with no legs. They rolled and tumbled in the surf until Zef pinned Yeti's powerful arms with his legs and sank his teeth into the shaman's throat.

The Hawaiian's pulse was strong, the heartbeat racing but steady between his teeth. He bit down until his teeth met and blood surged up in his face in a delectable red wave.

Yeti's arms crushed him in a spastic bearhug, cracking several ribs, before he went limp. He rolled off the corpse and most of the grizzled old local's neck came away in his teeth.

The retreating wave pulled Yeti into black shallows seething with gray fins. Sharks of every size, from fingerlings to ten-foot hammerheads and mako crawling half-exposed over the ribbed sandbar, converged on the mangled mancatcher in a frenzy so intense, the ocean itself seemed to eat him.

The rest of Yeti's thug priests hung back in a demoralized mob at the on of the beach, but slowly, they gathered the resolve to come after him. Kalei knelt amid the spoiled offerings, pressing a tapa cloth to her mutilated breast. She looked older than the islands.

With nowhere else to go, Zef waded into the ocean, trying to climb onto the silver road the rising moon painted on the water.

Wavelets played about his knees. The rocky bottom tripped him and he fell in the shallows. He felt sleek shapes bumping against him, curiously, lovingly. Their teeth not eating, but undressing him.

He thought, *This kind of shit only works if you believe in it...*

22

INNUMERABLE DARK HEAVENS

After all the shit he'd been through, all the obstacles he'd destroyed, you'd think the universe would've just given up by now.

Just lie back and try to enjoy it, world. Dr. Bill ain't finished with your fat ass by a damn sight.

Watching a big beautiful sunset and sipping a mai tai, he floated on a raft in the private lagoon at the center of his lowland estate on the Big Island. His erstwhile wife usually holed up here when she wasn't required for social appearances like his upcoming Celebrity Marriage Retreat Special for sweeps. He'd come to talk to her about reconciliation, and thus he was on the phone with the admiral of his legal armada, Mort Blaustein.

"Morty, she's fucking insane. I would certify her myself, if I was a real doctor. How many fucking honorary degrees equals one real one, anyway?"

"They don't convert, Bill." Morty had no fucking sense of humor. "She's pretty dug in, this time, then."

"You've never fucked her, have you? She's always dug in. Her own worst enemy, I tell you what. Her clit's as dead to pleasure as a tailor's thumb. I am trying to find a suitable enticement to get some civility out of her just through the fuckin' season…"

"Just let her go. Let our staff script the whole divorce. Sweeps in the spring, Bill. You play it right, it'll get you another Daytime Emmy."

"You don't understand, man. It's deeper than love, just take that at face value."

"If I have to." Morty's breathing sounded like a machine purifying air. "If I may ask, why now?"

"I don't know for sure, but she's got some crazy ideas, as usual. Paranoid. She sees a thing about a tidal wave in the Philippines and blames me for killing a butterfly in the backyard."

"Care to elaborate?"

"Some sort of crimewave over here. The locals are all bugshit. Some big nutjob native supremacist fell off his boat or something in the middle of trying to ratfuck our deal on Zweibel's holdings, and she thinks I'm to blame."

"You should feel guilty once in a while, all the lucky breaks you get."

"All the bad luck money can buy. I just wanted you to know what to expect."

"If she comes at us with anything nasty, I'll stiff-arm it until you can paper things over."

"I appreciate it, Morty. And let me know if there's any more problems with the mug thing. I want that shit off my plate. Bye now."

He felt salty, so he skipped the phone across the water, almost got it to the shore. Droids were the shit, they'd skip six or seven times. The lagoon was almost more of a pool, the narrow outlet fenced and filtered, with movable barriers to stop intruders above or below the waves.

Mitsy was giving him way more than his quota of shit. After every other obstacle he'd put down, if she had any idea how wet his hands really were, she was out of her fucking mind to get his dander up now.

He resented it, but he needed her now more than he needed his useless children, his shitty show or anyone he'd ever genuinely loved. He planned to retire here, and soon. He'd given all he could to the cause of healing America's septic, hypocritical soul. And he wouldn't have gotten where he was if he didn't always keep an eye on the big picture.

Though he invested heavily in oil and gas and backed Republicans and conservative social causes, he knew the world was fucked, and not by the Rapture. Dwindling oil, climate change havoc, famines, pestilence and human wave attacks of hungry, diseased beaner refugees were either here or coming soon. A zombie plague would be a fucking Club Med vacation compared to America's imminent future, and Dr. Bill had gone all in on where he'd be when it happened.

Sure, the waters would rise, but Hawaii was large and mountainous enough to weather the changes, but small enough to pacify—or cleanse of natives, if it came to that. Kinky-haired, smelly America could eat itself with its bad teeth and die, for all he cared. When the lights went out all over the world, Dr. Bill would have all the prime real estate, the weaponry and the resources on these islands, and so long as Mitsy couldn't retain a halfway competent lawyer, he had a fairly legitimate claim to the throne of the restored sovereign nation of Hawaii, should it ever come back.

He had no plans to assert it now, naturally. He'd look foolish, TMZ and *People* would have a field day with that kind of stupidity. Mitsy was only a quarter local, but it was all royal blood, and her white blood came from missionary stock that grabbed up plantations on three islands when the white traders deposed Queen Lilioukalani. He would quietly buy up Zweibel's operation and turn the undeveloped Maui site into a Marriage Rescue Resort as a front for an arsenal to shame the National Guard. Come whatever the fuck may, he aimed to retire in high fucking style.

And, it would all be just perfect, once he made sure that little shitbird from Vegas was well and truly—

The raft seemed to jerk a foot or two out of the water. Like someone stood up under him and tossed him.

Dr. Bill was not a small man—first-string offensive line in high school and college—but he got flipped out of his seat as if by a rogue wave.

Toes touched the soft imported sand on the bottom and pushed him to the surface. He gripped the raft, but it was already flat. What the hell? He flipped it over. The underside was shredded.

Jesus, something was in here with him. What did they say about sharks? They didn't like to eat people; they did it by mistake because they looked like seals or just spazzed out in the water. *Don't panic, big guy. Don't give him an excuse.*

Slowly, deliberately, Dr. Bill tip-toed towards the beach, where two big sides of beef who used to guard dignitaries in Iraq for Blackwater would be sitting and tanning, if he hadn't given them the afternoon off so he could have it out with Mitsy in private, and because one of them was a Jesus freak and the other one was maybe queer for him, so he was working on replacing them.

The water was up to his chin, and shit, if he had one of those headset deals he would look and feel like a fucking call-center operator for Time-Life Books or a suicide crisis center, but he could call for help.

Fuck help. A fucking blacktip reef shark or something must've blundered into the lagoon, and when he got out, he would have something more substantial to try the new autoloading crossbow on than his wife's surplus housecats.

Sport fishermen had pretty much wiped out all the big sharks anyway, and the fucking chinks were wasting the rest to make their shitty shark's fin soup. Shit didn't even taste like anything, but try and tell a chink that his #1 status symbol was a nasty, cruel, meaningless waste. You might as well try to talk them out of gambling.

Chinks. Jesus, but they had fucked him good, this time. For the thousandth episode of his show, he had the producers get these fancy coffee mugs for all the crew and staff—much nicer, apparently, than they could buy on their fat fucking union paychecks, because they all used them and lo and behold, the mugs had lead paint AND mercury...?

Somebody up there doesn't like me, Dr. Bill thought. *They gotta know one day, I'm gonna take over...*

He'd almost forgotten about the shark. The water was only up to his thighs when it bit him.

On the *Shark Week* shows, they always say the shark comes up and bites impulsively, and they often spit up what they bit, because we apparently taste like shit.

The whole back of his left calf was on fire and he got a head rush from blood loss and when he lifted his leg out of the water, he almost had a fucking heart attack.

The skin had rolled off like a sock and the bulging, fibrous pot roast of his calf was sheared raggedly off about five inches above his heel. His Achilles tendon, all the things that made his foot more than just a perishable kickstand, were torn out like so many uprooted weeds.

He tottered in a woozy circle on his remaining leg, wobbling and weeping and squeezing just above the knee, but he was still losing too much fucking blood and hopping like a fucking idiot and he saw someone on the balcony of the house…watching.

"MITSY!" He waved and hopped and screamed.

She waved and sat down, picked up something. A phone? No… a tall cool drink with a straw and an umbrella in it.

"HELP ME, goddam you… fucking… traitor…"

Even the most vicious sharks always took a bite and then hung back to wait to decide whether it was worth going back. With humans, they almost never came back. His Summer Safety episode told you to stay still and not to panic.

He didn't panic. He hopped for shore.

It came back for his other leg.

Howling, he fell onto a sleek steel-gray torpedo body that frictionlessly slid out from under him. He grabbed it the wrong way and his palms were torn wide open and the salt water in his wounds pushed him down into *shock*

and he tried to cling to the shark. It couldn't eat him so long as he could hold onto it. His face pressed against the flank of a young male twelve-foot great white with weird black scars all over it. Almost like… Jesus, Dr. Bill thought in disgust, who would do such a thing, putting *gang tattoos* on a shark?

The great white shook off Dr. Bill and plowed him underwater.

REPO NINJA, said the tattoo between its gills.

It was impossible. So unacceptable, he flung himself away from the shark and crossed his arms and shut it all out. *No, this isn't, no, not real*

NO

This was a night terror like the ones he had when his parents split up, or when the rumors got around campus in high school and college that he was queer, or when his first book got savaged by the APA…

In all his books, lectures, videos, TV shows and retreat camps, he always and endlessly said it was *will* that separated the victors from the victims. The will to change, the will to prosper and conquer, the will to shape reality to meet your needs.

And now, at last, he had to admit something. It didn't work. It was all bullshit.

The shark didn't care.

Its mouth yawned wide enough for Dr. Bill to sit down in it. The upper set of teeth dropped down into view and the triangular daggers in rows were not what held Dr. Bill's fascinated, repulsed stare right up until they bit him in half, but the writing on its gums…

It said WISEBLOOD.

Mahalo, Hawaii

Special aloha thanks to Mason Ian Bundschuh for his invaluable insights into island life and language; to Tori, Madeline, Joni, Ryan, Tina, Laura, Jenna and Daniel for all their tireless location scouting and research assistance; to Hailey for braving the road to Hana twice; to Cameron Pierce for convincing me to change the title; to Jeremy Robert Johnson for writing his own fucking books; and to J. David Osborne for publishing this one.

Photo by Hailey Goodfellow

ABOUT THE AUTHOR:
A part-time writer and full-time parking enforcement officer in Tarzana, California, CODY GOODFELLOW has never actually been to Hawaii, but he aggressively issues tickets to even legally parked motorists to save up enough bonus money to someday realize his dream of retiring to Maui to issue parking tickets in paradise on his own recognizance.